Forgotten Stories

Forgotten Stories

In the Shadows of the Son of Man

STEPHEN SHANLEY

RESOURCE *Publications* • Eugene, Oregon

FORGOTTEN STORIES
In the Shadows of the Son of Man

Resource Publications
An Imprint of Wipf and Stock Publishers
199 W. 8th Ave., Suite 3
Eugene, OR 97401

www.wipfandstock.com

PAPERBACK ISBN: 978-1-7252-5357-5
HARDCOVER ISBN: 978-1-7252-5358-2
EBOOK ISBN: 978-1-7252-5359-9

Manufactured in the U.S.A.   05/26/20

To my darling spouse.

Many thanks to my editor, Melvin (Trey) Bankhead III;
my commentators Rev. Ward Ewing, Rev. R. Cameron Miller, and
Dr. Jonathan Lawrence; Matthew Wimer at Wipf and Stock Publishers;
and those who have helped unwittingly and in the future.
Please know that any gross historical errors are mine alone,
as are the Biblical reimaginings.

Contents

Author's Note

This is the first novel written by Dr. Stephen Shanley, a retired Clinical Psychologist. Dr. Shanley is married, with two children, and four grandchildren. He is a lifelong, church-going Episcopalian. As a psychologist, he has witnessed some of the best and worst of humanity.

Dr. Shanley wants to thank family members, friends, editors, publishers, reviewers, and all who read the novel with an open mind. There is a mounting cost to blind adherence to religious dogma; all the good that Jesus did and preached in his lifetime is slowly being eroded by the beastliness that lurks in all of us. That beast is being fed, encouraged, and "weaponized" by those more interested in earthly power than heavenly reward, however defined. The battle for the good/God requires all our heart and soul, and I thank you for your efforts.

Introduction

WHEN DID THE STORY of the life of Jesus, born Yeshua bar Yosef, really begin?

When can we even say there was a beginning or an end, to a life that seemed to come from nowhere and yet stretches into our own time? Still, we might wonder how the story came to be.

A saga such as his was most likely nourished, shaped, buffed, and polished by the Apostles and other witnesses, until it shone for all to see. It may have been treated like a cherished family inheritance, one that was passed along to the favored believers, as from fathers to eldest sons. Over time, it may have formed the wealth of those most lucky and favored sons' estates, given that spot of honor on a mantle, say, in a main room, nearest the light. It likely was embellished and embroidered with even more stories, as the sons told their favored ones how the inheritance came to be, what it means to the family honor, and what the heirs must do to earn and merit the patrimony.

Down through the ages, and out through the spreading branches of the anointed believers it goes, buffeted by changing winds and fortunes. And all the while, each father tells his favored son, "We must keep this story in our family; it is our most precious inheritance, our past, our future, our reason for being. It is worth more than all the price we pay to guard it, and what we make others pay who try to steal or change it." With each retelling of the story, with each new set of hands upon it, the story hardens, becoming more sure of itself.

But there were other witnesses to Jesus' life whose testimonies were not included in the main narrative. What if their stories filtered down through the cracks of the next generations, hidden from authority and thieves alike? Younger sons and daughters, say, might have been told pieces of these Jesus

stories, keepsakes small enough to be ignored by the fathers as they collected the estate for the favored ones' share.

Or perhaps these smaller tales had not pleased the church fathers,
who did not consider them shiny or worthy enough. Perhaps they gathered bruises and scrapes from hard-traveling as they scattered to places
unknown. Perhaps they were forgotten in dark, dusty corners. Over time,
these nearly forgotten stories might have faded to mere whispers as they
moved farther and farther from the main narrative.

But if one could gather the lost fragments together, one can imagine
what these stories from forgotten witnesses might say.

I

Simon's Eulogy For Joseph Bar Jakob Of Nazareth

SH'MA ISRAEL, ADONAI ELOHEINU *Adonai Echad*,[1] Blessed be the Name of His glorious Kingdom for ever and ever.

Welcome, friends and family, and thank you, Rebbe Nathan, for hosting this memorial service. My father's family has been here for some generations, and it is only right that he should be remembered and respected by those he has served well. Looking around here today, I see his handiwork in many places that have required repair. While not a pillar of the Synagogue, perhaps he has been a lintel and a frame!

That is carpentry humor, friends, something my father always appreciated, especially in his later years.

---

1. "Hear O Israel, The Lord is Our God, and The Lord Is One." *Adonai* and *Elohim* are used in place of the English "God" by observant Jews, as they consider the full name of God to be too sacred to spell out. G-d will be used in this text to express this same thought.

It is perhaps customary on these occasions to look back on the deeds of the departed, as well as his or her character. My father's deeds were outstanding, and many of his roofs and doors still are! May his good works outlast all of us. But what can be said of his character? He was almost like two different men, the younger one stern and remote, focused as he was on providing for his family. He worked where he could, often traveling great distances and living rough in the countryside when harvesting wood. We saw him a bit in the slow seasons, but not in the building times. Even when I was old enough to apprentice with him, he did not speak much but would let his work be the teacher. He followed the rules of our faith and community, and enforced them on us children; he could have been a Judge with the Sanhedrin[2] under other circumstances. A good man, apparently, but we knew him hardly at all. We did not know what made him laugh or cry, did not hear any stories about his own childhood, and we did not know his dreams or fears.

Upon my dear mother Salome's death, however, he was almost reborn as someone completely different. Many said that he had lost his mind and become like a child again. I had to pick up work that he could no longer do and had to be very careful with what he tried to teach me. He still could provide somewhat for us if directed properly, but his general confusion was an embarrassment to us older kids. Many times I feared for our future, and the debacle at the Roman Census at Sepphoris was nearly our ruin.

I must confess that my sisters and I resented all these changes, made worse because they were witnessed daily by an outsider—sorry, Mary, but that is what you were, at first. Our resentments deepened because there was also another mouth to feed—that is you, Jesus, a crying one at that who sometimes kept us up at night.

But then, as Jesus got older, something almost miraculous happened. My father by then had let his beard grow long and white, and looked for all the world like one of the great Patriarchs of our history. And yet there he could be found on the floor playing horsey and doggie with Jesus. Father invented nonsense songs and told wild tales of flying animals, invisible spirits, and whole cities that floated in the sky. He let Jesus wrestle him to the ground. He tickled and held that boy as if he was the most precious being in the world.

Father was gentle in all ways even when Jesus would break things or throw a fit. He seemed to have a way of making Jesus understand right from wrong in the simplest terms. Mary was a loving partner in all this, as she fit seamlessly into our family. She always knew just what to do in those times

2. Assembly or council of Rabbis who served as a regional tribunal.

when Father's confusion got the better of him. So, slowly but surely, our little family healed and became whole again.

Not long after Mother's death, Father and Mary were formally married. The people in the village had protected our family's secret about Jesus' birth, but tongues had started to wag the longer Mary lived with us and acted the part of our mother. I do believe that it may have been Mary who asked Father to marry *her,* as he did need to be directed at times.

I gather that there was some awkwardness with her kinswoman Elizabeth and her husband, the Kohen[3] Zechariah. I do note that neither of them attended the wedding and neither is here today. If Mary cared, she never said, and instead Uncle Benjamin gave her away and spoke the prayers. Thank you again, Uncle Benjamin.

As Father got older, he of course slowed down, but he continued to treat all of us with the utmost kindness and love. He always seemed to think I was doing a fabulous job even when my work did not meet my own standards. His advice always seemed to echo things he had told Jesus as a child: "Love the person you are with and everything will be alright." He has been a wonderful father and grandfather to us, and we shall miss him terribly.

I sometimes think of my father as a building, one with a stolid and solid foundation that resembled every other building in town. When he changed, it was as if an entirely new structure was erected on top, one that was airy and often on the verge of collapse. In this upper story, there was always light, laughter, and a view of far-off imaginary lands where all creatures got along and all was at play. He never got to build this vision with his hands, but perhaps it is some place he has given each of us, in our hearts.

---

3. Hebrew for "Priest;" plural: Kohenim.

II

The Travails of Cyrus Of Gadara

I THANK YOU, KIND sir, for letting us graze our small flock on your pasture. The Fellowship of The Way will hear of your generosity. What? You have not heard of us? We are believers in Jesus of Nazareth in Galilee, a prophet, rebbe, and maybe even a Christ from Yahweh, what the Hebrews call their God. Yes, you can tell from my accent that I am not a Judean[1]—none of those 12 tribes am I, for by my name Cyrus you should know that I am a Persian! Yes, I am far from my ancestral home, but I have spent many years in this land. There is always a need for a tender of livestock. *Eirini se sas.*[2] Yes, I can speak your Helene tongue, for did not Alexander intrude himself into my country? And did not his successors

---

1. Relating to the Kingdom of Judah, with Jerusalem as its capital. Well before Christ's time, the northern Kingdom of Israel and its 10 tribes had been dispersed and broken up by invading armies.

2. "Peace be upon you."

invite their men to usurp my family's land, sending us uprooted onto this great road of life?

But I see that you are also exiled far from your homeland, and you also are under the domination of an oppressor, this Rome that thinks itself rightful heirs of Alexander. You Helenes had your chance on the world stage, I guess, as did my Babylonian and Persian ancestors in their day. You and I, friend, are like the dust stirred up by the marching boots of history—we scatter in the wind and soon forget where we came from or know where we are going.

Ah, did you like that phrase? You should know that we Persians are a great poetic people, just as you Helenes are the philosophers and deep thinkers of our world. I can see that you agree, so let there be peace between us, brothers in exile. A shepherd's life is lonely, at any rate, and it is good to have company.

A jar of water and a bite to eat, you say? Agreed!, for the road is long and dusty, and the day hot. Aaah, kind sir, you are indeed a godsend, and I know a few things about that. In fact, if you have time to spare, can I tell you of my own encounter with God? I thought that might get your attention! Let us sit a while in this shade and leave the goats and sheep to their munching. I will tell you that there is still godliness walking the Earth, despite all the wars and suffering.

As I mentioned, my family had rolled through many different lands trying to find a home for ourselves. After a time, however, most had drifted away, died off, or settled in a place I found unsuitable. Although I was born to roam with the sheep, goats, and other livestock I tended for various masters, the loneliness and lack of family slowly drove me mad. Yes, mad, and not just a little mad but completely untethered to this world! One pasture looked like the next, and I no longer could tell if I was in Samaria, Judea, or the Decapolis.

I would mutter to myself in all the tongues I had ever learned or even heard spoken. *"Alaiku dunpa stratikos blear,"* I would yell to the sheep and goats. I invented words unknown to any but myself, but I was terribly proud of them! I invented brothers, lovers, and friends to talk to, as the sheep and goats were not much in the way of conversation. I grew angry at masters and their stewards for not understanding what was perfectly clear to me. I did not need them! I had my imaginary family and friends around me.

As you can imagine, I soon lost all employment, and had to resort to the most primitive means of survival. I hated humanity, hated all the people who had driven my family so far from home, hated my fate, hated my hatred. Many times I was arrested and locked up, only to escape. Neither chains nor mere ropes could hold me, though I must admit that in those poor quarters the chains were rusted and the ropes worn and rotted. I hid in the tumbled rocks, tombs, and hills above Gadara, and ate what I had observed my livestock eating—roots, sweet grasses, berries. I wove grasses together and set snares for rabbits. I watched where the rock grouse laid their eggs. I wove stout rope from supple vines to snare larger animals. I made a kind of clothing from animal skins, but had no tools available to keep them knit together. I was covered with the scrapes, cuts, and rashes from rough living, but little else.

The pain of these thousand slices drove me even madder. I gorged myself when there was game, and nearly starved to death when there was not. I would steal into Gadara in the deepest night to rummage through the garbage heaps for food. Sometimes I was able steal from the camps of shepherds like myself, getting needed fire, food, and woven goods. Sadly, the shepherds soon learned to avoid the areas where I lurked. The blankets wore out and turned to threads, the fires always died, and I nearly froze many times up in the heights. Everything I touched ended in more pain and suffering. I felt cursed, but could not say by whom because I had no coherent thoughts about either gods or man.

It dawned on me during one of my more lucid days that I would not live long at this rate. In my madness, I asked all my imaginary company for advice. You cannot imagine the babel of voices and the many proffered solutions to my distress. I should kill an eagle, drink its blood, grow wings, and fly to a warmer clime. I should mate with a she-bear, who would become my wife, feed me, and keep me warm. I should learn to run on all fours so I could more easily catch the deer that lived in the copses and groves.

Finally, a quieter voice than all the rest seemed to say, "You must remember what and who you are." "What is that?" I said, and I meant it, having forgotten so much of my previous existence. The past is a luxury you cannot afford when your present is so perilous and the future non-existent. "You are a shepherd, find your lost sheep," this voice seemed to say.

"What, what, who, who, quo, quo. . .?" I kept repeating, for something in these words had struck a chord deep and long-buried within me. I raged, I screamed, I pounded my fists and then my head against the ground. With each blow, some nonsense would empty out, and the babel in my head slowly silenced. In a vision, I saw myself finding, trapping, stealing, and taming any and all sheep and goats that fell into my clutches. I would mate the males and females and raise their young. I would drink their blood to keep myself strong. I would slaughter them only as needed, and so stretch my meat supply over months and even years. I would be a shepherd again.

I knew how to hobble animals with vine ropes so they could not escape. All the pasturelands hidden among the rocks and high valleys outside Gadara were known to me. I was still mad enough to imagine that I would tame and herd the deer and gazelles that also populated these upland pastures, but, as you can imagine, that never came to pass. There are many beings in nature that Man has no command over, no matter how clever we imagine ourselves.

If I was to be a thief, however, I somehow knew that I must not be greedy! Only would I steal one at a time, for surely no one would search a mountain for only one lost sheep. I once played a wonderful game with a slow-witted boy who did come after a sheep I stole. When he went one way, I snuck around behind to his flock, left the one I stole, and picked another. This went on until he lost track of how many he had started with. Oh, but I imagined myself the cleverest of thieves!

In my madness, though, I worried that other thieves might come after me, being jealous of my gains. This fear bedeviled me for some time until I was nearly mauled one night by a small pack of dogs at a homestead I tried to rob. One of the faster but smaller brutes managed to clamp himself on my wrist as I scrambled up some rocks. Reflexively I began to beat him with a cudgel I carried for just such occasion. He released me, but I suddenly thought to grab him by the scruff and carry him back to my lair. It took a number of beatings followed by feedings of meat scraps to convince that dog that I was a master to be feared and obeyed. He was a young dog, and it seemed to me over time that he forgot his life in the pack. He became my ears and sentry at night, so I was finally able to sleep in some kind of peace. That alone took some of the madness out of my head.

So little by little I again had a herd to tend, a purpose, a reason to go from one point to another. I built myself shelters of stone and brush at each of the small pastures I found, and gathered wood for each in case I had fire. I ate better, and even the dumb company of the beasts and my dog took away some of my loneliness. I began to notice their different natures, moods, and comforts. I gave them names: Fang was the dog, for obvious reasons, but I also had Neb (for Nebuchadnezzar), and Adam and Eve, my favorite sheep.

The rhythm of my life started to return to what I had known growing up and in my early adult days. As the rhythm of the days evened out, so did something in my mind. I began to believe in a future for myself, especially when I had a full stomach, a fire, and animal friends around me.

One day in late spring I was checking my traps with Fang when I happened on some boar scat that was still warm. I knew that where there was scat there was meat to be had, so I put Fang onto the scent. It was not long before he led me to a kind of trail that led back towards some tumbled rocks.

We got about 100 paces from where I thought the den might be. Thinking fast, I resolved to use Fang as bait, thus drawing the boar out rather than risk cornering it in its lair. I leashed the poor beast to my hunting spear, which I then pounded into the ground. I set him alone on the trail while I crept above, staying downwind. Gathering a large, sharp rock, I waited, knowing that my dog's scent and whining would eventually draw the boar out of its den.

I knew that I might only have one shot at the beast as it charged. If I missed, I would probably need a new dog. Did I ask Fang's forgiveness or permission? *"Does the master ask the slave?"* I must have thought at the time, if I thought at all.

After a time, Fang's whimpering suddenly turned to howls. The bushes down the trail erupted into the blurred shape of a charging she-boar racing as madly as I had once done to shepherds in my domain. "I will show you mad," said I, rearing up and without thinking hurling my rock down upon the hairy-headed beast. My aim was true that day, but the beast's momentum carried it tusks and all right into the spear and my helpless, frightened dog. Leaping down onto the trail, I released all my own beastliness, and it was some time before I stopped howling and crushing its skull. I have never been in a human battle, thank the gods, but I felt like Goliath that day. I had a feeling of ultimate power, as if I controlled not just that animal's life, but all of life and death in the world. Oh, how I roared to the mountain, how the birds scattered at my voice, how I knew I was meant to be the Lord Eternal of the High Mountains! I was *mad*, as I have mentioned previously.

The next morning, I was still covered in some of the boar's blood from the feast before. As I surveyed my domain, it dawned on me as slow as the sun itself was dawning, that the she-boar would not have risked charging out of her den if she was not protecting her young. Sensing more meat at hand, I roused the dog, who most reluctantly accompanied me back to the den. Crows sang to my glory as they scattered from the blood and fur on the trail.

Slowly approaching the jumble of rocks at the end of the trail, I spied a small cave that was partly dug out and partly roofed over by the rocks. Leaning in, I could just make out the shifting and squirming forms of the she-boar's abandoned litter. Smelling their mother's blood on me, they seemed to show no fear, thus confirming that I was indeed the mighty lord over all creation!

I fondled the little pink balls for a time, and tried to sing to them in the grunts and groans I imagined a she-boar could make. "I am your new father," I grunted. "I will build a castle to protect you from the beasts." I set about making a kind of enclosure around the mouth of that little cave, stacking rocks in a wide semi-circle, and placing brush here and there between the rocks. I dug a small pit in the ground where water was dribbling down the face of one of the boulders; this would be a wallow and water source as the pigs got older. I pierced a hollow gourd, tied wool to the tip, and made a kind of nipple for feeding those infant pigs sheep milk. Did I not tell you I was a genius? Again, a full belly always helps solve the problems of survival. I recommend it more than any book or academic study.

Well, my new friend, all that changed one day after I encountered a man named Jesus. I had just obtained a ewe from the flock of a wayward shepherd who wandered into my domain. It had taken me considerable time to track this flock, and it was not until night approached that I was able to make my move. Grabbing the ewe, I dashed into the tumbled rocks of my lower domain until I found a cave I used for just such purpose. I hobbled the ewe with vines I had left there, and wrapped its mouth with a leather strap to keep it quiet. The hours passed without sounds of pursuit, so I settled in for the night.

In the morning, I crept out of my cave and found no one about. Hoisting the ewe over my shoulders, I began carrying the squirming thing up a trail to my sheepfold. Imagine my surprise when I saw this Jesus character coming down my very own trail, carrying what looked like a lamb on *his* shoulders. I was too shocked to remember my usual mad act, and sputtered out in a rusty mix of tongues (for I had not spoken to another living person in years), "Who are you? What are you doing on my mountain?"

This Jesus listened intently and replied haltingly in a mix of Aramaic and Greek, "I come in peace to meet the famous Lord of Gadara." But then he added in the same jumbled hash of words, "But can we speak in one tongue to ease our time together?"

You may imagine my confusion—I firstly feared that he was but a delaying tactic or a scout for an army of shepherds seeking revenge on me. My ears pricked up for any sign of such pursuit, while my eyes looked hungrily at the lamb on his shoulder. My thoughts fumbled through all my many disjointed languages, while my pride swelled to be called Lord of the Gadara. Deeper still, my heart started to ache in a strange way, having finally met another human being face-to-face. It is a wonder I did not shatter into pieces!

The hunter and thief in me—the part that had helped me survive all these years—soon got the upper hand. I asked him, in Aramaic, "How the devil did you find and get above me? And what are you doing with that lamb?"

Jesus told me that all would be explained in due time, but could we find some shade and put our burdens down so we could talk? He then said,

"I am quite alone, as your fine senses have surely told you. You are not being hunted and no one will steal from you while we speak."

Oh, even I could see that he was a clever one, praising me while somehow blunting my mounting fears. Perhaps I was secretly pleased to talk to a man as intelligent as myself, so I told him to follow me to where a small glen and pasture branched off the trail. Stooping and unburdening myself, I pushed my ewe towards the forage, and dragged a barrier across the mouth of the gully. With my prize thus secured, I turned to face Jesus. He had released his lamb, but to my surprise, it ran straight to my ewe, bleating piteously before attaching itself to its teats.

Jesus smiled at the happy reunion, for that was what it was. He had evidently brought that ewe's kid with him, hoping the mother-child bond would help him find the missing sheep. An odd feeling of something like respect bubbled up in me, a feeling I had not had in years, even before going mad.

I squelched the feeling quickly, however, as my animal instincts rose to warn me that this fellow might be a better thief and hunter than myself. He had already caught me off-guard on the trail and used a trick I myself had never thought to use. Narrowing my eyes into those of a hunter, and one constantly on guard, I examined him for signs of threat. I looked first for hidden weapons, then for scars or blood or other signs of having lived an aggressive, predatory, or even violent life. In short, I looked to see if he was like me.

He showed nothing, no fear, no marks of conflict or rough living, no weapon, no sly smirk or measured pretense, nothing but a kind of amused smile. For some reason, this infuriated me, and more words tumbled out of my mouth than I had spoken in years.

"Do you not know that I am mad?" I screamed. "I could bash your head in now and no one would hear your cry! How dare you come into my kingdom and act like some old friend here for a mere chat!"

This Jesus kept his eyes mild and fixed on my reddening face, then calmly answered, "But I *am* like an old friend. I have been a shepherd too, as have almost all country boys like us. I have seen your corrals, the care you take with your small flock, even your choice of this small pasture so that your ewe can be fed and watered. And I have even thought myself mad in my younger days, the first few times I heard the voice of The Almighty call my name. And I must say, I have also been spurned and misunderstood by men, and been banished to the wilderness. If you only knew. . ."

His head dropped and he turned away slightly; a sadness seemed to come over him as he drifted off somewhere into his own memories. His distress was so strong that he seemed momentarily vulnerable, lost in himself and unaware of his present danger.

Well, this glimpse into his life started a storm of conflict within me. On the one hand, I was filled with an unexpected feeling of pity for someone beside myself. This man seemed to have suffered rejection, madness, and maybe worse. I can tell you friend, this pity was the first time in years I had given even a scrap of regard to another living thing. I had spent my time on the mountain with only myself as audience and performer, subject and lord, victim and victimizer. Pity had stayed alive in me all through my harsh years, but only as something I gave to myself. More than anything, I was surprised that there was any tenderness left in me.

On the other hand, my instincts smelled his vulnerability and sensed that now was the time to attack, eliminating him as a witness to my hideouts and gaining a lamb for my own needs. Oh, how it pained me to be so utterly divided, as each feeling excluded the other with no apparent way between! Say what you will about all that I had suffered on that mountain, but at least I had a singleness of purpose—to stay alive. There was no room for regret or self-recrimination. There was only the pure animal focus on the hunt.

Being with this Jesus, however, threw me out of this role of hunter, for he claimed to simply want to talk as one man to another. He neither ran from me as prey might from a lion, nor did he seem desirous of a fight. I was being forced instead into something almost lost to me, meeting another human in peace.

But I hated being human! Humans were stupid, they were the cause of my starvation, they never understood or accepted me, they were in my way! It was too hard to be human, to live with loneliness, to organize thoughts into coherent sentences, to shape and bend myself to fit into society.

All I could do then was collapse on the ground and howl, banging my head in hopes that some kind of answer would come to me. I writhed in pain from this inner conflict, like Prometheus chained to a rock while eagles ate his guts. I howled until my throat burned and I could howl no more. I banged my head until nearly senseless. Pity once again flowed out for myself, but this time I had no answers how to proceed.

I heard soft footsteps approach, and a brown arm reached over my hunched and tangled limbs with a gourd half full of water. In a voice totally devoid of scorn or shaming, he almost whispered, "here is the water of life. I believe man is the only animal who can feel pain when his whole existence comes crashing down on him. You are a man, Cyrus, not a beast. I have learned some things about you and your true nature—you have never attacked or harmed anyone you have met, but have simply done what is needed to stay alive. And you have suffered, as anyone can tell by looking at your skin, which is weather-beaten as the animals you keep. It is perhaps through this suffering that you seem most human and most in need of understanding."

I did not dare look at him. I did not trust my eyes that had grown so used to seeing every living thing as either prey or predator. Had I really forgotten what it was like to meet someone who cared what I felt? A part of me could not bear to see his pity for my miserable condition. And in truth, I had no strength left to do or say anything anyway. I was exhausted with living.

We sat there for a time, and a companionable silence came between us. I felt no pressure to look at or answer him, and he must have felt the same. Little by little, I began to hear the little sounds in the glen around us: the gurgling water, the sheep munching, a few birds calling. The day was warming as well, with sunshine spreading across our little hidden pasture. I slowly roused myself, stretching my clenched limbs and breathing in the clean, sun-drenched mountain air that smelled of dusty rock and pine.

Jesus offered me some dried figs, a bit of hard cheese, and even some wine held in a stoppered bottle he had in a pouch he carried. Looking upward, he said, "Bless this food, O Father, to our strength and nourishment. May it be a reminder of the bounty of Your creation."

I must have snorted at that, for he then said, "I understand how that must sound to one who has had to fend for himself all these years. It must seem that life has not given you much."

"It has given me shit," I grunted at last, but I held my next thoughts so I had time to eat the food and drink the wine he had given me.

As I slowly savored this unexpected, and only dimly remembered kind of meal, a warm feeling started to creep over me. A pool of longing welled up in me, for all I had missed in my time on the mountain. Memories flooded in—of blood oranges, sweets, freshly baked, garlic-infused bread—and with these memories, the laughter, music, and companionship of those who had shared meals with me so long ago. Memories became tears, then, which quietly ran down my ravaged, sun-burnt, and hairy face.

It was then that Jesus continued. "I want to offer you a chance to rejoin the world of men. You will note the gifts I have brought to remind you of what that world offers—unexpected food, which comes not from your own efforts, but from one who understands your needs. Always give thanks to the unexpected, the feasts, the shared meals. A truly humble heart receives many such gifts.

"The second gift is someone like myself, a caring friend who does not judge but accepts you for who you are, a friend who may have been on the same journey as yourself. Loneliness can be a slow death, while a boon companion keeps all that is human alive in you.

"And the third gift is perhaps the most important, and was certainly the heaviest burden I bore on my way here—the love shown between the lamb and its mother. If God has created such tender bonds for these simple animals, just imagine what awaits you if you seek love. It was not a sly trick to bring that lamb up here, but rather a reminder of the work it takes to keep us connected to the ones we love. By the grace of God, that lamb has found its mother, who will nourish and bring it to fullness of life. By the grace of this same God, may you be healed, may you *also* find love and be brought to the fullness of what life can be for you."

My new quiet and respectful friend, have I put you to sleep with this long tale of woe and wonder? No? As the day is drawing to a close, so let my own encounter with a god come to its conclusion. Yes, I believe this Jesus must be some sort of agent of God, for who else could have reached into my barbaric, lost, and twisted soul, and fed the little spark of humanity that was left in me? Not only were his gifts exactly what my broken heart needed and wanted, but the very fact that he sought me out—me, a lost and lunatic, raging madman—meant that I mattered. He was the door back to the world of men, the light, the love, the father, the brother—all the things that I had always wished to have.

All these feelings flooded through me. As best as I can describe it, something in me turned itself inside out. I clung to him as all my bestiality, madness, anguish, and loneliness screamed out of me. I was truly the lion whom he had taught to lie down with the lamb.

What is that you say? Yes, you must know by now that I am the very Madman of Gadara you may have heard about. I am glad you have not run away, for I am not so fearsome, yes?

You want to know if Jesus indeed put my demons into a herd of pigs? I truly do not know how that rumor started. I can only tell you that Jesus convinced me to release all my wild animals.

"As you have freedom and release from the bondage of your isolation here, so should they be free," he said. That made sense to me, so I released the piglets—now fairly grown— from their pen. This happened just as some of the villagers were creeping up the path to see if he had gotten their ewe back from my clutches. No doubt the pigs were panicked into confusion by the whole scene and their unexpected freedom, and they did scatter in all directions. I do believe Jesus was much too kindly a soul to inflict my pain onto animals even as lowly as those pigs. I do admit, however, that it did feel as though all my many demons had left me.

The villagers were terrified of me for a time, as you might imagine, although I bought back some good will by returning all of the livestock I had stolen over the years, keeping only the offspring for myself. A man has to make some kind of living, yes? Now I follow his disciples with my herd, supplying them with wool and meat. I am just the humble shepherd you see before you. Well, maybe not so humble, but surely thankful to be here today.

As the Sabbath approaches, you are welcome to hear this Jesus speak. No, please, do not trouble yourself to get all clean or to sacrifice anything before you come—we will like you just as you are, a good and patient listener who is willing to share time and sustenance with a stranger.

III

Susanna's Tale

THANK YOU, SISTERS, FOR taking in this tired woman. Do not think I am ungrateful for even this small fire and thin soup. I have had better and I have had worse, let me tell you. A woman alone in this world must take what she can get. Do not think I am bitter—well, think what you will, for I have been free to think for myself and would grant the same to you. Freedom is a thin blanket in a cold world, but I would not give it up no matter how hard the winds of fate might blow.

It is not fate, however, which has brought me here to you. I know how much you esteem the Magdalene, and hope my tale might win me a place by your fire. I knew her well in the early years. We worked, laughed, drank, and travelled together, and I was with her with she first met Jesus. Yes, yes, I have met Jesus too, but please allow me to set the stage for that meeting so that you may know I speak the truth. I do hope this is a fair exchange, my story in payment for your kindness.

Shall I go on?

Good.

Mary had come to Jerusalem after the death of her lover or husband, I cannot remember which and it makes no difference. Let us just say that she had some experience with men! He had died fighting the Romans in one of our many ill-conceived uprisings, and I guess she had no immediate means of support. She had been shunned in her village due to her association with that man, and had come to Jerusalem seeking work. Not knowing anyone, she more or less drifted into the Duck, an inn where I worked at the time. She and I served the gentlemen their food and drink, and she kept her eye out for that wealthy man who could free her from her labors. She could sing a pretty tune and was quick with her wits, which came in handy when fending off unwanted advances. Her beauty and spirited nature were a magnet to many, but trouble soon found her.

She had some success, you might say, as a 'special friend' to some of the traveling merchants. She would ask them for mementos of their friendship and time together, and had begun to attract some valuable possessions. One night, however, one of her suitors got quite drunk and beat her up badly, having discovered that she had other admirers. How he could not recognize her generous and flirtatious nature is beyond me, for it was plain for all to see and was part of her charm. This man was well-known and well-protected due to his business dealings with both the Romans and Sadducees[1] and was not a man to cross. Unfortunately, I had to break a chamber pot over his head to stop his assault. That insult brought a roar of approval from the inn crowd, but signaled the end of our employments.

I gathered our belongings and whatever wealth we had managed to hide in our room, and took her broken and bleeding away to a cousin of mine out by the northern gate. He was none too glad to see us, I can tell you, fearing the merchant's displeasure. Jerusalem was but a small city, and it would not be long before news of the salacious women and the chamber pot assault spread to all quarters. (I heard later that the merchant had spread awful rumors about our immoral characters, but, of course, he had omitted his role in the affair.)

Mary was clearly in a bad way, however, and my cousin must have taken pity on her. He may also have had other thoughts in his mind from the way he kept staring at her, and I knew that our time with him would not be long.

The same market that had brought the ill-tempered merchant to Jerusalem also attracted a large number of farmers from the surrounding countryside. I thought we might to join them as they departed the city, hoping to

---

1. A Jewish priestly aristocracy

be lost within their numbers. I covered my hair and finery with an old cloak and went looking for our salvation.

In the market stalls, I kept hearing both women and men remark on a man named Jesus from far-off Galilee who was attracting notoriety as a preacher, teacher, and healer. A few had heard that he had cured a man of leprosy, another that he had actually revived people from the dead. Several talked of taking their remaining goods north in search of him and his followers, for both profit and prophesy. These folks seemed as good as any to join, I thought, as Galilee was far from perilous Jerusalem; this Jesus also might prove healthful for my Mary.

Feigning a similar interest in this man, I begged a comely woman who seemed part of this pilgrimage to allow me and my friend to accompany her. I added that my friend had accidentally fallen on some jagged paving stones and would greatly appreciate a ride in her farm wagon. I showed her some shekels[2] to let her know our gratitude and ability to pay for her help. Although she was hesitant, her husband had a good eye for business and for my not-inconsiderable womanly charms. We agreed to meet at dawn on the morrow at their stall.

Much heartened by this development, I slipped back through the market to tell Mary the good news. She was staring blankly at the wall, and would neither eat nor drink. Some kind of spark seemed to have left her, and she merely shrugged when I related our impending escape. I was alone with my fears for our future. I slept badly, and could hear Mary moan and keen softly to herself throughout the night.

To shorten this tale, sisters, I will not describe our near-disaster at the gate, nor the grueling trek over rough roads up to Galilee. Mary rarely spoke during our journey. She was in pain physically and mentally, and barely looked up from the road beneath her feet.

As we neared the Sea, we joined up with some followers of a preacher named John who were also on their way to hear this Jesus. Their man had just recently been arrested and beheaded by the Tetrarch Herod Antipas, all over some comments John made about Herod's wife. I rather wished Mary and I had such a protector, but knew that it was our lot to be the ones crushed by the mighty rather than avenged.

These followers of John, who called themselves Baptists, seemed of nice enough character despite their grief over the death of their rebbe. They talked freely with me and our train about the need for baptism, inner cleansing, and forgiveness of sins. As we were traveling along the shore of

2. Jewish unit of money, worth about $2. Greek coins, such as the lepton (1 c.) and kollybos (25 c.), were also accepted currency.

Galilee by this time, I took them up on their suggestion, and had myself thoroughly dunked and baptized. I recommend it highly, ladies, both for the hygiene and the marvelous sense of leaving your dirty, sinful ways in the past. Words are not enough to describe the liberation I felt due to this cleansing of body, mind, and spirit. I truly felt reborn. After having failed to properly keep all the myriad Kosher rules and rituals, it was a blessing to simply and physically feel clean and worthy before The Almighty.

But back to Mary, who still was in some dark pit despite the apparent healing of her cuts and the knitting of her bones. She showed no interest in her traveling companions, nor in baptism or our future prospects. She continued to only eat and drink enough to sustain life, but let her hair, clothing, and indeed her whole demeanor tumble into disarray. I began to fear that she would soon just crawl into a hole and die from grief over the loss of all her dreams. I did not have long to find someone to bring her back to life.

As we neared the town of Na'in, we joined a large crowd who had gathered to hear this Jesus teach and preach. He seemed a gentle, humble, yet firmly rooted man who deftly handled some difficult questions thrown at him by what looked like high-caste kohenim. He sounded as learned as they, yet also stopped his teaching long enough to engage some children in his lessons. The children were frightened at being singled out by a stranger, but soon warmed up to him and he to them. Here was a man comfortable in his own skin, I thought, and with all classes of people.

Unfortunately, I could not follow many of his parables and lessons. He claimed the greatest were the least, the last first, and children justified wisdom. What I did remark, however, were the many stories of those healed by him, the blind, lame, deaf, and dying. This was the man for Mary, I thought, if I could only reach him through the throng of all his disciples and admirers. I resolved to follow behind him and his disciples as they took their leave of the crowd, hoping not to be noticed lest they rebuke me and send me away.

Keeping to the shadows, feigning interest at the market stalls, and generally shrinking my flamboyant self, I tracked him to a lodging close by the Nazareth road. There were still considerable numbers of followers with him, and some commotion broke out between them and a small group that seemed to have just arrived. I asked someone on the fringe of the crowd who they might be, and she answered that these were his mother and siblings come to speak with him. It appeared that even they could not pierce the protective wall of his disciples; my spirits sank when I compared my own prospects.

Having come all this way and with Mary's very soul at risk, however, I was not to be deterred for long. I sat back into the shade of a nearby stall and watched for any gap in the defenses of his retinue. Towards dusk, a rather self-important-looking messenger arrived, making the crowd part before him. I heard the man announce to one of Jesus' men that his master requested the honor of Jesus' presence at dinner that evening. He gave a location and his master's name, but did not enter the lodging to speak directly to Jesus, nor did he look at anyone in the crowd. Jesus' man left to consult with his master, and returned a short while later to say that yes, Jesus would be pleased to sup with the notable Pharisee.[3]

The messenger merely nodded and turned back the way he had come, taking care to leave as quickly as was seemly. There followed an awkward and uncomfortable silence, as the mere presence of the haughty messenger seemed to cause some anxiety to ripple through the crowd. They began to drift away, and I realized that few would dare to follow Jesus to this dinner.

I did not know much about Pharisees, as few ever deigned to frequent the Duck, so I felt no such trepidation, only opportunity. Here was a small window of time where I might approach Jesus without his disciples, but I had to come up with a strategy to get into the Pharisee's house.

Ladies, you must know that in this life, we women have usually had to give up something for what we get. There, there, you know in your heart of hearts that this is so. Although I had seen a few women in Jesus' retinue, I had seen none of the preening, sly glances, or physical hunger that would indicate that he was that certain kind of man we have met so often. I did not think feminine wiles would work, or even be appropriate. I played different schemes through my mind, as I am wont to do, until suddenly I felt them slip off me like a snake shedding its skin—that clean, wondrous feeling from my recent baptism must have filled in some hole within me and I suddenly knew what to do.

The realization hit while I was crouching down in the shadows like some gnome or coiled snake. I did not want to be that person any longer. I was human and thus a valuable daughter of Adonai! I needed to be truthful, not scheming. I needed to be real, not play a part ill-suited to my new sense of self. I wanted to give, not give *up* something,

I stood up then and walked with new purpose and even confidence back to the market stalls I had passed on my way to Jesus' lodging. I found the seller of ointments and perfumes whose scents had momentarily delayed me while I stalked my target. He began his set speech, which was as full of flattering emoluments as were his wares. I merely smiled at his obvious appeal to my vanity, so he switched to a conspiratorial tone, suggesting his goods would help me best my rivals for the favors of my heart's desire. Again, I gave the smile that revealed nothing of my character or intent. "I have three shekels to

---

3. Lay person who took a pietistic, strict view of the many laws and rituals of the Jewish religion.

spend," I said, "and I know that that is enough for a small jar of pine-scented ointment. I have enjoyed your efforts, but I know my own mind."

Well, that stunned him a bit and he opened his mouth for another try, but my direct and unflinching look into his eyes must have assured him that he was dealing with a woman who was in possession of her wits.

At another time, ladies, we might discuss further this art of doing business and bargaining when you feel free of past limitations and expectations placed on you as a woman. I thanked my baptism and Adonai again as I walked away with my prize, being careful not to feel smug or cocky—we all know where that word comes from, do we not, ladies?! Suffice it to say I presumed nothing about my chances, but felt in control of what I would do for effort.

I had asked the vendor for directions to the abode of said Pharisee and had managed to say nothing after he smirked broadly at me. I found my way to the house as dusk fell, with lamps and the smell of roasting lamb guiding my way. The aroma nearly deflected my purpose, as I had not eaten in some time. One must be in control of all our senses if one is to survive in this world! Collecting myself, I applied what little I knew of such Pharisees to the problem of getting into the house.

I knew that an unaccompanied woman could never be seen at the front door of an observant household lest the neighbors remark, so I followed a low wall around to what looked like a servant's entrance. It was poorly lit, so I felt with my hands for some kind of bell, rope, or knocker. As luck or fate would have it, a house servant soon came out carrying the remains of the first course of food. I coughed gently to warn her of my presence and wished her a good evening as she stood in the doorway.

Looking directly into her eyes, I said, "I am Susanna, come from my Master Jesus' lodging with ointment for his tired feet. I would be grateful to perform this small service while he reposes at table." You can see, ladies, that this was on the truth side of the fine line I had to walk to gain the greater good for my Mary. We are not asked to be perfect, but we do need a worthy goal to justify any misdirection.

The servant first disposed of her burden, then said that she would check with the house steward. I waited outside the gate for him, and again tried to stay in full possession of my inner calm, which had thankfully started to grow and become a more permanent part of me. The same messenger who had summoned Jesus appeared at the gate, and stared at me with some distaste showing on his rigid face.

"Yes?" he said, giving nothing away.

"Master Steward," I said, and this time I looked only briefly at him before lowering my gaze to the jar of ointment in my hands, "As your servant has told you, I come to anoint my master's feet, to ease his tiredness from his long journey. It is a practice well-loved by him, and I would be most pleased to perform it with your permission."

He stood there for the proper time to let me know that nothing spoken by a woman was granted immediately. He then gave a small roll of his eyes, as if the affairs of such an odd one as Jesus were beyond his caring. He gave a slight nod, then turned away while gesturing for me to follow. He directed me impatiently into the kitchen, where bustling servants were preparing the feast I could hear just beyond another door.

I understood that I was to blend in with them so as not to draw any attention, but on impulse, I loosened my considerable mane of hair. Was it to distinguish myself from those tightly constricted, even cowed women who were so plainly dressed and spoke only in whispers? Was it to appeal to Jesus' vanity, for that is where much of men's sexual pride originates? It may have been some of these things, but rather I believe it was only to show the steward and all the others that I was a free woman.

So, in I walked with the serving women and went straight to where Jesus lay on pillows beside the feasting table. I did not look at any other but him, and again noticed his deep, soulful eyes that showed only a hint of surprise when I knelt at his feet.

"If I may, Master," I asked, while showing him my jar of ointment. I looked right at him until he gave a nod, and then began massaging and anointing his feet, which believe me needed all the kneading they could get. They were rough and calloused, but firm and finely shaped. I could feel him tingle to my touch, and I had to again control that hotter part of my former self that knew just how to please a man. This was to be an act of respect and service, and not of conquest or feigned submission. Unexpected tears began to well up inside me, of relief I believe at no longer having to play the flirt, or maybe I was relieved to simply have gotten this far.

In my memory of that moment, I can sense all kinds of things that may have been going on, but it is like trying to pick apart a river to identify the very streams that have fed into it.

With my hands full of ointment, I dared not wipe my eyes, so used what was closest to me, my hair, to dry my eyes and the many tears that had fallen on Jesus' legs. He made no move to rebuke or encourage me, but just accepted the pleasure I was offering. This only added to my tears, as never before had a man simply met me as I wished to be met, without presuming more than was offered. I continued my anointing until the job was properly done, and waited for a chance to speak with him quietly.

After a short time, the Pharisees at the table began some long theological discourse, and Jesus turned to me with that same steady gaze. I blinked back my few remaining tears and said, "I have wished to give you something as thanks for all your words, work, and very presence among us. Please receive this gift as it is offered. I do, however, have a friend who most needs your healing touch, if and when you have time." Seeing him smile and nod, I added, "We are staying with an encampment just on the other side of the Nazareth road from where you reside. I would be most honored if you could visit us." With that, I bowed once to him and made to leave.

Jesus reached out a hand on my shoulder, then made a kind of cross on my forehead with his fingers. "Blessings and thanks be to you, my sister, go in peace. Your transgressions tonight are forgiven."

This touch traveled through me from top to bottom, and side-to-side. I cannot do justice to how it felt, but it filled me with an intense but quiet joy.

I straightened myself and left through the door from which I came, again not daring—or was it deigning?—to look at his company. I could hear a low, somewhat angry murmur follow my departure, then Jesus' calm voice in reply. I left before the steward or any other could disrupt my feelings of accomplishment and hope regarding Mary's well-being.

I returned to our encampment in the dark, guided by our fires and a half-filled moon. Mary sat just where I left her hours previously; a half-empty cup of water and most of her scant dinner were spread out before her. She barely lifted her eyes at my approach, and I controlled the temptation to tell her of my marvelous evening lest my joy widen the yawning gulf between us. If she waited for anyone to help her, it would have to be a man, to undo the damage caused by her male attacker. Of all men, I believed it would be Jesus, whose very touch seemed to bring tingles of life into the soul. I had done what I could and the morrow would have to prove its own worth.

The sounds of the awakening camp reached me a bit before the sun rose. These farmer families certainly had their own rhythm, one set by their animals and need to get as much work done as possible before the heat of the day set in. I was about to steal back to sleep when one of them approached our simple tent, which was nothing more than a blanket tied to a wagon and stretched over our heads to keep off the morning dew. This Tzviya announced that a visitor was asking after us, and I could tell by her excited smile and expectant eyes that this was Jesus.

I roused myself, threw a cloak over my sleep garments, and shook Mary, telling her we had to get moving. I asked Tzviya to tell Jesus we would be with him shortly, and could she find a place where we could talk privately with him? Mary was none too happy to awake, perhaps thinking that the day offered nothing to her but more grief and humiliation. I persisted gently but firmly, and she made some half-hearted effort to make herself presentable.

Tzviya returned and pointed us to a cluster of palms some twenty paces away. I led Mary there, and she was too disinterested or perhaps just foggy-headed to resist. There sat Jesus cross-legged on the ground, alone for once, and engaged in a kind of rocking motion that I took for prayer. Mary startled at the sight of him and started to back away, but I held her firm and said, "Mary, this is the Jesus of Nazareth that you have heard about. He has come at my request and out of the manifold goodness of his heart to restore you to your true self, if you so wish."

Mary looked momentarily dazed, then something of her old temper reared up.

She looked first at me and then almost glared at Jesus. "Who will bother to help one as lowly as me? And what will you demand in return?"

Jesus nodded slowly, as if admitting that the world could be cruel. He lowered his voice so that only Mary and I could hear, and I knew he was not preaching to the crowd for effect. "I see that you have been ill-treated, sister, and it is My Father's wish that I help restore His creation to its true beauty. It is a new day, so let me help you leave whatever has harmed you in the past, where it belongs. If you will join me in the quiet of these trees, I believe you will feel the better for it."

Mary teetered a bit on her feet, as if pulled in all directions, but she eventually sat down with a resigned shrug. I took this as my cue to leave, and bade them both a goodbye. "I will go prepare some breakfast for both of you to have once you are finished." And with that, I left them to their ministrations.

Ladies, I must confess to many anxious moments while I awaited her fate and prepared a simple breakfast. Was this Jesus what he seemed? Could he reassemble the broken shards of her soul into something like the Mary whom I knew and loved? And what of my own role? My new faith had given me the courage to enter the Pharisee's house and secure Jesus' help, but I knew almost none of the prayers the Baptists used to plead before God. I felt helpless to intercede any further on her behalf.

After a decent amount of time, Mary came back alone to our eating area, saying that Jesus had needed to return to his lodging to prepare for the day's preaching. Her steps were lighter, her shoulders higher and square, and her eyes no longer were the lifeless sockets that almost dragged along the ground.

"I do not know how he did it, Susanna, but he coaxed my whole life story out, like spinning yarn from rough and tangled wool. He listened as if he really cared. At every major turn of my fortunes, he would ask gently how I got there and had I learned anything? He remarked on my love of golden trinkets, and how that tied me to the Duck and the pursuit of men who had no real love for me. He gently rebuked me for wanting these men to give me a life of ease, saying that each of us must find the work that Adonai has prepared for us to do in this world. To be always at leisure leads to sloth; it pushes our duties onto other unfortunates, who must then carry our load along with their own.

"He also remarked on my beauty, and I braced myself for his advances, though I did find him handsome enough, for a country boy. Sensing my discomfort, he still chided me.

'Why should I not remark on something which is plain for all to see? Beauty is not something you have earned, created, or bought. It is not something you own or should use to your advantage, to lord over others or bait them into giving you favors. Nor is it something that men should covet and try to possess as their own. It is simply a gift from The Almighty, like a beautiful sunset or flower. Hold it in your heart, but not in a mirror.'

"I must say, Susanna, that his words flattered me, but they also cut me to the quick. How was I to succeed in this world if I could not use my main advantage?"

Here Mary did seem truly confused and even defeated, as if his words had pierced all her pride and defenses. I feared for a moment that she would collapse into her previous lifeless shell, and that all my work for her would be in vain.

Thankfully, she merely shook her head, gave out a deep sigh, and continued. "Slowly it dawned on me that I had paid too steep a price for my beauty—men had fought over me and beaten me for denying them what was really mine to keep or give as I chose. I was not innocent either, as I had burnished my beauty, like a golden snare, to trap more gold. I had fooled myself into thinking I wanted love, but he had seen right through that self-delusion. I thought, 'Who is this man who can hold a mirror to my vain and selfish soul and not despise or reject me?'

"I did not know how to proceed. Was I supposed to make myself ugly? Swear off men entirely? Jesus said simply to accept the gift of my beauty as a blessing. I was to be thankful but to wear my looks with humility, as if they were nothing more than daily dressing.

"That word, 'humility,' jarred something deep within me. I pictured all the downtrodden and beaten women I had seen throughout my days. I heard all the demeaning words husbands and even priests used when speaking of the women in their lives. I felt a kind of anger that this Jesus—who had seemed so understanding—would want me to be submissive, a slave to all.

"I must have sputtered out a dozen angry thoughts at once before I caught myself, fearing that my effrontery would garner rebuke and condemnation from this man whom I admired. Instead, Jesus gave a delighted laugh, clapping his hands together and looking me straight in the eye.

'Well said, sister, always keep your fire burning against the injustices of this world. We all could use more heat and light in these dark times, but I fear I have not been clear in my words. True humility comes from being who you truly are, no more and no less. To be less is a rejection of the gifts that our Father in Heaven has given you. It is a kind of defeat, a shrinking away from your proper place in life. To act bigger than you are requires that others around you surrender something of their own humanity to keep you bloated and fat. A humble person is a servant, not a slave; she is one who senses what is needed in a situation, and freely gives what is required.

'Humility is like that tenon up there in the corner of the roof—that peg, though small, fits perfectly into the mortise and by so doing upholds the entire roof. When you know your own proper size and place, you will have strength, purpose, and beneficial impact far beyond your imagining.'

"Finally, Susanna, Jesus picked up a handful of dust. He had me put the names of all those who had abused or disappointed me into his fist. Then he blew the dust away, reminding me that they were too small to bother me. I felt a great weight and tension leave me then, as if I was retiring from an exhausting sport that claims many more victims than it grants winners. I sense more clearly than ever that I have played a losing part in a man's world, where the rules are stacked against me and where I have been required to continually change myself to suit those with more power and wealth. I have willingly played the role of princess-in-waiting, and have wasted much time being jealous and resentful of any other woman who got more attention or favor than I did. O, how foolish and vain I have been!

"I told all this to Jesus, who simply got me to laugh at myself until I cried. He held me in his arms and let my tears dampen his tunic. It was as if all my poisonous memories, hurts, schemes, and fears were drained away, one by one. I am now ready to go on, Susanna, whatever this life may hold. It is so strange to have felt so dead but now to feel so wonderfully alive! And I owe so much to you, Susanna, for your friendship and for all you have done for me during my dark days."

You might say, sisters, that Mary was reborn that day. I thankfully have never seen a golem[4] or any others from the land of the dead, but my friend Mary could easily have been mistaken for one after her beating. She had been a mere lump of flesh with little or no will of her own. This Jesus had relit the fire in her eyes, and a warm, steady glow of life now surged in her veins.

---

4. Mythical human-like creature made from mud.

She would say later that Jesus had helped her repent of her sins, but as time went on others claimed that he had driven demons out of her. She took great offense to that, as if she herself was not responsible for the many poor choices in her own life.

"I was much too tired and spent from my troubles to suffer any exorcism, Susanna. Jesus was as gentle but as firm as anyone I have met. He gave me time to let go of my painful memories until they were just like the dust he had held in his hands. His regard for me was so warm it was like, like . . . having a hot, soaking bath after a long journey."

Not a very exciting image, I grant you, sisters, but there you have it. No lightning bolts, no thrashing of demons, only something that each of us might go through, with help from a loving friend.

It was obvious to both of us that we should start to follow this Jesus. We had no family responsibilities, only a general desire to remain far from Jerusalem, at least until our faces faded from the memories of our enemies. Each of us had had a life-changing experience thanks to Jesus and his cousin John, but we somehow knew that our old ways would creep back into our souls if we did not stay on the right path. We therefore said good-bye to the farmers who had remained with us in Na'in, but were now returning to their fields. We joined up with those of the Baptists who now wanted to follow Jesus. The rest of their group went on towards Damascus, intent on establishing their own community somewhere.

We had never followed anyone before and were unclear how it was done. One of the Baptists explained that it helped to have a sponsor who paid for supplies in return for securing the blessings and favor of the rebbe being followed. As there was much talk about Jesus being more than that, being a prophet no less, there were a growing number of possible sponsors in each of the cities and towns through which he traveled. Most of these sponsors, however, tended to have kinship ties with those on the pilgrimage, for only in this way could the sponsors ensure a spiritual return on their investment, as it were.

This was no help to Mary and myself. We had no kin in this area and did not want to return to our old habits of currying favor with a lonely, rich benefactor whose interest in us would most likely not be spiritual.

So, I looked at Mary and she at me. "The Lord help us," I said, "but we shall have to keep using our wits. There may be small jobs we can do around the camp as it travels and rests, and we both have a store of money laid up for our adventures."

Well, I will not bore you sisters with the shopping and other preparations we made to become proper pilgrims, but we soon blended in with the throngs who followed Jesus and his disciples. Each town he visited seemed to have heard his name, and our numbers increased after each sermon and lesson he gave.

At one point, he must have grown exhausted from having to meet and speak to so many people hungry for his word and touch. He took a few of his disciples and boarded a small boat across the Galilee. We were told there would be no preaching that day, so we kept to our camp. We dutifully went around greeting people and asking if there were any domestic duties we might perform in return for some food and drink. This occupied us for some time, until a storm arose out of the northern mountains, compelling us to return to our shelter.

The next day proved fair, and about midday, a murmur ran through the crowd that Jesus was returning. While he was still some way off in his boat, the crowds started moving down to the lakeshore, there to greet him, receive his blessing, and perhaps hear more about a place he had called the Kingdom of Heaven. We moved with the crowd, whose murmurs had risen to an excited pitch as Jesus and his companions made their way up from the shore.

The throng parted, and there he was, looking as bedraggled as if he had been outdoors throughout the entire storm of yesterday. He literally shook himself into readiness and climbed aboard an over-turned boat in order to see the multitude, and have them see and hear him. He began his preaching about the Kingdom, The Holy One, and what each of us needed to do to enter into His protection. He was exhorting the crowd to show their fealty to and appreciation of The Almighty Father by treating His creation with all the love and care that He had showed to them.

I was not sure what this meant, as I cannot say it was love that Mary and I had received at the Duck. Looking around, I saw mostly peasants and farmers in the crowd who, like our former travel companions, most likely had just returned from nearby markets. They did not look like The Almighty had showered them with very much of anything either, and what little extra they had probably had gone to the Temple, landlords, or the Romans.

Perhaps sensing their skepticism, Jesus spoke about many of the beautiful things that Adonai had created all around us for our simple pleasures: lilies, birds, gentle rain, and the like. He spoke about the good earth beneath our feet, how it yielded food for our nurturance without our knowing how or why.

"There is plenty for all," he said, "and in thanks for all the blessings we receive, should we not share our blessings with each other? Not only should we love our Lord with all our hearts, but we should love our neighbors as ourselves. What matters love if it does not propel us to feed the hungry and welcome the stranger?"

He reached down from the boat and pulled up what looked like a string of fish that had been smoked and dried. He beckoned to one of his disciples, who brought over what looked like several loaves of bread. "This is what I and my friends have brought with us this day, and it is only right that we share it with you, our new friends and companions on the road of life." He proceeded to break off a piece of fish and a chunk of bread and offered these to those standing in the front rows. They seemed quite hesitant, for it was unlikely that anyone, let alone a stranger or a religious man, had given them anything for free, asking nothing in return.

It was then that Mary surprised me by striding right up to Jesus. Turning to the crowd, she announced in a loud, steady voice, "I have tasted of this abundance and love which Jesus freely shares with those he meets. As he has given to me, let me also give to you." And with that, she added her own store of dried figs and fruit to his supply and began coaxing the nearest listeners to take some nourishment for their needs.

This seemed to awaken the crowd, who could see that this Jesus and his beautiful helpmate were sincere. They slowly began filing past the boat, which soon was piled with vegetables, fruits, nuts, pieces of dried meat, dates, and other kinds of food. The throng just kept coming and coming, and none went away hungry or untouched by this outflowing of generosity. The food on the table kept growing and ebbing, but never seemed to run out. It was a near miracle that these simple folks had heeded his message, as they must have laid down some of their own precious travel food while sharing in what others had left before them.

Jesus had hopped down from the boat in order to be on the same level as the crowd, and he and Mary greeted and blessed each member of the multitude as they passed. Her beauty, as he had assured her, seemed as much a gift to be shared as was the food, and Mary for once seemed entirely comfortable and at peace within herself.

Watching the two of them working so seamlessly together, however, I could feel the snake of jealousy grow within me. I am only human, sisters, for I had given Jesus much of myself at the Pharisee's house and felt responsible for introducing him to Mary in the first place. I must have wanted some of that glory, attention, and, yes, divine love that was so evident between them. But with my newly clean soul, I also knew that I had to kill that jealous snake before she ate all that was precious, godly, and newly alive within me.

It took some time, but by the grace of The Lord above I do feel free of that invasive, cunning beast. Jealousies, like snakes, are part of creation, as are all the emotions—good and bad— that pervade and surround our days. It is not fair or right to hate oneself for being human, as each emotion has its place. Snakes also have a purpose, to kill vermin and be food for other animals in need. Yes, the snake tempted Eve in the Garden of Eden, but then it paid for its sin by forever after eating the dust of the Earth. Even so, it is not right to hate what The Lord has created. The issue is to recognize whatever turns you away from God and your neighbor. Repent, remove the impediments from your soul, and move on. Remove the impediment, but rarely should you take it upon yourself to kill and destroy it. Even having hate in your heart does more damage to you than to whatever is in your way.

And that is preaching enough for one day. Let me rest, sisters, but perhaps I will remember more on the morrow.

IV

Susanna's Second Tale

GOOD DAY, TO YOU sisters, and thanks be to our Father for a blessed night's sleep. I had some worry that my narrative might displease The Almighty, who then could have visited me with frightful dreams. One should not presume to speak for Adonai or about His ministers. It is meet to speak with humility in hopes that the truth of your words finds favor. Of course, every fruitful tree, flower, or garden will have its share of weeds, and it is probably so with any narrative as well. I will try to keep my words clean of such weeds, of petty emotions, distractions, and evasions.

I did end last night with my own jealousy over how easily Mary had allied with Jesus at the feeding of the multitude. I had hungered for his attention, and had caught myself just in time before that snake of jealousy bit me. It was the very next day when Jesus came again to our campsite, and asked both Mary and myself if we wanted to join his personal retinue. He looked at me with full recognition and thanked me again for my service to him. When I was done blushing and stammering out my acceptance of his offer, I had to laugh at myself for being so needy the day before. I have since learned to trust that good things usually come to those who wait.

Mary, of course, readily accepted the invitation as well, and soon we were introduced to all his male and female disciples. There was a woman who followed Jesus who bears some particular mention. She was an attractive, well-dressed young thing named Johanna who was with us for a considerable time before her husband Chuza forced her to return to his household. This husband was steward to the Roman King Herod Antipas, and this no doubt led her to try to put on airs around us. She was initially aloof with us former maidservants and clearly seemed intent on positioning herself as Jesus' favorite. She was full of blandishments and material favors for him, taken no doubt from her husband's treasury. While Jesus welcomed all gifts that would allow us to eat and survive, he paid her the same mind as all his disciples.

It eventually dawned on her that such courtly ambitions and wiles would not work in her favor. We found her crying one day off by herself, and both Mary and I indulged in a quick smile at her distress. We steadied ourselves, however, and approached her with some compassion. We had seen such misguided women oft times before, and indeed had played many of those same games ourselves. Mary knew that she was not the one to comfort Johanna in her suffering, as she was seen by Johanna as her main rival for Jesus' attention. I therefore stepped forward and as gently as possible asked if I could help her in her distress. She struggled to control her tears and feign a control she evidently lacked, but soon my soft voice and tender gaze convinced her to confide in me.

"I do not know what I am doing so wrong that Jesus hates me," she said in a most self-pitying tone. "He only has eyes for that one," she said, glaring at Mary, who thankfully was some distance away, waiting for her cue to enter the drama. "See how Mary gloats at my distress, and does not even deign to look at me," she added. The poor soul then burst into more tears, which were now tinged with anger. These tears and her feeble attempts to wipe them dry ran the kohl and other emoluments from around her eyes, giving her the unfortunate look of a civet.

"There, there, dear," I said, using my most motherly tone. "I have asked Mary to stand watch so that we might have this private moment away from the ever-present eyes of his disciples. I am sure you would not want Jesus to learn of your suffering. You must know by now that there are several among the disciples who do not approve of women being in his retinue, and they would gladly make you appear weak and unfit for his ministry." I offered her my napkin for her tears and streaked face, and this she took as shyly and gratefully as the young girl she actually was.

Once she had composed herself somewhat, I went on. "Please know that being around Jesus can be as painful as it is liberating and joyful. We all have had to shed many of our old ways and fit ourselves to new, like exchanging our robes for shirts made of hair. These tears of yours may be part of that struggle to leave your courtly ways behind and adopt this new soul, as a free woman who is now burdened with the requirement to love and be loved equally."

As she continued to just stare at me, I went on. "What do you make of his saying, "The first shall be last, and the last first?""

Johanna arched her eyebrows and flinched a bit, perhaps fearing that this was some kind of test for which she was ill-prepared. After a polite pause, I went on.

"I believe he no longer wants us to strive to put ourselves ahead of our rivals, or even to have rivals at all. He has already strongly rebuked some of his male disciples for competing to be his favorite. We are not to compare ourselves to each other, to say one is better or worse, as we each have our gifts and limitations. There should be no jealousy to interfere with our loving each other as we love ourselves. Or put another way, compared to The Lord of creation, we are all equally small and our earthly ambitions insignificant.

"The question is, what will you do with this new time and energy you have if you are no longer wasting it on petty rivalries? I believe there is more than enough work to do spreading his gospel, and that is where he wants our efforts."

Johanna had leaned forward to hear what I had to say, then she looked to the heavens as if waiting for a fatherly voice to confirm my words. She sighed deeply, closed her eyes, and went into the gently rocking, inward-looking prayer mode that Jesus had taught to us all. Mary chose this time to join us, and we three sat in a respectful silence for a time.

When Johanna emerged from prayer, she startled slightly at the sight of her rival, then relaxed and smiled. "I am sorry to have treated you so, Mary. Please forgive a young girl her foolish infatuation. This is all so new to me, and I need older sisters like you two to translate what Jesus says into words I understand."

Mary smiled in reply, "You must know, Johanna, that the desire to please and fulfill what men expect or want of us can be a great distraction to us women who seek to form our own friendships. I can only hope that we try to look out for each other in these unsettled but exciting times. Believe me, I have been slow to learn this, and so has Susanna despite all her apparent wisdom."

Here she gave me a teasing glance, which I thankfully received without flinching. It would not do to take offense from a dear friend or undo what had taken so long to build between us. When and where there is love, sisters, there is little need for offense or defense.

Having arrived at this understanding, we gave each other the kiss of peace that Jesus had also taught. I took that moment to retrieve my napkin and to gently daub away the remaining tears and smears that had turned her perfectly formed face into something much less flattering. Perhaps it was my imagination, but she seemed even more beautiful then without her carefully applied make-up. Her lovely childish innocence could shine more brightly without the constricting layers of paint, scent, and lotion she had used until then to attract or even command Jesus' attention. Her face relaxed and lost all traces of the forced smiles, jealous glances, scheming intensity, and bitter resentments that must have consumed her days at court and in Jesus' company.

Ladies, I suspect that we would all love to have her money for such beauty treatments, and there probably is a time and place for such in life. But, simply put, godly and sisterly love, along with forgiveness of one's foolishness, can make all of us more naturally beautiful!

We chatted for a time, exploring our childhoods, travails, and the various paths that had led us to Jesus' side. Johanna, of course, knew nothing of our time in Jerusalem, nor of the salacious rumors that had followed us around that city. She had been almost cloistered in the King's palace, with her main occupation seeming to have been to keep her husband satisfied and guards from cornering her in dark rooms. We questioned her on palace life, but she was initially reluctant to gossip, fearing, I suppose, that Jesus would disapprove of her unkind observations. Nevertheless, we persisted and soon we were all giggling and trading stories like young maidens.

After a pause in the conversation, Johanna looked around for any prying eyes and ears. She leaned closer to Mary and spoke quietly, in a near whisper. "I do believe we shall be lasting friends, and I hope you will forgive my curiosity. I have seen the wonderful, warm, even loving ways that Jesus looks at you and you to him. Have you yet. . . do you think you will. . . has he ever. . ." Her hands fluttered in a kind of helpless pantomime, while her eyes darted all around, lest her imagined audience condemn her. She finally just blurted out, "Oh, do you know what I am getting at without my having to say it?"

Mary gave a delighted laugh, and said, "Yes, I know what you mean, but no, nothing *intimate* has happened between us. However, I must say that I have reasons to believe that he wants to. We have exchanged the usual kisses of peace, and I can feel his lips on my cheek even now. And it is not so strange that you ask, for even I have done so myself. . . to him."

Johanna and I both gasped at that, for I could not believe that Mary had been so bold as to talk to a prophet of The Most High about such sensitive, personal, even base matters. Johanna leaned closer, and with hands held in unconscious prayer, whispered, "Please do go on, Mary, as you must know that every woman who meets him wonders what he is like as a man."

Mary gave a rather serene smile, and looked off into the near distance of her memory. "He smells like any other man who walks the fields and roads, but his eyes up close have a depth and warmth to them that is impossible to exaggerate. I can hear him breathe more heavily when we are together, but I sense that he is careful not to brush against me or look me in the eyes for too long a time. For my part, I am careful not to sway my hips, soften my voice, or do any of those little gestures that all men are able to read, but not resist. Having finally felt free from my own past, I do not want to impinge on or bend his freedom to my will, although Lord knows I have been sorely tempted!"

To that, both Johanna and I gave our own knowing but guilty glances. Both of us had evidently thought the same and probably had gone so far as to plan our approach. Mary laughed at the faces we made as these thoughts escaped us.

"Do not rebuke yourselves for being the women you are, for these wishes are surely natural and shared by any woman with a pulse! Even last night, as Jesus and I walked by the seashore, I was swept away by the moonlight and lost a bit of my own resolve. I came right out and asked him what our future together might be. His face was in some shadow, but his voice remained steady and warm.

'Mary, you are dear to me in many ways, and I have delighted in your company. I have been with women in my younger days and know enough about myself to believe that you and I could fall in love and have a life together.'

Both Johanna and I gasped aloud, and instinctively clutched each other in girlish shock, mingled with the excited anticipation that accompanies being on the verge of one's deepest secrets. We barely heard Mary say, "Let me tell you, I nearly crumbled at that admission, but some inner strength allowed me to bide my time and hold my tongue. Jesus' quiet voice went on, now seeming to float out from the evening gloom.

'You must know, Mary, that I have been put on a path that requires me to give and not take, to be someone for all people and not one woman's special man. I have come to proclaim My Father's love for all creation, but I dare not divide that love into something private for myself and above all that I give to others. I also do not want you to be an object of other's resentment and jealousy, nor do I want to tempt you to protect, possess, exalt, or defend me. I can have no intermediary between My Father and myself, nor between myself and my followers. It grieves me to say this so bluntly, but I believe you already understand.'

"And I did, and I do somehow. I respect his great self-control and commitment to his calling, which is certainly bigger than my personal desires and wishes. I would not want to deflect or distract him from doing his Father's will. I could not live with myself if he abandoned all that he had done just to be with me."

Mary released a sigh that seemed to carry all the thwarted longing in her soul. Johanna and I could both sense how much this understanding of hers had cost her. I had never been close to possessing anything or anyone near as precious as Jesus was to her, and could only imagine the depth and intensity of her struggle. Yet here she was clear-eyed and more wistful than grieving. I stood in awe of how that same shattered shell of a woman had healed so completely in body, mind, and spirit. She now seemed to have her own well-spring of love and life-giving confidence. She was a woman in bloom who seemed capable of surviving any disappointment or loss. The Magdalene was to keep this intense confidence and self-possession all the time that I knew her.

I do want to relate one additional story from our time with Jesus and his disciples. There was considerable tension between us women and the men, as I said before. At first, we women were not even called disciples, as that title was reserved for the men who had followed him from the beginning. Some thought we had no place in the Kingdom except as bearers of children and as their own personal handmaidens. There were also more than a few veiled comments about Mary and my so-called sordid pasts; these hovered in that foggy realm between condemnation and come-on. Many of the men had come from observant households where sexuality was closely monitored, if not outright feared. There were more than enough stories in the Torah to make men leery of the female species: Samson lost his hair and virility because of Delilah. Salome had bewitched King David with her alluring hair and dance. More recently, John had lost his head.

A few of the country boys seemed more at ease with us, but that created its own tension. The situation was not helped by Johanna's youth, as the poor girl could not help but flirt and seek male approval, all despite our recent talk. I could see that old habits died hard, unless one were already broken, as was Mary before she met Jesus.

This tension boiled over one surprisingly rainy day, when circumstances required all of us to squeeze into the common room of an inn that had been reserved for us by one of Jesus' sponsors, a man named Joseph from Arimathea. As you know, it has always been the custom for women to be separated from the men during services, and so it was with us. But on this occasion, we were forced into close proximity, with latecomers having to sit wherever they could find a spot. I suppose any change is unsettling, but the mood was made more uncomfortable by the humid, sweltering air and the dampness of our clothing. Many of the men had loosened their robes, and soon after that, we women joined them by removing our headscarves. More than a few of us also removed our wet shawls.

Mary had removed scarf and shawl, and was unconsciously loosening her beautiful hair to aid its drying. All conversation stopped as the men stared, and I believe it was Judas of Iscariot who was the first to protest to Jesus that such behavior had to stop or the women made to leave. This brought hoots of protest from some of the country boys who much enjoyed the show, while some of the sterner disciples leapt to their feet, pointing rudely at Mary and the rest of us women while calling us vile names.

Jesus let this commotion continue for a time, perhaps to let all the pent-up frustration and disapproval run its course. It showed no sign of stopping, however, as we women also joined the fray, defending Mary and calling her defamers several unmanly names we keep in reserve for such occasions. Judas pretended to be mortally offended and made to approach Mary, who leapt to her feet, faced him, and clenched her fists in preparation. Simon Peter had to grab Judas by the scruff of his robe, nearing stripping him in the process, while Simon's brother awkwardly restrained Mary, being loath to touch her bare skin. Several similar confrontations erupted throughout the room, but Jesus seemed merely to take note of who was allied with whom and who remained neutral.

His silence gradually began to weigh on us. Perhaps we were waiting for a sharp rebuke, and when it did not come, some became curious, while others were merely confused. Soon enough, we stopped our accusations and threats, and many started to shift nervously on their feet, awaiting his judgment.

"Well, that was interesting," Jesus finally said to nervous laughter. "I can see that I have not yet written on your hearts that women are equally children of The Father. Did not the rain today fall on man and woman alike? Should not the women here have been able to be as comfortable as the men? Can they not be themselves without you men howling that they should be just as you declare? Yes, yes, do not protest, for it should be obvious to all that man requires a woman even to be born, and woman requires a man to have children. In all of creation, there are male and female of the species. Our Father in Heaven has made it so and thus it always will be. There is a purpose behind His design, and it should be for Him to determine and proscribe, not mankind.

"You may say that Eve came from Adam's rib and thus is secondary to man. As I have said so many times, what is first and second to The Lord of all creation? Do you imagine that He has fingers to count? Others may say that it is custom and habit that women should be chaste, modest, and covered at all times, lest she entice men into sin. Even this day, we saw how the mere sight of Mary's hair inflamed those men of a certain nature."

Here Jesus paused to hear protests, but none dared speak. "I say, let the men douse their own flame, for they are the ones who surely set the fire in the first place."

Now there was grumbling from some of the men, and it was Judas again who rose to speak for his contingent. "Master, we who protested certainly did so out of respect for your own chaste and proper nature, you who have eschewed the intimate company of women. It is meet and right that we who hope to follow in your footsteps do the same, and that any stumbling blocks on this path be removed."

From my seat only paces away I could detect a rather pleased, even smug smile escaping from the corners of Judas' mouth. How smoothly had he moved to deflect responsibility and adorn himself with feigned emulation of Jesus' celibate nature. Several of his like-minded friends rallied to his words, adding their own calls for a return to strict separation of women from the men.

Alas and sadly, none of the men who had leapt to our physical defense spoke up against this rather well-worn stricture. All kohanim, rebbes and other religious authorities were men; women worshipped separately and usually behind a screen lest the men be distracted from their devotions. There were countless restrictions in *Halakha*[1] governing the relations between men and women, few of which favored women, at least in my opinion. None of our new defenders were prepared to offer an alternate vision that might defy the thousand years of our tradition. Jesus himself must have known to tread carefully once Judas' followers invoked *Halakha*. More than once he seemed to glance our way as if to convey his own helplessness in the face of such orthodoxy. I could feel my newly won freedoms slipping away as the cold, confining walls of tradition closed in.

The Judas faction would have continued their indignant posturing if Jesus had not started rocking and even moaning in prayer. Even Judas knew to stop his protestations.

"My Father in Heaven surely loves His daughters as well as His sons," Jesus said at last, his voice rising into something like irritation. "Our squabbles are like that in any family between siblings who fight for the love and attention of their parents. Rather than fight, however, we are called to love and to make the earth abundant and fruitful. It is only women who bring forth life, who largely tend our gardens, who make our feasts joyful with their preparation and service. There should be honor enough in all our hearts for our brothers *and* our sisters, our fathers *and* our mothers. Why it is not so in our laws and customs is not for me to say, but, my brethren, we who are gathered here are trying to discern and follow The Holy One's laws, with due respect for those of man."

Here he paused and looked at each of those he had identified as allies of Judas. "As for the matter of intimate relations within this assembly, know that my path is not necessarily your path, although you do me honor to accompany me on my journey. I bear the yoke of celibacy so that I show no

---

1. The collection of Jewish laws and jurisprudence, following the Talmud.

partiality in the love that I give as gifts from My Father in Heaven. Some of you may be called to bear this yoke, while others may be called to engender and provide for children, who indeed are a blessing from The Lord. And some of you may be called to be as the eunuchs, a womanly nature in a man's body. This calling may be from birth, or through your experiences and travails on this road of life. Whatever the source, it is not for you to declare what others should or should not do, for in this you are to listen to what Our Father intends for you alone."

Looking around our small circle of women, I could see tears welling in thankfulness that Jesus had not abandoned us to our low estate. However, we dared not show any other emotion lest it reawaken the newly subdued beasts that lay in many of the men's hearts. If they felt chastened or even liberated from the strictures of the past I could not tell, as no man spoke in rebuttal and no hosannas were heard. For generations untold, our men had felt uniquely responsible for keeping and honoring the covenant between Israel and The Holy One, with all its many laws and rituals. This covenant bound them as severely as we women felt ourselves to be bound, but instead of making us sympathetic to each other, history or mere habit had decreed that we women were only slightly better than house slaves. Certainly, female modesty and service were virtues to be emulated and honored, but, to quote Jesus, perhaps we were to await our individual calling to these command-ments rather than have them foisted on us by mere mortal men.

I must admit, the very idea of equality with men was both exciting and daunting. It was like looking at an alien but bountiful land that lay just out of reach. How would we even talk to each other? Would each of us have to quickly pray to our Lord every time an issue of primacy, control, or ben-efit arose? Would decisions come down to who was strongest, or richest, or most needy? How could we even determine such things? We have been told all our lives to follow what the religious authorities, or the kings, or our husbands and fathers say; who would have authority in a land of equals? I could sense a dark chaos wherever I looked in this landscape of equality, despite the beauty of the concept. Instinctively, I knew that all of us women needed to cleave to Jesus' side if we were to be guided through this new but dangerous territory.

I also had learned which disciples to avoid and which to approach, in hopes that the latter would be more sympathetic to Jesus' vision of equality before The Lord. Simon Peter and his brother Andrew were some of the country boys who clearly delighted in the company of women. They had come to our defense this day, and I resolved to deepen our friendship in hopes of discovering how this idea of equality would play out. But perhaps that is a story for another day.

What more can I say about the Magdalene? She was there that cruel day of his crucifixion and for his glorious resurrection. I cannot give testimony to what she saw, said, or heard, as I was ill with a deathly fever that almost brought me to Heaven's gate at the same time Jesus was to arrive. She told me once I recovered that he looked like death itself when he rose from the dead, and that he needed weeks before he was filled with life once more. She was with him when he appeared to several of his disciples, but she mostly just tended to his wounds, gave sustenance, and enforced rest on him in the face of the many demands to explain what had happened.

Despite being much depleted by his ordeal on the cross, he did tell the brethren that he thought he was to be a sacrifice to atone for the sins of mankind, but this did not make sense to me. He had already opposed the Temple authorities for demanding sacrifices, saying that his Father was not pleased by them. Mary simply believed that Adonai was cruel to Jesus, as if he were some Job used in God's eternal battle with the Evil One. She was angry at Him for several years, but did not waver in her commitment to Jesus' message and mission. She surely was in love with him and this may have fueled her anger over his pain and suffering. The Father in His mercy did not punish her for her wrath, and it gradually faded as more pressing problems presented themselves.

After Jesus' ascension, the other disciples more or less ignored her and me both, although, to be fair, all were being persecuted and had to look out for themselves. We travelled with Simon Peter for a time, but lacked a sponsor to pay for us to accompany him to Rome and the other outlying provinces of the empire. It was becoming increasingly dangerous to declare ourselves Nazarenes. We spoke of equality, love, and forgiveness with all the women we met, but were careful not to mention Jesus by name unless we were sure of our reception.

I cannot tell you ladies how fraught it has been to be filled with joy and fear all at the same time. It is a wonder we did not go mad. We heard no stories that any of our martyred brethren had risen from the dead as Jesus had, yet many of them had gone to their reward with a smile on their lips. I hope to be as brave, sisters, although I do pray not to be put to the test.

Mary and I finally separated soon after Simon Peter left for Rome. She decided to continue with another of the disciples, a man named John who had been particularly close to Jesus. This John initially had been a bit jealous, I believe, of the attention Jesus showed Mary, but they had resolved their sibling issues, as it were. They recognized their common love for him, and by traveling and preaching together, perhaps they hoped to keep him alive in their hearts. Just by seeing their excited reminiscing, joint laughter, and ease with one another, I knew that I had to leave their company. We had many a tear at our farewell, along with prayers that Jesus' spirit of love would stay with us for all of our days.

In the years since, I heard various stories about how she had fared, with some saying she had been abandoned in a cave in far-off Gaul, while others said she had married this John and kept house for him while he evangelized. Whatever befell her, I hope she has truly reconciled with the Father and continues in His favor.

I myself have walked lonelier roads, sisters, one of which has brought me here. I am on my way to a community east of Damascus that was founded by followers of the John called the Baptist. These were the ones who had baptized me years ago and cleansed my soul of my former, sinful ways. They have a powerful new preacher there also by the name of John, who is one of their ruling elders. I go in hopes that my faith will be refreshed; perhaps I will find kindred spirits with whom to share my remaining days. I have been too long among the wolves of this world and, by the grace of The Lord, have survived. I now seek the sheep who live in the peaceful valley of love.

I thank you, sisters, for your welcome and the care you have given out of the goodness of your heart. Know that there is great freedom of spirit to be had from the words of Jesus and his disciples, even if that freedom must be kept close to your bosom, where no man can touch or steal it.

V

The Gospel of Benjamin

MY FELLOW DISCIPLE JUDAS of Iscariot has urged me to write down some thoughts on the events surrounding the rebbe we both follow, Jesus of Nazareth. Why he asked me, the least and youngest of the Disciples, I dare not ask him, as he is not someone to upset. His is a delicate nature formed from intense study of Torah and Mishnah.[1] The finest points of Midrash[2] are not beyond him, and his voice has often been heard within the Fellowship refining points of difference between us and the *goyim*[3] who surround us.

Judas studied for a time with a noted rebbe from the *Beit HaMikdash*[4], but I believe he became somewhat disillusioned about his lack of

1. Oral history of religious stories and sayings, forming first part of Torah.
2. Rabbinic commentary on Torah and other scriptures, held to be of nearly equal worth.
3. Non-Jewish inhabitants of Israel.
4. The High Holy Temple, most sacred site in Israel.

advancement within the Temple hierarchy. It is often thus, in my opinion, that a brilliant mind such as his can glare too brightly for those grown too comfortable with their own dim knowledge. His great scholarship has been a blessing to me, and I am honored to be considered worthy of his trust.

It was he who first recognized that Jesus indeed may be a prophet of Adonai. It was he who saw the parallels between Jesus and Isaiah, he who saw the value of recording the wonderful deeds of healing and the prophetic words that flow from Jesus' every utterance.

"I shall content myself with drinking in his every word," Judas told me, "while you, my worthy scribe, shall be as a mirror to record all we do."

Judas then provided me with parchment, stylus and inks, as I had none of my own. From that moment on, I have stood back somewhat and observed, while my dear friend and mentor Judas cleaves to Jesus' side, the better to drink in his words I guess.

Oh, there have been so many examples of wonder, of the power of The Most Holy at work in this very generation! It has been Judas again who correctly understands how uniquely important it is to be a witness ready with pen and ink.

"We shall be the first to truly describe a prophet at work," said Judas. "All stories of the prophets of old relied on the fading memories of the elders, and that of those they told. Only the simplest and broadest outline of events survived enough to be included in Torah and Mishnah. There was scant mention of all the other actors in the drama, of their words and contributions. You will do us disciples honor and be the first to describe Jesus' deeds of glory, for all generations to read and remember."

Oh, that such as I from the nearly lost tribe of Benjamin could be included in Torah! I shiver with trepidation at such a prospect, for as much as I fear displeasing Judas, I am more fearful by far of displeasing The Lord.

This job has been harder than it looked at first. I sit here while Jesus goes up into the hills above Gadara on some errand or other. I am most upset to have nearly lost all my parchments during a fierce storm on the boat ride over. I hesitate to say, but my mentor Judas was absolutely no help to me as the boat we were in started to swamp. He mostly screamed and prayed while the Zebedee brothers furiously bailed and Thomas handled both sail and steering oar. My case with all my completed parchments washed right out of the boat when a great wave hit us, and Thomas would not turn around to help me retrieve it.

When we finally reached the shore, Judas then had the gall to rebuke me for the loss, as if I was to throw myself overboard and pray that Adonai would bring me safe to shore! Perhaps Jesus and Judas are right that I lack sufficient faith to do such daring and risky acts, but I am a scribe and not a prophet! I almost told Judas that I did not want to put The Lord to the test, as Jesus himself once preached, but he would have only drowned my puny excuse in twenty other scriptures.

I did find my case later in the day when it washed ashore, but by then the parchments were a sodden mess, with ink having run away with the waves. I offered to rewrite my lost pages from memory, but Judas just scoffed, saying that I would then be no better than the elders of old. He complained about the cost of replacing the ruined parchment and inks, but he among all of us disciples seems to have money when he needs it. Sure enough, he somehow procured new supplies while we awaited Jesus' return, and I am back in business!

But I am still a little confused about what that business is and exactly how to do it. For example, I did not know what to make of Jesus when he eventually returned from his adventure. He said only that he helped a man regain his senses. The excited villagers who accompanied him to our camp told quite a different story, however, of how he had driven demons out of a wild barbarian and forced the unclean spirits into a herd of pigs, who are unclean to begin with, as everyone knows. Certainly, unclean spirits seek out each other, while the good and divine spirits seek out their own. These villagers were not entirely clean themselves, but that is another story.

Judas, in contrast, makes much of keeping himself ritually clean, and urges all of us to attract divine favor by doing the same. He asked me to get out my writing implements and said, "We are a chosen people whom The Lord Most High has separated from the unclean. Why Jesus consorts with the unclean is beyond me, although perhaps it is to drive out their unworthiness so they can be more like us." I have a collection of similar brilliant sayings of his somewhere, but I will need time to locate and organize them.

Anyway, who was I to believe and what should I write down about this encounter with a madman?? I talked with several of the villagers who claimed to be eyewitnesses, but each had their own story. While they all agreed that this barbarian had tormented them for years, by stealing their sheep and scaring their shepherd boys, none could say where the pigs came from or what Jesus actually said to the mad man. One man thought that Jesus had waved his hands in a special way, casting a spell over the man and compelling the demons to enter the pigs. Another said that Jesus spoke an unknown tongue with the man, perhaps a language known only to G-d, but his neighbor laughed and said that it was just Greek. Another said that Jesus walked arm in arm with the man as if they were old friends, and wondered perhaps if the mad man was kin or someone known to Jesus from before.

Another opined that the man was a Nubian, another that he was merely filthy from his years living wild.

I had believed Judas' insight that direct witness was required to keep wild speculations from growing into perceived truth. But now the thought hit me that each of these simple villagers had thought themselves direct witnesses, yet each came away with a different story. Like the Talmud stories of old, these tales might now spread in all kinds of directions. I was right back into my confusion over who to believe, and what to record.

I have endeavored since then to be as faithful a witness as possible, hoping that my advanced education (for I can read and write) makes me more reliable than those uncouth villagers. I have tried to write down events almost as soon as they happened, to prevent time from eroding my memory. Let me relate what I think happened soon after all of us lodged at a believer's abode in Capernaum. Judas and the Zebedee boys had been arguing on the long trek to this house over who might be the greatest amongst all of us disciples. Judas of course thought that he was due to his great learning and obedience to the laws of our ancestors, while John felt that he was most like Jesus in piety and adherence to his precepts. James thought he was the strongest and most zealous in defense of the poor.

After we settled into our lodging, Jesus drew us to him and asked what we had been arguing about. I was about to speak up for once, having listened carefully to the three others in hopes of recording some useful formulation that would help me understand what it takes to be great. One look at Judas, however, discouraged me from speaking. Jesus already seemed to know, however, and then gave one of his confusing speeches about the first being last, and the ruler being instead a servant. I cannot imagine Judas, for instance, being a servant, as he spends most time studying Torah and supervising our meals and food purchases. He makes a point of keeping his hands clean, and usually cannot be found when labor is required. I am saddened, therefore, to think that he will not be able to achieve the leadership he so richly deserves, if what Jesus said about servanthood is indeed ordained by his Father in Heaven.

I hope I am not being unkind or ungrateful to Judas by mentioning that he asked that I remove his name from this last incident when I write up my final gospel. He did this a few more times, once when some unruly children in one of the houses we visited broke through the circle that usually surrounded Jesus. I supposed they wanted to see this man about whom so much had been said, but Judas rebuked them for daring to intrude on adult matters, or maybe just for their bad manners.

He and I were both surprised when Jesus turned and rebuked *him* for rebuking them. Jesus said that anyone who welcomed children welcomed him, and that it was necessary to be as children if we hoped to inherit the Kingdom of Heaven. I knew that Jesus had a soft spot for children, not having had any of his own, but I did not understand why we disciples should act childish in order to get to Heaven.

Judas seemed a bit upset to be rebuked, not being used to it, I guess, but he patiently explained to me that Jesus must have meant that one had to be sinless and uncorrupted by the world in order to ascend to the throne of Heaven. As I said, Judas had a particular focus on cleanliness, propriety, and obedience, all of which he felt were required in order to separate us from lesser folks. These children showed none of the virtues Judas prized, yet here was Jesus praising them and rebuking him.

"Perhaps it would be best to remove my name from this little set-to until I understand it more fully," he told me, nodding gravely and reaching for the Torah scroll to immediately gain further insight. I let the matter go and again marveled at his desire to understand the truth of Jesus' every utterance.

But then it happened two more times, once when the disciples and our camp followers were on our way to Jericho to preach to the people. The Zebedee brothers, having been chastened for trying to be greatest among the disciples, had shifted to asking Jesus to let them sit at his left and right hand in Heaven. Jesus had rightly rebuked them, and Judas had been listening intently lest the brothers indict him as another disciple who also wanted to be granted an exalted position. He then began talking to Jesus about some fine points of lineage, kingship, and the ranking of angels in Heaven when some blind beggar on the road kept interrupting. "Have mercy on me, Son of David," the man repeatedly cried, until Judas finally lost his temper.

"Can you not see that The Master and I are talking? We are discussing the Kingdom and you would bring our attention down to you, a lowly creature of the road?"

Jesus had rebuked Judas for his intemperance, and the Zebedee brothers had seized the opportunity to redeem themselves by inviting the blind man to approach. The man threw off his mantle and ran straight to where Jesus was standing, despite his alleged blindness. It was a bit suspicious, if you asked me. I am beginning to agree with Judas that something is peculiar about all the people that Jesus seems able to cure.

Despite his hurt feelings about being rebuked in front of his fellow disciples, however, Judas retained his dignity and modesty.

"Please remove my name from this as well, Benjamin, as your focus should be on Jesus and his marvelous works. As he has said, we disciples are mere servants; this gospel should not be about us. Perhaps you can mention the beggar by name, as this will please his kin who then might be well-disposed towards us." A good and forward-thinking man, that Judas.

I mention a similar incident when a sick woman intruded into our Sabbath discussion and prayer, right in front of some important Pharisees who Judas had hoped would bless our cause. Judas told me later that he was most upset that Jesus healed her right then and there.

"I cannot believe that someone chosen by Adonai himself would violate the Sabbath like that. He is supposed to set an example for the rest of us, but instead he is showing off his so-called healing abilities. Oh, he had his reasons and quoted some scripture, but if you could have seen the look on those Pharisees' faces, you would know that we have lost our chance at some important allies."

Judas then did his best to mollify the Pharisees, pointing out Jesus' kindly but impulsive nature. When this did not remove the look of horror and condemnation from their faces, I thought I heard him say that Jesus had been drinking heavily lately due to his many preaching and healing responsibilities.

When he saw that I was close enough to hear him, he drew me aside, and again asked me to remove any mention of his presence at the entire scene. Looking most bereft, he added, "I am aggrieved, Benjamin, and scared for the future of our mission. The less I am reminded of this, the better."

As an aside to anyone reading this, I must ask forgiveness for my inability to be a proper, or at least fully honest scribe. I have wanted to be an accurate witness, but I learned from that episode in Gadara that each witness sees events in their own way and with their own perforce limited access to the full story. Even when I have been a direct witness to events, I have not been allowed to use the names of all the other participants who might vouch for the accuracy of my notes. Is it kindness or cowardice that has me erasing Judas' name from what might be important moments in the religious history of our people? He is my sponsor and a man I once greatly admired, but lately I have wondered if I am but a tool in his employ. The more time I have spent as a disciple, the more I see where love, mercy, and servanthood pave the way to the Kingdom of G-d. I suspect that Judas may be more interested in gaining the earthly rewards offered by the Pharisees, having given up on the ambition to be Jesus' most prized student and acolyte.

I prayed on all these matters, and some things that Jesus said came to me in answer. He had rebuked Simon Peter—he who has been like a rock throughout our travails—for seeming to put his heart and mind on earthly concerns and not heavenly ones. He also said another time that he spoke differently with us disciples than to the great masses of those simple but trusting folks who follow us.

I put these two ideas together and decided to keep separate journals, one 'official' and the other with my own personal reflections. The official journal will serve the needs of the men around me, while my own thoughts shall be known only to The Lord and to those whom He may appoint to read them after I am gone. If I be a mirror, I may be clouded and even cracked, but at least I will strive to be truthful before The Father. If I take Judas' money and patronage, bowing to his requests and nodding to his pronouncements, that amended report will serve my earthly needs. I lack my own money for supplies and have a practical desire to remain on Judas' good side. If I use the parchments and inks to bear witness to what Jesus and the various named disciples and others actually say and do, that will serve my heavenly aspirations. May The Holy One forgive any duplicity, but it is Jesus and his Father who are my masters, not Judas.

This decision has led to a most unexpected and strange transformation, but one that has given me much inner peace and even a kind of certainty. Once I decided whom I served, I lost most of the fear, timidity, and vain desire for acceptance that had dogged my days. I no longer have to describe all the nuances, drama, conflicting accounts, and possible interpretations that surround Jesus. I now just know in my heart that he is an agent of The Lord Most High, and that all he says and does is designed to prepare us body and soul for Heaven. It is a knowledge beyond words, although words, images, and parables do help us understand what is asked of us.

My official accounts—those read and screened by Judas, that is—have been getting shorter and shorter, but with a greater emphasis on the exact words Jesus uses. If I adhere to verbatim wording, hopefully there will be less chance of human interpretation, bias, and doubt. In this, I hope the mirror is as clean and unbroken as possible.

My personal reflections, however, grow ever more complex and cloudy, as there are dark forces swirling around us. There have always been tensions amongst the disciples, and most recently they broke out on a damp, dreary day between some of the men and the women. Judas, as usual, was in the thick of it, representing shall I say the more pietistic, ascetic faction. He has grown fond of quoting Jeremiah and complains that the Pharisees and Sadducees are too accommodating to the Romans and too loose in their Midrash interpretations. He wants to return to the strict separation of men from women, as first articulated by the ancients. He generally views women as unclean, messy in their emotions, physically weak, and altogether too forgiving of transgression. I believe he had hoped that Jesus was some kind of prophetic voice for the scourging and purification of our religion, a mighty task for which the "softer" sex was ill-suited.

On this day of conflict, Judas was rebuked again, although fairly gently in my opinion. It must have galled him when Jesus proposed that sexuality be a matter of personal conscience and discovery, rather than something determined by the dictates of a supreme religious authority.

It occurs to me as I write this that there may be something of a pharaoh still lingering in Judas' mind and soul. He seems to want a supreme god-like figure at the head of a religion where all laws and habits fit like finely-cut blocks of stone into a giant, coherent edifice. He had been prepared to worship Jesus as this god-like figure, for whom he would shape himself into precise, controlled habits out of piety and obedience. He would then be snugged within a level of similarly controlled believers—in his case, in one of the top tiers of the pyramid. The world would be orderly, everyone would know his (and her) place, and the entire construction would be monumental, solid, unmovable, and visible from afar. The edifice would also house the dead.

It is a pity that he chose the wrong prophet to follow! This Jesus is not a creature of stone, but of water, of nurturance, of the very stuff that sustains life. He comes not to build up to the heavens, but to bring The Heavenly Father down to the humblest soul. This is what I believe Jesus is getting at when he brings in children as exemplars of those worthy to enter the Kingdom. He wants all people to realize that The Holy Father knows them by name, as did their own fathers. He wants even the humblest to talk to The Father and listen to what He wants of them. Judas and his ilk would have their god be fierce, remote, appeasable only by piety and sacrifice, and reachable only through the efforts of specially ordained priests (like himself). These two visions cannot live side by side or near each other without a great war erupting.

I can see a change in Judas as he perhaps senses these same fatal differences. He no longer jests, although truth to say he was almost always sober and serious. He has stopped dropping by for casual conversation, and has stopped caring what I write except to have me no longer write his name in any account. He complains that he is running out of money and can no longer afford to supply me with parchments and ink. He now talks in low voices with the few other disciples who supported him against the women, and grows silent when either women or the other disciples pass by. He spends long hours in a kind of tense prayer that involves binding his arms and thighs with rough cords, tightening them until he nearly cries in pain. He is doing something below the surface that smells of rebellion and betrayal.

And what is my responsibility now that I have had these observations and images fly through my brain? The timid part of me has shrunk considerably, but still has a voice in the assembly of my mind. It urges me to do nothing, but to keep both sides of this divide happy with my work and devotion. "Do not be a casualty in the war to come," it seems to say. "At least wait until it is clear how the sides form and who seems to have the stronger position."

I tell that little voice that I cannot unsee what I have seen, or unthink what I know in my heart of hearts. I tell myself to have more faith, that love and The Holy Father's favor are with those of us who truly follow Jesus with all our hearts.

The timid voice grows bold to say, "What is love against the evil that is in the world and in man?" I tell that voice that we shall soon see, for I serve The Lord of Love and will go into battle for His sake, whatever the odds and whatever befalls.

With my heightened alertness to danger, I could almost see storm clouds gathering over the brethren as we approached Jerusalem for Passover. Jesus continued to defy expectation by entering Jerusalem on the back of a donkey, rather than a war elephant or horse. He dared to trash the moneychangers and has brought condemnation down upon both Pharisees and Sadducees alike. He is almost in a fever of preaching, going in and out of Jerusalem and staying at various houses of men who are sympathetic to his prophetic voice. I have not found him alone to tell him of my terrible forebodings, and yet I dare not show my worries on my face lest Judas remark on them and question my loyalties.

I could not help but notice that Judas did not partake in the cleansing of the Temple, claiming to have had family business to attend to. Two days before Passover, he again claimed family matters and left our inn. Seeing him depart, on instinct I told the brethren that I needed to refresh my writing supplies. I followed at a safe distance, my long-established timidity coming to my aid. I knew how to shrink myself and pass unnoticed through the throngs of last-minute shoppers, soldiers, and Temple personnel. I had some vague sense that Judas might try to contact those at the *Beit HaMikdash* whom he knew from before, or, even worse, he might make for the Roman praetorium. At the central square, I could just make out his haughty stride as he veered towards the Temple.

I had been within earshot when both the Pharisees and Sadducees had questioned Jesus, and could hear the note of falsehood in their supposed concerns. The Pharisees had asked about paying tribute to the Romans, about which they should not have cared, and the Sadducees in their turn had asked clarification of an obscure matter of resurrection, they who did not believe in it. Jesus had deftly parried all their questions and had turned the tables on them, accusing them of being hypocrites and worse. This was among the harshest I had heard from him, and showed that he had not fully expelled the spirit of indignant anger that had led to the cleansing of the Temple. It did not sound as though he was preaching to convert, but to punish and bring The Father's wrath down upon them. They had left his company muttering darkly, with fists clenched and eyes on fire. Judas had no business going into that angry Temple wasp's nest unless he already believed himself to be a kindred spirit.

I needed to confirm my suspicions without bringing the same anger back on myself. I assumed the proper posture and actions of a penitent, and had but a little difficulty entering the Temple grounds. The guards were nervous and rough with the throngs entering the *Beit*, as if fearing further attacks by the Nazarenes. I also acted frightened when I should be frightened, and indignant when others around me were. In this way, I mingled with the worshippers and it was not long before I spied Judas speaking to some of the very kohenim who had questioned Jesus.

It is a curious thing, but scribes and spies both have heightened senses that seem to arise within them without conscious thought. Just as I could hear a particular conversation from across a crowded room, the better to record accurately, so I could just look at the faces surrounding Judas and read their intent.

I arrived just as the kohenim were venting some kind of frustration at him, perhaps thinking him allied with their adversary, Jesus. Judas had adopted something like a penitent posture, almost lowering his head in shame. He began speaking in a low voice I could not hear; this seemed to startle the others, for they abruptly stopped their harangue. Hungry, avid looks came into several of their faces, for it seemed Judas was delivering something tasty and unexpected for them to consider. Much excited speech followed, with the kohenim talking rapidly with each other and smiling at Judas, like a rebbe to a prized student. Above the prayers and murmurs of the worshippers, I thought I heard one of the kohenim say, "You would do this for us?"

Judas was no longer hanging his head, but seemed to be looking them all right in their eyes, speaking to each in turn. I heard snatches of his speech, including, "false prophet," "threat to . . . authority," and "No Son of . . . "

The kohenim began nodding their heads in agreement; they soon drew closer to Judas and lowered their voices below what I could discern. My spying was over. I made one fervent prayer to Jesus' Father in Heaven to protect him against the evil of such men, and made my way with solemnity but some speed out of the *Beit*.

I really cannot say I was shocked or surprised by Judas' actions. I had sensed his disaffection ever since the incident with the wet women disciples. Looking back, I could almost count the number of times he had questioned Jesus' interpretation of scripture and his choice of those whom he favored. His tendency to scold the children, women, lame, and poor had led to numerous gentle rebukes from the Master. Judas had only appeared to be humble and of service, believing that that was what Jesus wanted. What Judas really wanted was to advance in this world, and he had clearly decided to change his allegiance.

Many of the Master's sayings sprang into my thoughts as I worked my way back to where the disciples and Jesus were staying. I did not think this a time to turn the other cheek, nor could we take up the sword against the combined might of Jerusalem without bringing death onto ourselves and on our largely unarmed and defenseless followers. It is not enough to love our neighbors as ourselves if that neighbor wants our death. It occurred to me that even Jesus could not prescribe how to behave in every instance; he was human after all. He had been talking during our trek to Jerusalem about the Son of Man having no home in this world, and about how generation after generation had spurned and even killed those prophets sent by Adonai. That possibility had certainly been on his mind the larger his following grew, but he had still hoped to move the hearts and souls of those in power. Even as my own heart ached with the thought of his coming confrontation, I was fairly certain that he already sensed the outcome.

And so he had. When I finally reached the house, I sought him out, while all around me our women helpers made preparations for our meal. I found him on the roof, and waited while he finished his prayers. He finally looked up at me, and perhaps he was a bit surprised that I, almost the least vocal and most unobtrusive of disciples, should be seeking a personal audience. I thought for a second that I might have to dig deeply for courage, but found that his eyes were gently fixed on mine. He seemed to be welcoming me as an old friend, and I accepted the invitation.

"Master," I said, "it is as you feared, for one of us has betrayed you to the very kohenim who treated you so poorly this week. Some foreboding compelled me to follow him to the *Beit HaMikdash* this afternoon, where he did shameful business with them. I shall never forget their look of almost bestial anticipation, like lions licking their lips while stalking a lamb. Judas was a mentor and even a friend to me, but his heart has closed against you and all you stand for. Tell me what you wish of me and all those who love you, for no one should face their trial alone."

This was the most I had ever spoken with Jesus in all our time together, and I stood there in a kind of stunned amazement that I had even spoken coherently. He gave me a look I had never quite seen before; if I had to put words to it, I saw warmth and love mixed with an edge of fear and some kind of steely determination.

He then gave out a sigh, and said simply, "I know. Thank you, dear and brave Benjamin, for confirming what I have been suspecting."

He may have wanted to say more, but a call came up to us that the meal was ready to be served. He slowly got to his feet, and shook himself, almost like a wet dog after a storm. He gestured for me to precede him down the ladder to the upper room where we were assembled. Looking back, I thought I saw him wipe a tear from his eye, but it could have been dust.

Coming down into the room, I had only a brief time to resume my guise as a simple scribe and quiet disciple, for there was Judas close to the head of the table. He was talking amiably enough with John and barely looked at me as I passed him. I assumed my normal place at the opposite end, and waited for Jesus to take his seat. He always eschewed pillows and any kind of platform that might elevate him above his friends, and this evening he reinforced this notion by sitting in the middle, amongst his friends and angled so that he would not have to see Judas off to his left side. After a brief prayer to thank His Father for another day, Jesus wasted no time in venting what was building up inside him. He startled the disciples by announcing that one of us would betray him, as was foretold in scripture.

"Woe betide he who betrays the Son of Man," he added, again not looking directly at Judas but clearly warning him of awful condemnation to come. After a shocked silence, many of us, perhaps fearing we had inadvertently uttered something incriminating in the market or to an acquaintance, started asking, "Is it I, Lord?"

Judas made sure to raise the same question amongst a host of others so that his voice did not stand out, but upon hearing it, Jesus said clearly, "You have said so."

This gave no clarification to the disciples, for they did not know to whom Jesus had spoken. How I yearned to leap up and accuse Judas directly, so that the disciples could rip him to pieces! One look at Jesus, however, made me stay my hand. He remained almost serene, so I quickly reasoned that he must have had some reason not to name Judas out loud. By sparing the snake at that moment, perhaps he was still hoping that Judas would have a change of heart, confess his wrongdoing, and avert the planned disaster. No such hope, I thought, as I knew Judas to be a man sure in his own judgments and ambitions.

There continued much commotion and furtive looks around the room, with James, son of Zebedee, and some of the more militant disciples venturing names of those they suspected or simply disliked. This led to more angry denials and counter-charges, with many accusing James of always provoking friends and enemies alike with his aggressive speech. The peace, companionship, and sense of united purpose Jesus had so carefully nurtured over the past several years seemed broken and shattered, with each disciple now cast adrift in a sea of doubt and mistrust.

Jesus must have intended this test of our faith, perhaps as a foretaste of the ordeal that he himself would face in the next few days. If indeed he was to be sacrificed like some unfortunate Isaac, we would be left to our own devices, now with intimate knowledge of the evil that was in and all around us. He had held us together through many confrontations with the principalities, ignorance, pain, and joy of the world, and now it seemed we were to be released.

Jesus waited for the anger and dismay to die down, and indeed a few of the wiser heads had already started calming the other disciples. I identified Simon Peter and Jesus' brother James as two who seemed capable of healing the rifts that were revealed amongst us. Even in my distress, I saw some hope that through them some of Jesus' work might continue. Jesus had remained sitting while many around him had leapt up in defense or accusation, and he soon motioned that all should return to their seats. There was much muttering, stifled sobs, and quick exchanges of glares, but eventually a certain order was restored.

This indeed was a night like no other before it, and Jesus surprised us once more by claiming that the bread for our meal represented his body, while the wine represented his blood, shed for the forgiveness of mankind's sins. We were to be nourished by remembering his substance, his words, and his physical presence among us; and we were to celebrate rather than grieve his bloody sacrifice. The cup itself was to hold our memories of his sacrifice and our new understanding that His Father was Our Father. Jesus was giving us a new ritual and rite for the new covenant he was trying to create between mankind and The Holy One, a covenant built on love more than obedience, on service rather than rule, on caring for the least rather than building up the powerful.

So we duly ate the bread, drank the wine—too much of it in several cases and assuredly not in celebration. We finished our meal in a tense silence. At Jesus' request, we ended with a hymn of praise to The Father, with Jesus reiterating what he had said just a few days before.

"You will not have me with you always, but there will always be hymns and devotions to be made. Earthly matters may go for or against you for a time, but you must keep faith with what is eternal and everlasting. Even in grief there can be joy, even in death there will be new life, as it is My Father's wish that life be abundant and joyful."

To emphasize and demonstrate his point, he took us all to the nearby Mount of Olives. There on the heights, we saw clearly the full gamut of life and death, the bustling city stretching in the distance and the necropolis of the dead filling the southern slope.

"This is the scope of life as you have known and heard about from the ancients. To this known, I want to add the mystery of God and Heaven above. In me you have lived with the flesh-and-blood embodiment of God's love, a mystery revealed."

We were a bit shocked to hear the sacred name of The Holy One spoken aloud, but Jesus only smiled. "Yes, it may be difficult at first, but as God has made Himself manifest in me, so has He consented to be known to you. You can be familiar with God, who indeed knows each of you by name, even the one who has betrayed me."

Jesus next took us to the garden called Gethsemane just as the sun went down. "I would have you sleep within this place of beauty and peace, in hopes that the very essence of this verdant, colorful, and varied life would enter and remain with you after I am gone. It is my fervent wish that you be gardeners of souls, weeding out all that would choke and disturb the beauty that God intended for His creation. Your words must be the water of life, your hands be in service to The Lord of Life. Mark well the places where there is sun for those who need it, shade for others, even damp and dark for those best suited to that pocket of nature. Learn what each soul can bear, and what they offer in turn. Some may yield fruit, some medicines, some sheer beauty and simple delight. Some may be irritating, even poisonous for now, but their ultimate role in the great mystery of life must needs await future revelation. Pass your knowledge, caring, and love of life to each succeeding generation, in The Father's and my name. May future generations add your names to mine. I do not know—in the human sense—what awaits me upon my coming trial, so it will be my faith alone that will carry me onward. If I be sent to Heaven, there I shall await you, my dearest friends and companions. May God bless and keep you on the path for which you have been chosen."

He then made some kind of gesture, like a *tav* as written by the ancients, a kind of cross that he finished by holding his hand against his heart. His words and gesture seemed to give us a kind of momentary serenity despite the seriousness of his purpose. We made our farewell blessings in turn, each of us walking up to him and mumbling whatever came to us in this most unexpected of moments. Many wept and tried to fall at his knees, but he firmly held them upright so he could look them in the eye.

"Have faith," he said over and over, and by the end of our farewells, we had absorbed some of his dignity and resolve.

It was not long before most of us were asleep, the emotional upheavals of the night having sapped us of our energies. As I drifted off, I could not recall whether or not Judas had been among the disciples at the garden, and if so had he dared to say goodbye to Jesus. By then I was too exhausted to weigh these matters, and so fell into a disturbed sleep.

I dreamt of vultures swooping over and around Jesus' head, where they took turns taking vicious bites out of him. All the while he calmly fed them pieces of bread that seemed to come right out of his body. Blood came out of him in fountains; his body gradually disappeared, until only his arms were left. They gathered the blood into a cup and offered it to the carrion birds, but they only laughed harshly. One whose face looked suspiciously like Judas' grabbed the chalice out his hands and carelessly flung it to the ground. Out of the blood grew beautiful flowers, fruit-filled trees, and indeed an entire Garden of Eden. Up and up the garden grew, forcing the vultures farther and farther up into the heavens. As they touched the highest clouds, each disappeared in blazing lightning bolts that seemed to come from every direction. The birds' scattered feathers became a gentle rain, and the lightning bolts swirled in and around each other, forming a sun that shone throughout. Small creatures came out from under the bushes and undergrowth once all the commotion had died down, and all turned their faces to the sun.

I awoke all too soon and with much regret at leaving this prophetic dream. Sounds of a great disturbance came to me from but a short distance away. I could hear the angry voice of James, the son of rage, then yelps of pain, and then indignant voices raised to a pitch before Jesus' calming tones seemed to wash over the affair, whatever it was. In the dim light of dawn, we disciples were groggy with sleep but could see armed guards and Temple authorities through the branches, with swords drawn and of a number to brook no opposition. The other disciples took but a moment to collect their wits and measure their choices, and all but me fled as quietly as they could.

I am no warrior or hero, but I believe strongly in direct witness and the truthful testimony that can come from it. Even though I was dressed only in my loin cloth on this very warm night, I made for the clearing where Jesus, Simon Peter, and the Zebedee brothers had slept. "What is going on here and why have you accosted the Son of God?" I said.

The kohenim erupted in anger at this mention of the sacred name, and many in the entourage turned to me. "Be gone, little one," said one of the soldiers, who then made a half-hearted sweep at me with his sword.

I stood my ground for a moment, yelling, "shame, shame upon you all!" All my righteous indignation and scorn were leveled at them, and if ever there was a time for Adonai to come to our rescue, this was it.

Unfazed by my anger, the lout and his companion made a lunge at me. They got a hold of my cloth, tearing it from me as I bolted out of the clearing. Naked as a gazelle, and just as fast I might add, I sprinted out of the garden and headed for our lodging to get dressed. My eyes were filled with tears of rage and a kind of shame that I could not do more to thwart their capture of Jesus. In that fraught moment, I cared not for the petty rules governing modest dress, nor for what others might think of me in my naked state. I felt an unexpected kind of freedom in that race home that has remained within me, a most curious gift in a most tragic time.

I was to learn later that Simon Peter had been the truest and most loyal of all, trailing behind the arresting party all the way to where the High Priest held court with other dignitaries. After what seemed like forever, he returned to our lodging shame-faced and weeping. We could tell that it had not gone well with Jesus, but Simon Peter was at a loss for what had actually transpired, as he had not gained entry to the court to hear the testimony. Instead, he said, "I am the most foul of friends, for I denied even knowing Jesus, lest they arrest me also. My very accent gave me away as a Galilean, as are most of you."

Many of the Brethren tried to comfort Simon Peter, but he could not be consoled. Without our rock to anchor and encourage us, and for fear of our own lives, we felt we had to remain hidden from the public until we learned Jesus' fate.

His brother James could not accept the shame of doing nothing, however, and felt obliged to attend whatever trials and punishment the authorities meted out to our Master. "My kin are in town and I will join their party, whatever befalls. Under the Law, we have our rights and obligations to attend to his needs. I pray that these rights will be respected and that I will be safe from arrest. I will send word about Jesus' fate, and our own."

With Jesus and the Zebedee brothers arrested, Simon Peter collapsed in misery, Judas banished in disgrace, and Jesus' brother James gone to his kin, we remaining brethren felt puny and insubstantial, adrift in a stormy sea without captain or strong oarsmen. Thomas, perhaps the most cynical of the Brethren and most apt to see the worst in people, thought that Jesus was doomed and that we should all scatter to the winds rather than suffer the same fate. He wanted to leave immediately, but the majority believed there was still hope that God—how strange to write His sacred name—would intervene to save Jesus, and ourselves.

Andrew and Philip stepped forward to lead us in a kind of spontaneous prayer, reminding us of our many past trials and all we had learned about community, love, forgiveness, and hope. They reminded us that there was a Holy Spirit alive in each of us that would and could sustain us even without the physical presence of Jesus. At the mention of the spirit, Bartholomew spoke up, offering to bring out bread and wine as a means of binding us in common faith, purpose, and ritual observance. We proceeded to repeat from memory as many of the words Jesus had so recently used during our last supper together. These prayers seemed to calm our fretful and fearful souls as we awaited the words we dreaded to hear.

News dribbled in during the day, first from John, who had been released from the *Beit HaMikdash* as somewhat of an afterthought to their main purpose of arresting Jesus.

"I acted the part of an innocent and they must have felt I was no threat to them," he said almost apologetically. "James got roughed up a bit for injuring the slave, but he will be released once he receives bloodmoney from our parents to pay to the slave's owner. That is, if he does not further incur their wrath due to rash, threatening behavior. You know my brother!"

We welcomed John like one of the lost sheep Jesus always talked about, but he had little to tell about Jesus' punishment. He and James had been held far from the Court, and John could only tell us that the soldiers had shackled Jesus and treated him poorly all the way to his trial. "I kept praying for some kind of rescue from Adonai, or at least some sign that He was watching over us. I could see no supporters, and there was nothing in the sky but dark clouds." These words sobered us and some of that darkness returned to our souls.

The next day, Jesus' brother sent us word that Jesus had been sent to the Tetrarch Herod Antipas for trial, and then had inexplicably been returned to Jerusalem. The messenger raised the hope that the Roman authorities might simply release Jesus, for indeed he had offered them little that might incriminate himself. He had upheld Roman rights of taxation and preached a gospel of peace and forgiveness, not war and rebellion. Our hopes were rekindled, but were dashed only hours later when yet another brother or cousin of Jesus' came with the news that our Master had been condemned to death at the urging of the *Beit HaMikdash*.

"There was one final hope that Jesus could be pardoned at the whim of Praefectus Pilate, but when he asked the crowd, they screamed for a man named Barabbas instead. Why our followers were not there in force, I cannot say, but I did see the Temple soldiers stationed at every entry to the square where the trial took place."

It is clear that the religious authorities have thought of everything, have planned and organized a trap from which Jesus cannot escape. In my grief and anger, I nevertheless take note of how cunning they have been; we ourselves will have to match that cunning if we are to survive long enough to see Jesus' gospel sown, nurtured, and harvested amongst an oppressed people hungry for a new covenant with The Lord. There can be no doubts, timidity, wishful thinking, or false hope. It will be a life and death struggle from now on against the rulers and powers who oppose us.

As a scribe, I have to be prepared to shape and sharpen the words that convey Jesus' deeds and message, so that they might penetrate the hardheartedness of the people threatened by his life and example. These words also need to promise what the current jumble of religious rules and sanctions cannot: a simple, direct way to experience God's love and favor. As a named scribe, I also know that I will most likely draw the hateful attention of these enemies of Jesus. All these thoughts flit through my mind as I await Jesus' execution.

Joy, rapture, disbelief!!! Great surging love of God and Jesus! He lives, undeniably he lives after death!!!!

We have just heard that he has risen from the grave and will meet up with us again at the mount secretly known to us from our time in Galilee. (As part of my new awareness of the forces arrayed against us, I will not put certain names, locations, and acts in writing lest they fall into the wrong hands.)

The first news of this came through our women brethren and then a drunken fellow who lives below the hill where Jesus was crucified. Many refused to believe them, but his resurrection has since been confirmed by his kin. Great floods of joy run through my veins, and it is a wonder I do not burst like some volcano into a thousand songs of praise and thanksgiving!!!

Oh, dear reader, I must calm myself and attend to the tasks at hand. Our new day begins and we must be about the work that Jesus has set before us. I will end this journal on this note, as the battle against the evil forces of this world has been enjoined. This war requires that I assume a new name, to protect me as a shield and cover, and to signal my new purpose. I shall be Mark,[5] dedicated to the war of good versus evil, of love against hate and power, of the lambs of God against the lions of gold and blood.

---

5. Mark is derived from Mars, the Roman God of War.

VI

Gospel of James, Son of Zebedee

My brethren and friends, harken to me, who was with Jesus from the beginning along with my brother John. Fishermen we were before our Lord and Savior called to us. We left our father Zebedee's house to be with The Lord, forsaking our share of his patrimony and traveling the road of baptism and new birth. How we thrilled when The Lord said that he came not in peace, but with a sword!

"I will cleave sons from fathers, daughters from mothers; each household will be divided into sheep and wolves," he said.

"No, James, that is not exactly what he said," interrupted my brother John in his usual pedantic way.

"You are wrong again, brother," I insisted, "Many times he talked of sheep and wolves and this was one of them. Besides, I was making a point about swords and cleaving, how those who believe in him will be separated from those who do not. Surely you want to be among those select who are saved?"

I knew that this would shut him up, as he, more so than all of the disciples, thinks himself closest to Jesus and thus most likely to be saved. John
is the one who most emulated Jesus, from chastity to obedience to claiming
to have spoken personally with The Father. While the rest of us would gather
food for the evening meal, secure shelter, or organize the crowds to hear
Jesus speak, my brother could be seen nodding his head up and down and
back and forth as he had seen Jesus do in prayer. Nod, nod, nod, bow, bow,
bow, but nothing came of it except softer hands than those of us who worked!

My little brother was the one who whined to our mother that Jesus had
not yet named him the likely heir of his ministry, despite all his piety and
slavish emulation. She then had done what she always seemed to do, which
was to curry favor for her little boy. She had gone to Jesus himself to ask that
we *both* be allowed to sit, one at his left and one at his right hand, when he
ascended to his throne in the Kingdom. Clever woman that she was, she had
added my name to take the sole focus off John. The other disciples had laid
into us, rightfully so, but this only caused my temper to boil even more than
had my brother's naked ambition. I had to practice turning the other cheek
until I was dizzy with the effort.

Let me admit that this temper has gotten me in trouble more times
than I can count. In my time before being called by Jesus, I had taken out
my disappointments on numerous fish, our leaky boats, uncooperative sails,
and the occasional disrespectful drinking companion. My first encounters
with Jesus led me to believe him to be a zealot too, what with his claims to
come with a sword and not peace. However, I soon realized I was only seeing him through my own anger at the Romans and their collaborators. He
jokingly called me his "*bene reghesh*," or "son of rage," but I suspect in his
heart he always welcomed my strong right arm and willingness to confront
those who would disturb, assail, or even arrest him.

He tempered my anger with his many parables and examples of love,
forgiveness, and mercy towards the poor. He gathered the lost, forgotten,
and discarded sheep of Israel into his embrace. He rebuked those who
sought to make him King, saying the first would be last, and the last first.
He appealed to the mothers in the crowd by showing favor on their children
and holding up the little ones as an example to us all. He healed many, and
after each miracle his following grew, as did his reputation. Many were now
convinced that he was at least a prophet sent by Adonai, and some among
us began to believe he was more, a savior, a messiah sent by The Holy One
to redeem Israel. We all believed that he would present our righteous grievances to the authorities. G-d-willing, he would soften the hard hearts of
both the Romans and the Temple elite who set the tone for how the poor
were treated.

As much as we tried to preach on our own, we were no match for Jesus' oratory and healing gifts. We had particular difficulty with those outside our faith, who were naturally suspicious of us. Although Jesus made occasional, sympathetic mention of the Samaritans[1] and *goyim* in the towns we passed, he left the preaching for these folks to some of us disciples. Indeed, one Samaritan village refused to let us enter their gates, even going so far as to throw manure on us from their guard tower. My brother happened to be with me this day, for once abandoning his desired position at Jesus' right hand. He was hit directly on the head, and, after I stopped laughing, I threw curses back on the unbelievers in the most threatening language I could summon. I was expecting the heavens to erupt in punishment, but not a thing happened.

When we returned to camp, I told Jesus that our attempts to bring Adonai's wrath down upon them did not work. I feared that my faith was too weak to attract His divine notice and sense of justice. My brother and I asked Jesus to smite the Samaritans and avenge John's shame, but to our surprise, Jesus rebuked *us*.

"They did not heed the call because they are not yet ready to leave behind what has taken them so long to achieve. They are surrounded on all sides by those hostile to their faith. You of all people, James, should know how hard it is to feel love when your heart is hardened for battle."

'*How well he knows me*', I thought to myself, for indeed Jesus' calls for love and mercy had often fallen on the rocky ground of my soul, where they were choked by the thorns of my anger. All around me, I saw soldiers, battlements, walled cities, and the occasional corpses of those brave souls crucified for their beliefs. '*This surely is a land at war with itself*,' I thought. Perhaps I hoped that all his talk of love was like some Trojan horse, inside of which lay the swords Jesus promised to obtain justice for the poor and an end to domination by our oppressors. I could see the hunger for freedom in the eyes of the peasants. I could see how they clustered around him as the sheep surround the shepherd to obtain protection from the wolves.

Even as we approached Jerusalem, I still saw him as some kind of general or king leading his troops into battle, only he chose to arm us with righteousness, faith, and hope, rather than sword, shield, and spear. Despite my hopes, however, I feared that the authorities' hearts were well-guarded by both gold and power.

On this last trip to Jerusalem, Jesus confided that he did not know exactly how he would be received. He knew that many prophets before him

---

1. An older sect of Judaism, discredited and demeaned by current religious authorities.

had been abused, rejected, or even killed. He was ready for that fate and was prepared to ransom the soul of Israel with his sacrifice. He hoped, however, for one further miracle from His Father, who had already blessed him with spellbinding speech that could move thousands. If it be God's will, the powerful would repent and justice would flow like a river down from the hills of Jerusalem.

My hopes were buoyed with the size of the crowds who greeted us as we approached the city gates. They gave us food and drink along the road, some waved aromatic branches in the air, while all around there was singing and loud hosannas. Jesus sent Andrew and me to secure a mount from a man who lived just outside the gate we were entering.

"At last," I told Andrew, "he is acting the part of a real king and leader;" but imagine my surprise when the man could only produce a small ass or colt on which to parade Jesus before the gate!

"I guess he does not want to appear too haughty or regal," I complained to Andrew, but in truth I felt that such modesty would only encourage the Romans and religious authorities to dismiss his importance. Nevertheless, up Jesus went on the ass as people continued to sing his praises and decorate his path through the gates. The crowds were unarmed and in a jubilant mood, so the Roman soldiers just stepped back, many with bemused looks on their faces. I heard one soldier gibe that this must be the Judean Festival of the Half-Assed Man, and Simon Peter had to grab me roughly to keep me from repaying the insult.

Jesus took the crowd to the *Beit HaMikdash*, where he dismounted and went up a few steps to better deliver his sermon. He had chosen quite a backdrop, for there behind him were all the many things wrong with our current religious authorities: The vendors hawking their wares, the animals meant for sacrifice with their piteous calls and copious manure piles, the doors of gold shut and guarded by stern looking Temple soldiers. It could not be more obvious that the poor were not welcome and that the Temple was in the business of raising money for its own aggrandizement.

I believe all this greed and earthly vanity finally got to Jesus, for it was not long before he turned his words into action. He let out a loud cry and ran through the market, tumbling the stalls and thrashing out at the moneychangers and animals alike with his staff. How I rejoiced to follow his example, as did the many among us who looked to him as our general and king! We released all our frustration on those despoilers of Adonai's house, and I for one was glad to no longer turn the other cheek. Many in the crowd gathered up the coins and trinkets spilled in the melee, and I knew that these poor, downtrodden souls would finally eat and sleep well that night. Here was a moment that served both the needs of Adonai and man, and that showed the authorities that Jesus was not a man to be trifled with. Would they now listen to his message and change their ways?

Well, as it turned out, they did listen for a few days. They let him into the Temple to preach and answer their questions, despite what he had done to the moneychangers. All have heard by now his parable of the vineyard owner and the selfish, disobedient tenants. He called for them to repent and warned that all their efforts to build a physical monument to God would crumble to nothing if their souls were not aligned with God's purposes. Many animals can build houses for themselves, he said, but only man was made in God's image and could make his soul into something worthy of The Creator. He simplified Torah for them, emphasizing love for Adonai and our neighbors, and cutting through all the welter of Kosher and other laws that served mainly to separate man from The Father. He deftly parried obscure hypothetical matters of Mishnah, and cleverly avoided a direct confrontation with Roman authority. Jesus had been careful not to antagonize the Romans, and never preached about their occupation of our ancestral lands.

"Render unto Caesar," he said. (I would have liked to render them with my sword, but we had no army to back me up!) Jesus was no zealot, but he did take direct aim at the hearts and souls of his own people. For the briefest of times, I thought that he might have reached them.

Alas and woe to us all, but peace, brotherhood, and simple love for The Father were crucified, exactly as Jesus had predicted. That bastard son of ha-Satan Judas waited until Jesus was out of hiding and resting unaware in the Garden of Gethsemane. He brought the Temple soldiers and religious authorities to where Simon Peter, John, and I slept while Jesus prayed. To my eternal shame, I awoke too late and could only take a swipe at a lowly servant before my arms were grabbed and my sword taken from me. This shame eats at me even now, eased only by the witness of Jesus' resurrection and promise that his sacrifice was ordained by The Father. But I still ask why The Father could not have softened the hard hearts of those who arrested and tried Jesus. Why could Jesus not have been allowed to live out his span of days, spreading the gospel of love and raising up the poor?

It is a wonder that my heart has not burst with a murderous rage, or that my head has not split asunder with doubt and confusion.

It is only my love for Jesus that has kept me whole these many years. Against this rage, I have built a dam from all the parables, acts of mercy, wisdom, and love that Jesus showed to me and his followers. I would not betray him twice by gainsaying his sacrifice, but my heart is not big enough to forgive those who killed him. This generation did not and does not respect a prophet of love, and I cannot be as soft as many of the other disciples. I preach the gospel of love, but not forgiveness of true enemies. I feed the grievances of the poor so that they know that, through me, The Father also hears their cries. Everywhere, I urge listeners to care for the children, the poor, the weak and oppressed. I then urge them to press their rebbes and kohanim to do the same, hoping some day that the hearts of these so-called agents of Adonai will finally heed Jesus' prophetic voice.

I confess that I also practice my swordcraft until that day when a righteous army is armed and ready to march on Jerusalem. As I wander the hinterlands of Israel, I note those hot-blooded men who also balance love and revenge on the edge of a sword. Hatred by itself makes us no better than those who killed Jesus, and I must pray every day to keep that beast chained and locked within my breast, where love holds the key.

But yet I need that fire to keep me going. Water and fire, love and hate, the cunning of snakes and the gentleness of doves. Oh Lord, how is it that our nature is bounded between our animal and our spiritual, God-given selves! Jesus appealed to all that was sweet, loving, nurturing, and peaceful within us, but he also upended the tables of the moneychangers when he had had enough desecration of the house of The Lord. We all have our limits.

LETTER OF JOHN TO HIS SISTERS:

Greetings my sisters, and may the blessings of our Lord and Savior Jesus the Christ be upon you. I write to you from Patmos, where many are heeding the gospel of love and turning to Jesus as the true Son of God. I am saddened to tell you, however, of the death of our dear brother James, who has joined our Lord in Heaven. James died as he lived, with a sword of zeal in his hands. He was preaching in a village just outside Jerusalem when Roman soldiers came to harass the listeners and arrest James for his incendiary speech. Although they put up no resistance, the crowd was roundly beaten and many dispersed. Several refused to leave and rallied around our brother, trying their best to shield him from the soldiers. He, ever merciful, urged his protectors to leave him to his fate and then faced the soldiers alone. Witnesses in the crowd told me that he drew his sword from beneath his cloak and challenged any soldier who dared attack a man sent by God. "I can send your soul to everlasting darkness, or show you the light," he said, but the soldiers hesitated but a moment before setting on him.

No longer a young man, he parried their spear thrusts as best he could, but the soldiers only toyed with him. Little by little, their thrusts struck home, and blood could be seen running down his cloak and pooling on the ground. As he tired and weakened, the soldiers mocked and derided him, much as our Lord was mocked. He finally slipped on his own blood and fell, whereupon the soldiers disarmed him. Trussing him like a hog, they bound him for presentation to Herod. One of the faithful in Herod's court reported to me that Herod then delighted in ordering James to be decapitated with his own sword, fulfilling our Lord's rebuke that all who live by the sword shall die by the sword. Woe that it should be our brother who failed to heed this admonition.

I am certain that Jesus will receive our brother when he reaches Heaven, as Jesus loved him and chose him above the other disciples to accompany him several times in prayer and ministry. Jesus knew the zeal that lived within James, calling him a true *bene reghesh*.

Like a sword, however, this rage cut both ways, both kindling ardor in the faithful but also causing his enemies to seek his death. By the grace of God, I have been spared the same fate, and live to preach the Gospel. It is not for us to say who will fall in the battle for the Kingdom and who shall live, but it is for us to honor their martyrdom. I shall build a room in my heart in his name, and hope that his deeds will live throughout the generations.

VII

The Moneychangers' Prophet and Loss

To the Most Esteemed and Honorable Zacharias, Kohen of the *Beit HaMikdash* Office of Treasury:

We, the duly licensed moneychangers, most strongly protest the recent disruption of our legitimate business by one Jesus of Nazareth. He and a small group of his followers came on Sabbath past and proceeded to harangue all who had assembled in the Court of the *Goyim* where we have our shops. Accusing us of foul misdeeds, untruths, impiety, and worse, he presumed to upend our tables, scattering all the people's monies, our weights and measures, and our account books. As you can imagine, a great tumult ensued as beggars, worshippers, soldiers, moneychangers, and more scrambled to regain or steal as much as they could find.

As our licensor, you are obligated to uphold our rights and safety, and we wish that you intercede immediately and forcefully with this Jesus and his ilk before we are driven to poverty and worse! It should not have to be stated, but if we cannot keep our monies safe and cannot provide our service to the people, we cannot pay our Temple rent. There will be no more special favors granted to your Office if we have no money at our disposal.

In short, this Jesus is a grave threat to all the traditions of our forefathers, and to all the comforts to which we all have grown accustomed.

Let me add that we consulted with a learned kohen of our own, as well as a lawyer of undisputed piety and learning. We firmly believe that your Office is liable for the losses suffered on that day, as your soldiers did nothing to stop the assault or control the crowds once the tables were turned on us. I have consulted with our members regarding our losses, and believe that the figure owed is well over 2400 shekels, not including the documents that were destroyed by the trampling mob. We discussed the value of these ruined documents and account ledgers, and will add another 400 shekels to our claim. We must pay scribes for the hours it will take to interview all the moneychangers and have them recall the transactions, loans, deposits, and exchanges made before Jesus tried to destroy our livelihood. It was only by the grace of the Most High that we had already sent the morning's receipts to our vaults before this riot broke out, or this loss figure could have approached 20,000 shekels.

Finally, we request recompense before Sabbath next, and well before the Romans gain access to your Passover tax receipts. Such recompense will lower the amount you seemed to have taken in, so their tax on receivables will also be less. Let us make something good out of a bad situation, and prepare ourselves so this assault on our traditions never recurs.

As ever, your humble and faithful servant,
Abel bar Reuben, Scribe to Temple *Shulhanim*

FROM THE MEMORY OF ARI, SON OF DAVID, PURVEYOR OF KORBAN ANIMALS[1]

Silence, you fools! You are as stupid as your sheep if you keep bleating and arguing amongst yourselves! We must have some kind of order if we are to make demands to Levi, Kohen of *Korban* animals, about our losses from that Temple riot. It has been difficult enough to find and bring you all together in one place. Fortunately, we all drink at the same three inns who are unlucky enough to host us, so it was not too hard to find you! Of course, with all the livestock we lost, it is a wonder we have any money at all for drinking.

What is that? You are right, Barak, we drink when we lose *and* when we gain, but no matter!

---

1. Ritually designated, approved, and prepared for sacrifice.

I have heard that the moneychangers have already hired lawyers to plead their case at the Temple. Those clever bastards will squeeze all they can out of the Temple Office, leaving us with the dregs. It is bad enough we have to clean up all the shit from our own animals, but we are going to be shit on by the Temple if we do not stick up for our rights.

And we must all work together, whether we sell the fattest rams or the scrawniest pigeons. You ram princes think you can cut a better deal with Levi just because you know some rich people? Do you know who runs away from controversy and trouble the fastest? It is the rich, and they will suddenly forget your name and claim they never gave you money for those lost rams. They know how to hold onto their money—How do you think they became rich? You may think because you have bigger stalls, finer cloaks, and more slaves than the rest of us that you will be first in line for recompense; but I tell you that you will be first to have the door slammed in your face! And while you face that door, the rest of us hungry and angry lot will be sneaking up your backside to get what we can out of your hides.

As for you pigeon, sparrow, dove, rat, and mouse sellers, you might think because your losses were as small as your animals that you have no part in this complaint. Wrong! We know that those lost leptons and kollybos are as dear to you as are the shekels of the ram princes. Those thin coins are all that separate you from the beggars on the street, and we your brothers and sisters want to keep you alive a while longer. Many of us started out selling as you do, and we do not disdain you. Besides, we need your many numbers and loud voices to swell our crowd, and your strong arms to confront any Temple soldiers who may try to block our way.

So, all of us who husband our *korban* animals, who follow the rituals, who haul the feed and manure, who tend the stalls at Temple, who bargain with the multitude of worshippers—be they foreigners or neighbors—who provide the means for the sacrifices demanded by Torah, may we all join with one accord to present our just grievances to the Kohen Levi. Just as it takes many stakes driven into the soil to create a sturdy and safe pen, so too must we stand together to protect our livelihood.

A number of us have discussed how best to proceed. We propose that a delegate from each family clan be sent tomorrow at first light with a request for the Temple to either help us regain our animals—which no doubt have disappeared into every back alley and holding pen of this hungry city—or help pay for our losses. My scribes Ephraim and Elon here will go through the crowd and record your losses.

What's that?

{Lengthy mumbling}

Ah, Barak, you may have drink in you but you retain your wits. He thinks it best if the scribes retire to some more private place so that we each individually relate our losses. It would not do for us to overhear the prices our neighbors charge for the same animals, else we restart our arguments. Such discord will surely splinter our efforts, so that we all lose. We are not wolves to ravage each other's flocks, but rather men of honor and service, at least all but Barak there, who once sold an old piebald donkey as a fatted calf to a half-blind merchant from Phoenicea! What is it that the Romans always say? *Caveat emptor?* Something to live by as sure as the great Torah, The Lord be praised.

{Muttering from crowd}

I hear you, friends, there are some among you who want to take our revenge on and recoup our losses from those Nazarenes and country boys who caused this trouble in the first place! I have to say by the looks of them that they did not seem to have two leptons to rub together in the first place. For all I know, they had their hungry fellows waiting in the shadows to grab our animals as they passed! What? Speak up!

(Samuel): I know some of those men, and they seem honest to me, despite their dirty hands and ragged cloaks. I cannot vouch for that Jesus, but I have bought fish from Simon Peter and his brother, and they always gave me an honest weight of fish.

(Another voice, perhaps a seller of pigeons?): I agree with Samuel there. Although I wish them to stay away from my animals, I would sooner eat and drink with them than with all the kohenim combined! Though they are troublemakers, they are working men just like us, while those kohenim strut their divine selves all through Jerusalem, as rich and haughty as any Roman merchant. Yes, yes, I know that we all make money off the same pilgrims, but at the end of the day, the kohenim retire to their inner sanctum surrounded by all our people's gold and silver, while we return to our shit-filled pens. The kohenim say this is the divine order, but where in Torah does it say that the priests are obliged to get fat on our animals and wealthy as well? Have you ever seen a starving kohen? I have seen plenty of my neighbors having to sell off their herd, their children and even their birth-rights in order to simply live!

(Yet another man): Whatever the truth of what you say, do you think it wise to say so aloud? Who amongst us is a secret ally of the Romans or the Temple? We are a subject people, and the powers above us work hard to keep us so. This is the way of the world; our people's history should have taught us when to submit and when to fight. This is not the time and not the place. I am only here to get paid for my lost animals, not to tweak the tails of the ruling beasts!

(Abram): Someone should tell that to Jesus and his followers! He is going to bring down the Roman soldiers into our Court, and they will also want a cut of our profits or of our animals, supposedly for our own protection. Zealots have no idea the harm they do to us innocent bystanders!

(Barak): You are not so innocent yourself, Abram, with all your girlfriends!{Laughter}

(Me): Perhaps Samuel should go to his friend Simon Peter and find out if his mob feels compelled to repeat their performance. Despite his questionable character, I am persuaded by Abram that we should smooth over any trouble as quickly as we can, so as not to give a pretext to the Romans to stick their big noses into our business! Perhaps Simon Peter can talk his boss out of further mischief, especially when he realizes what harm it is doing to our families, who simply want to eat from the little money we make at our trade.

(Another voice): If Samuel is such good friends with that crowd, maybe he should tell the Temple soldiers and Judges where they live so that they can be removed from our city! Punish them! That will teach them a lesson and show the Romans we have everything under control!

{A clamor erupted, with many parties giving their opinions.}

(I continued): Friends! Friends! Calm down before we attract the authorities to our own gathering! Simply by meeting in numbers like this we are a threat to the Romans, although heaven knows we are more of a threat to each other with the way we argue over every little inch of courtyard and prospective buyer! . . . That's better. Have we heard from all the families? Yes, you, sir, of the turtle dove tribe.

(Jacob): It is no wonder, Master Ari, that you do not know my name, because what are we bird sellers compared to you mighty titans of business? I am Jacob bar Jacob, of Beth'el. I have listened well to the other speakers, but in all this talk of grievance, reparation, and strategy, no one has remarked that this is only the second time in all our nation's history that anyone has interfered with a sanctioned sacrifice. It took an Angel of The Lord to release Isaac from the hand of Abraham; what do we know of this Jesus? By what authority does he enjoin us to leave the Temple? By what authority does he claim that our *korbanim* and moneychangers foul the House of The Holy One of Israel? What if he is also some agent of the Most High, sent to rebuke us for bringing our business, our haggling, our jealousies, our animal shit, and all those money matters right into the near-Court of the Holy of Holies? Maybe he *is* some prophet, like Jeremiah, scathing us and scourging our animals due to our corruption, greed, and Roman-like behavior.

We have all heard the angry voices of those complaining about the new exchange rates. Maybe the moneychangers think, with Roman soldiers only steps away, that the people dare not raise a grievance. Are we so innocent, apart from Abram anyway? {Laughter} Imagine what would happen if all of us and the moneymen heeded his condemnation and abandoned our businesses, or at least took them far from this sacred site. Yes, imagine—The kohenim would soon lose weight! They might have to work for a living rather than feed off the people. The gold and silver would gradually dwindle away, and the lust for it might fade from all of our hearts.

You purveyors of the larger *korbanim* will not starve, for your animals will then simply be diverted to the public market. It is us dove and pigeon raisers who may have to find new work, but no matter! I ask you to imagine something that seems unimaginable—that Adonai is sending us a new prophet, right in our own time! Who are we to resist?

{A great silence fell over the crowd, and all motion seemed to cease.}

(Me again): Well, you have taken all the wind out of our sails, Jacob bar Jacob, and I am at a rare loss for words. Your thoughts may yet save us from a severe beating by the Most High. Maybe there are other options. Barak, are you sober enough to propose how we should move on from here? No? Where did that slippery fellow go anyway? Back to the inn? Someone go fetch him, please. While we wait, perhaps we can break into our families and discuss what each would have us do next. Choose your delegate carefully so that he speaks with the family's authority. Consider that Jacob here speaks as one of us, not as some angry kohen on his high altar telling us that it is the will of the Most High that we should up our taxes. I am as eager as the next man to make a living, but all my ambition is humbled by the thought that a new prophet may be among us.

Let the delegates reassemble here when that tree's shadow reaches the inn's door. As for the rest of you people here, keep your own counsel and speak none of this to those outside our company. There are many hungry men out there who would see us lose our licenses so they could have our stalls for themselves. The Romans want their pounds of flesh and the Temple seeks more of our silver to build a bigger shrine to Adonai. The less they know of our troubles, the better.

O Lord, we are beset by hungry and powerful men on all sides, and now must we contend with You also?

VIII

The Soldier's Tale

FILL MY CUP AGAIN, Marcus, and I will tell you truly what happened to that stupid Nazarene we crucified. Yes, yes, I have already told you I was there on duty that day; you can check the log if you must. How many of our company now say they were there too? If they are to be believed, there was an entire phalanx armed and alert to put down an army of angry Zealots. But in truth, there were maybe six of us on duty during the hearing. The priests and their men were quite capable of controlling the crowds. At best, we were there so our Principale[1] could show himself off to Pilate without costing himself much money.

Surely you want to know the truth? No, not the kind of truth our commanders tell us to gird us for battle; not even the kind of truth you tell yourself afterwards. Just the truth of what I saw with my own eyes, and what I myself did. To hell with those who came late to that party, but boast of their starring role!

1. Equivalent to platoon leader or sergeant.

There, now do I have your attention? Aah, thank you for the wine—it washes away the dust from this god-forsaken post and lubricates the throat so I can sing your praise. All hail Marcus Priore, true boon companion and shield mate! It is only because you have money and that we are both likely to die in this dungheap of a desert that I tell you what I have told none other.

First, let me assure you that this Nazarene was a scraggly, filthy thing, a real country boy with callouses on his hands, and years of dirt on feet and neck. I gather that he begged all over Judea and had no proper job. He could have used a few good meals to put some meat on his bones. It is laughable that he could be any kind of king, or indeed any kind of threat to us. During the hearing, he rarely raised his eyes from the ground and seemed the mildest of men, but then, all the Judeans lower their eyes when we are around.

Yes, yes, as they should, for are we not Romans?! Toast!

Here, woman, another cup, and all hail Marcus Priore! And you, be quick about it, for my throat gets dry with such truth-telling.

Aaaah, thanks again. Where was I? Yes, the preamble. This Nazarene was nothing to look at and nothing to fear, I tell you. At most, we could have had him lashed for taking an ass from some poor fool living near the North gate. You and I have marched for leagues without getting tired, but this scrawny fellow could not make it up the hills and into Jerusalem without hitching a ride. Ha! No wonder these Hebrews lose to everyone who wants to own a piece of this shit-filled desert, although I do not even know why we are here.

Anyway, Pilate was half-drunk and irritated that his lunch had been disturbed by the priests. He tried to throw the scrawny fish back to the sharks so that he could finish his meal, but they were in a mood for blood, even if it was dirty. Oh well, killing is what we do best, is it not so, Marcus? Remember that campaign against. . .against. . .?

Oh, right you are, buyer of drinks, no more digressions, marching straight to the point I am, though another cup would keep my aim true. . . .Aaaaah, you are a living god, Marcus!

Well, I had a bet going with the other men that the Nazarene would carry the *patibulum*[2] all the way to Golgotha, just to show off his might to his followers. But no, he stumbles halfway and some poor fellow has to jump in to carry the load. Some king—he cost me half a day's pay! Double or nothing for his tunic, says I, and the gods smiled on me finally with a lucky dice throw. And why waste a good shirt on a dying man? Why should those carrion birds get a mouthful of cloth rather than rotten Judee meat?

---

2. A crossbar to be attached to a permanently embedded pole, thus forming a cross.

The boys were angry over my getting the shirt, for some reason, even though it was a dirty thing itself. "You do the final deeds," they said, and left me there after nailing him to the cross.

I was supposed to make sure he was good and dead, or at least had his legs broken so he could not run. Just for sport I broke the legs of those two bastards next to him, all the while saying, "I am coming for you, kingy, here I come!" I just wanted to see him flinch, but he just whined and said he was thirsty. Someone from his family did give him some nasty wine that was lying around. Wine for a whiner. . .

I am being funny again, Marcus, in spite of myself! This wine of yours has made me a wit as well as a witness! Ha!

Anyway, he took a good long drink of that foul wine, not nearly as sweet as what we have here, I can tell you. And why should a man not get good and drunk before diving into the great darkness beyond? I would have joined him for a drink myself if the brew had not reeked so. I must be getting soft in my old age, because I just stood there while his family or whoever gave him the wine and said their good-byes. He mumbled something in reply, but after a while his head drooped down and the family thankfully shut up. I tried to shoo them away, but one of the women—a pretty little thing from what I could tell—begged me, "Oh, please, do not hurt him, sir."

I almost laughed, as if driving nails into a man's hands and stretching his arms until they nearly break is not bad enough.

"Would not think of it," said I, but just for fun I poked the man in his side with my spear to see if he was alive. He did not move or cry out, so I just left him there. No need to exert myself and break his legs—he was not going anywhere. Dead is dead, and I was eager to get off duty.

You know what they are saying in the streets now, that his blood gushed out like water? But I tell you, friend, I had to come up with something creative to make it seem like I had done my duty. The Principale knew I had not broken his legs like I was supposed to; there was no way to hide that. I got docked plenty by him, leading to my current penurious state, I might add. Yes, it was me who started that little rumor of the bloody fountain, thinking fast I was when the Principale grilled our detail when no one could find his body.

"I speak the truth," I cried, "or else let the gods strike me dead. I have seen enough death in my time to know dead from alive, and that man did not move a muscle when I speared him. All his life water just gushed out, and ran off into the rocks and sand. Dead is dead, and doubters be damned." I looked up to the sky as if expecting lightning to strike, but none did. Gods come in handy sometimes, I must say.

Ah, the missing body. Lean in close, friend, for here is another matter I do not wish to get back to anyone. After menials from some rich merchant were done wrapping and entombing the body, I finished out my duty shift and thought I was done with the whole affair. I am at our favorite inn when here come several Temple guards tromping past me. Turns out one of them is a drinking companion of mine—one of many, of course. I have made some money off him in the past for what might be called private duty, so I hoist myself up and join him for a bit.

"Well, this is something, you fellows being released from bondage to the Temple," I say, being conversational but keeping a keen ear out for trouble or opportunity.

My friend grumbles that his superiors sent them to guard the Nazarene's tomb to prevent any mischief. "We will have to stand in the hot sun with only the stench for company," he says, sounding disgusted.

"Well," says I, feeling the weight of my empty purse, "I can arrange for me and some friends to stand a watch in your place, if you want."

I see him pull back a bit, so I add, "Not to worry, friend, no Temple priest will go near that foul place to know the difference. You can reach me here at the inn, for the usual fees of course." And then I wait to see if he takes the bait.

And what do you know, Marcus? Here he comes the very next day, which is his Sabbath. "It is not right for me and my friends to, um, work on this day, Cassius, so we have pooled our money for you. But where are your comrades?" he says, looking around.

"Do not worry," I reply, "I will send word and they will meet me at the Tomb." For of course I will pocket their share and do the duty myself. "Please do not trouble yourself further," I say. "You are a good and righteous man to keep to your faith, and we are only too glad to help."

You see, Marcus, he needed to hear some flattery to ease his guilt, as I eased his money into my own purse. A fair trade, I would say.

So. . . off he and his companions go on their way, and I back to the Tombs, but with a few more drinks and coins in me than before. How I have learned to love their Sabbath! Most folks are at Temple or home with their prayers, leaving none to bother me. I slept for a time in the heat of the day, but by evening I was sore from lying and sitting on the stones, and both hungry and thirsty. The coins in my purse were telling me how to handle my problems, so I waited a time until it was quite dark, then made my way back to the inn.

And as all Jerusalem knows by now, all hell breaks loose soon after when no one can find the damn body. Even with a sore head from a night of celebrating my good luck—a head which's feeling jus' fine now but maybe a bit tipsy, all thanks to you, Marcus—Well, I figgered only my Temple friends knew I was even *at* the Tomb. They was not gonna tell anyone or accuse themselves. They musta roused themselves early to be at the Tomb before the Temple bigshots arrived. My friend claimed a mighty force came outta th' Tomb, and knocked 'em all senseless. At least he had the brains not to tell th' truth.

It was jus' our bad luck this all happened 'round their Sabbath. They shoulda just let the dirty basturd rot out in the open, like a good criminal should. Nothin' like a pile of stinkin' bones to keep the crowds quiet.

Aaaaaah, this wine 's good, Marcus, only the bess for us, eh?

As to who took the body, maybe it was his cult, tryin' to steal his bones so they could sell 'em as relics or somethin'. Maybe hiss fam'ly took him, but I 'da bet on that rich guy, Joseph of sum place. He paid to wrap the body, but he coulda paid someone t' drag kingy's bones back t' his own home. Ev'ry once inna while, these Judees do th' righ' thing, like givin' their dead a good send-off and makin' 'em feel at home. Fat chance we 'll make it back t' Rome, righ' Marcus? Here's t' dying old an' in our own beds!

Toast! Thas a good lad. One more cup should do it, while I cun still stand. . .

I dont see wha Pilat 'sso maddabout. With all th' dead bodies we lef' scattered b'hind us, I cant see makin' a fuss over tha' scrawny nobody. . . .Oh, what'ya know, *another* joke, Marcus! No body!!

But this 's no joke—where there 's fuss, there 's trouble plenty and iss us fools gotta pick up th' pieces. I dont mind knockin' heads, but iss the knife in th' dark tha' scares me. Lemme face a honess en'my tha' knows t' play by th' rules, but spare me from th' mob!

Pox on the Judees, an' Pax on us Romana, says I, . . .

Shtill witty, thanks t' you, Marcus! All hail!

Ah well, all this 's th' truth, *in vino veritas*, dead iss dead, an' all that.

Juss dont tell th' Principale, eh?

IX

Testimony of Joseph of Arimathea

I, Matthias bar Shimon bar Judas, a duly sworn officer of this Sanhedrin Tribunal, having heard the testimony of said Joseph bar Joseph bar Ari of the prefecture of Arimathea, in the matter of the disappearance of one Jesus bar Joseph bar Jacob of the village of Nazareth, do offer this sworn record, may it please the Tribunal and The Holy One that I speak the truth.

The offenses in question involve the desecration of the dead through removal of said justly crucified Jesus (to be referred to as the Nazarene) by means not known to or sanctioned by the proper authorities. Said offenses having been perpetrated by persons unknown, this Office, in its authority and with just cause, has conducted several and various investigations of persons most recently in contact with the aforementioned Nazarene. Joseph of Arimathea, being of uppermost significance in the testimony of those interviewed, is our main defendant. Should this Tribunal, in its divine wisdom and just cause, require supplemental testimony from these other persons interviewed, I, Matthias, will duly comply.

But, may it please the Tribunal, several of this Nazarene's compatriots would not present themselves to the proper investigative authority of this Tribunal, while others of his associates were deemed of insufficient moral character to be worthy of the time and attention of this duly constituted Tribunal. One Cephas of Golgotha was most eager to testify, but was considered an inebriate, while several women of the Nazarene's acquaintance were known to the Temple authorities to be of dubious and even fully immoral character. One Mary, said to be the mother of the Nazarene, and a brother, Joseph, did comply with the summons issued by my office, but offered few useful details under thorough questioning. Both denied knowledge of said desecration and broke down into rather unseemly emotion. Neither seemed capable of dissimulation in my opinion, may it please the Tribunal. Finally, one of the Roman guards, having been assigned to the Nazarene's trial and crucifixion, did provide useful insights into the workings of the Nazarene's sympathizers and was instrumental in leading this Office to said Joseph.

This process thus leaving Joseph of Arimathea as the main interview subject, my Office conducted a thorough, even pointed interview over several days, stopping only for brief periods in order that the subject should regain his health and restore his memory to a level deemed sufficient by this Office. At one point, this Office thought to bring in his wife and children for thorough questioning, hoping they could supply missing details. This threat indeed increased the quantity, though not the quality, of his remembrances. The facts appear to be as follows:

Said Joseph of Arimathea has been a member in good standing of the synagogue located in said city, being a merchant of fine linens and dyes with frequent travel about Judea. He possesses an estate of some three hectares in land, a main house of some eight rooms, a sizable warehouse, with four house slaves, and numerous workers under contract, none of whom are known enemies or malcontents of the religious or Roman authorities. A younger half-sister of this interviewee's wife was said to be an associate of the Nazarene, but this Office was unable to re-examine the author of such observation. It is unclear what role this woman may have played in the present events.

Said Joseph reports that he is a "generous," "open-minded," and "ethical" man, employer, husband, and friend. Upon being interviewed, his wife and children used most of the same words Joseph used to describe himself, adding only "kind." This Office firmly suspects them of having been prepared and coached to give similar descriptors. One member of this Office suggested that we interview his house slaves and workers to verify these claims, but this idea was dismissed, as their responses would be unreliable due to his patronage hold upon them. This Office believes it noteworthy that he failed to use any of several long-established and respectful terms ("devout," "pious," "observant") to describe his character. A check with his synagogue purser did confirm that he pays his assigned tax but, again, this Office has not been allowed to ascertain his wealth to verify that his tithe is indeed accurately reported.

Said Joseph reports being in Jerusalem some weeks before the trial of the Nazarene, this reason reported by him as a "business trip." Independent observers of his business behavior have come forth at the urging of this Office, and report that he has been accused several times of false weights and measures, but no legal claims could be verified against him. In their words, "He is too clever to be caught outright, but one is not as rich as he without gaining at others' expense."

This testimony must be weighed as somewhat light on facts, but accurate in character assessment, as this Office also had difficulty extracting definitive answers from him about his business dealings, his associations, his beliefs, and any seditious or blasphemous behaviors before, during and after the events in question.

Several friends and trusted confidants of this Office reported that said Joseph did not attend any known services at the *Beit HaMikdash* or other sanctioned Midrash activities this Passover. They added that he had not bought any sacrificial animals nor used any of the sanctioned Temple moneychangers, despite his many so-called business dealings. This Office wonders if he purposefully avoided Temple authorities for reasons unknown. He himself stated that he was "too busy," which this Office considers an evasion.

This Office made several attempts to place said Joseph at any of the many reported sightings and activities of the Nazarene both before and during his time in Jerusalem. Joseph made several statements that could not be independently verified:

- "I may have unwittingly sold some cloth to him or one of his followers, but it is hard to tell one bearded countryman from another."

- "If it was not the Sabbath when he supposedly fed the multitudes, I was no doubt working. If it was the Sabbath, I would not have done such a long journey to hear him, as that would violate the proscription against work. Believe me, with my big belly, it would have been work indeed to travel so far."

- "I have not been to Cana or near Gadara in years. The trouble to reach those towns is not worth the small amount of trade I might have with them."

- "I have done business with three Samaritans, all male, and none living near a well."

(This Office did confirm the identities of these business contacts, and each Samaritan denied even having heard of the Nazarene. Although one can never trust the Samaritans, these particular men were clearly traders and seemed to have no political or religious deviations relevant to our hearing.)

This Office had learned from the aforementioned Roman soldier that the Nazarene was suspected of having stolen a colt from a citizen [name withheld by this Office] in the week before his trial. When questioned, said Joseph did finally admit to being involved in that situation:

- "I did send my house steward to buy a donkey so that my wife's half-sister [name withheld by this Office]—who is pregnant—could have some comfort and ease while visiting with us here in the city. I gather he did tell the man, 'My Master has need of it,' as the fellow was reluctant to sell. My steward was authorized to pay up to a certain price and no more. I gather he bought a sickly colt instead, but what happened next, I cannot say."

This Office attempted to further interview this steward, but said Joseph stated that he had sent the man back to his estate in Arimathea to tend to his business there. This Office, having expended more time and money than expected in investigating these assertions, wisely chose not to pursue the matter.

This Office, having diligently verified through our confidential sources that said Joseph was at his market stall throughout the trial of the Nazarene, asked him directly and firmly how then he had come to be involved with and pay for the burial preparations for the blasphemer and criminal Nazarene. Let the Tribunal know that we were vigorous and pointed in our questioning, even so far as suggesting some of the many sanctioned, righteous, but somewhat unpleasant consequences he and his family would face for dissimulation. Said Joseph appeared unfazed and altogether too calm in this Office's estimation when he answered as follows:

- "As you know, I am a dealer in linens, dyes, and other materials used in many activities, including burial preparation. I was simply approached by a member of his family—a younger brother, I presume—for enough cloth to make a burial shroud, as well as certain ritually-approved spices and other unguents needed for cleansing and body preparation."

Let the record state that said Joseph added the following impertinent qualifier:

- "If it please the Tribunal, I did not 'pay' to bury Jesus of Nazareth, but did extend credit to his brother, who had failed to bring sufficient money with him for such supplies. He could not know, I presume, that his brother would be tried and crucified. As I have been a 'guest' in this Tribunal's prison since the disappearance of Jesus, I have not been able to pursue the brother for payment. I sent a house slave to the man's lodging, but he found him and his family gone to parts unknown."

Let the record show that said Joseph was not able to produce any letter of credit, receipt, or ledger entry to verify this loan transaction. When questioned about this seeming irregular business practice, said Joseph answered as follows:

- "I took pity on this fellow who had lost his brother in a most unexpected fashion. He was grieving so deeply that immediate payment seemed indecent to mention."

This Office feels that these statements by the interviewee were out of character for one purported to be so clever and even ruthless at business. It is this Office's experience that a truly just and righteous man would have insisted on his due under the Law. When confronted with this well-known fact of human nature, and asked to thus explain himself, said Joseph responded,

- "I still have a heart."

When probed as to the meaning of this most cryptic and evasive answer, said interviewee did not respond or elaborate further, nor did he add explanatory details when we returned him to his cell for further vigorous examination. It is this Office's learned opinion that "heart" was some kind of coded message to the Nazarene's followers.

As this confirmed this Office's suspicion that said Joseph of Arimathea was indeed a follower of the Nazarene, we pushed him further to describe his direct role in removing and desecrating the Nazarene's body. A brief summary of our examination follows:

Office: "Do you know the whereabouts of said Nazarene's body?"

Joseph: "I honestly do not know."

O: "Do you know who may have taken it?"

J: "I do not know if any living person did."

O: "Please explain yourself, as it is common knowledge that a physical body must have been moved by a physical being. Remember that you are under oath and subject to punishment both divine and ecclesiastical."

May it please the Tribunal to excuse our human limitations, but this is where said interviewee finally broke and erupted in speech, so the following transcript is not verbatim:

J: "You claim to speak for The Holy One and to be men of religious learning, but your minds are fixated on the physical. You are like the worms that crawl in the earth, and knowing only earth you assume that all activities are physical. I can barely stand to talk to   you, as I can barely formulate a coherent thought! I believe I have witnessed Adonai breaking through our earthly life, and taking His Son home with Him! Can you even conceive of such a thing? O, to be alive at this moment! My joy explodes at you! I laugh at your petty concerns! O Adonai, O Adonai, forgive me for doubting You, O Adonai, I rejoice to be so near You! Alleluia, Adonai, Alleluia . . ."

At this point, the interviewee fell on the cell floor and was incoherent for several moments until physically restored to his senses by the examiners. He continued thus:

J: "All our lives we heard through Torah how Adonai spoke to the people of Israel. Generation after generation we heard how He cared for Israel, but we have heard nothing in recent times. Where was Adonai when the Romans invaded? In my grieving heart, I worried to the point of doubting. Did He forget His People? And then. . .and then this Jesus brings hope and word from above! The Lord of Hosts has not forgotten His people, He is speaking to us still!

"You small functionaries and bureaucrats, you ants and worms, you care only for the tittles of the Law and the so-called violations of the body, but your minds are closed to The Holy One—He can do what He pleases with Jesus! The physical is nothing to Him, as all of us are like as nothing to Him. He can snatch Jesus up and for all I know put him down again. Who are we to say what Adonai can or cannot do? Why are you not in awe that He was here? Why are you not groveling and asking forgiveness for accusing and killing His servant and prophet Jesus? The time must be at hand where your great sins—and mine—will be weighed by The Lord Most High against your pleas for mercy and forgiveness. O Lord, I am your servant, I am your servant, I am your servant . . ."

This continued despite several attempts by the examiners to again restore him to his senses, and the interview was deemed over, as it no longer bore useful information.

The insults uttered by said Joseph of Arimathea against this Office and Tribunal, along with his obvious involvement in this Nazarene cult led this Office to judge him complicit by means and manner unknown in the present charged offenses. We might have wished for more direct evidence, but will have to make our judgment based on character, which is well-discussed and justified in Midrash. Our recommendations for a measured punishment under the Law is contained in a separate document, may it please The Holy One who sees and knows all, and please this Tribunal, The Holy One's duly recognized representative of justice upon this blessed land.

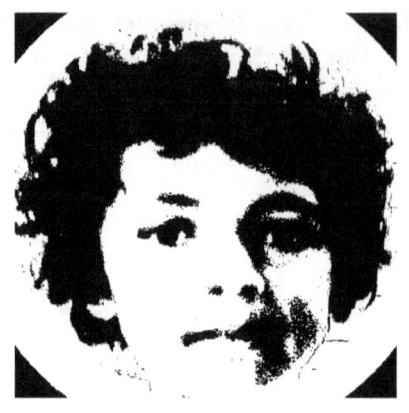

X

The Squirrel's Tale

MY GIVEN NAME IS Abram bar Joseph bar Joseph, but my family has always called me *Sna'i*, "the Squirrel." I was born small, thin, but wiry, with quick hands and feet, more like my mother's side of the family than my father's. My father was a carpenter and maker of all things useful, like his father before him, and it was my task—and my joy—to cut or break off the useful branches out of my father's reach. These smaller branches we made into baskets or fencing for the sheep or shade for sitting outside during the day. I gathered eggs from nests, and served as lookout to alert my father to approaching business.

If I may say so, I was so good at these small duties that I felt I owned the trees of my village. I knew them all, and some I gave names to: The Tangle, The Broken Man, and The Temple of Eyes. The trees were my joy and my refuge from the bigger boys of the village, who delighted in practicing their slings on me and my family. My father would say to turn the other cheek, take the pain, and show dignity; but as long as I could run and climb,

I chose escape. My pride always healed much quicker than the cuts and pain from those angry stones.

And what dignity or pride could my family have in our village anyway? Everyone knew that my uncle Jesus had been crucified and declared *koferim*[1] by the chief priests and rebbes. If my father's family had not been the only carpenters in the village—and the only ones with the proper tools of the trade, passed down by our fathers and the fathers before them—we no doubt would have been forced to leave. My father rarely lifted his eyes any more when walking around the village, rarely smiled even to us children, and could not say he had one friend upon whom he could rely. We already lived on the outside edge of town, the farthest from the synagogue, both wells, and the main market road. A few of the *goyim* would talk to us, and I did have a friend of sorts for a few years before they moved. Mostly, however, we kept to ourselves and I kept to the trees.

My family had stopped going to synagogue ever since my uncle's death, and especially after Jerusalem replaced our old Rebbe Nathan with a young firebrand right out of the *Beit HaMikdash*. This zealot held my family up as unclean and even dangerous to the faith, although it seemed to my young self that my quiet and unassuming father was not a threat to anyone. He seemed as harmless as our donkey, who shuffled meekly from harvested trees to my father's workshop.

My mother kept the Sabbath and observed all the rituals, but with fewer and fewer visitors, even these ties to the Faith slowly eroded. My older brother Ephraim also carried the family shame, having gone to our synagogue for several years before our uncle's death. He had followed all the teachings of the Torah, he had heard the sermons from Rebbe Nathan and believed in a stern but merciful God. Now he knew the difference between acceptance and rejection. He could count the friends lost and could feel the glare of a judgmental god. He was in a kind of perpetual pain, and a line began to form between his brows. He withdrew into his duties, leaving me even more alone.

I, being only six when we were expelled, only knew that I would no longer have to sit for hours on the dirt floor of our synagogue. I had little sense of this god who seemed to control how the rest of the village acted and thought. With time, my family drifted into a steady rhythm of our own little habits, and seemed cut off from the history and fabric of our faith. I was free from the social restraints of my village, but always on guard.

What does a little squirrel do in such a time? He learns where to find the smallest tidbits of joy, and develops a keen eye for predators. I could

1. Heretic.

creep through the trees and eavesdrop on the villagers passing below. I was small and almost invisible, a person of no account but with keen eyes and ears. I knew when to run, where to hide, and what bits of knowledge could be traded for protection and escape.

One day, as the sun was setting, distant cousins of my mother came for a visit, having travelled the 30 mils[2] or so from Jerusalem. After the usual greetings, the men settled in the front of our house while the women worked on the evening meal. I of course grew curious about these rare guests, and about what they might know about that fabled city. I had a favorite listening spot up the tree that shaded our fire pit, and I made myself comfortable while they cooked and chatted.

Adah, my mother's cousin, was all excited about our Uncle Jesus, but instead of admonishing my mother for the family association, she seemed full of admiration. Did my mother, being a married woman, ever get a chance to speak to Uncle Jesus? Did she ever hear him preach? Was she at any of the healing events—all these questions seemed to gush out of her at once, and it soon became obvious that this cousin had made the long trek from Jerusalem just to pump my mother for as much as she could tell her about my uncle.

At first, my mother maintained her modesty—and probably her native self-protection—by denying any real contact with Uncle. Even I knew this was a stalling tactic, as he had frequently eaten with us. He and my father would argue over religious and other matters while my mother would flit about serving food and drink. I was too young then to know what they were talking about, but I still remembered my mother hanging in the shadows under the eave while the men went at it. She was good at disappearing when need-be, a trait I soon developed as well.

Mother must have thought she had dampened her cousin's curiosity, and soon went about her meal duties. Cousin Adah was not to be denied for long, however, as she must have sensed that my mother was holding out on her. After the meal was finally served and completed, all was cleaned up and preparations were made for bed. My brother and I, of course, slept in a loft above the main room. Over time, I had worked a hole in our loft floor where a knot had been, and had placed my sleeping mat where I could easily listen. Nothing significant happened for a time, as pleasantries and family gossip were exchanged. The men said their goodnights, but the women kept up a low murmur.

As the voices grew softer, I must have dozed off myself, but a creak of the back door tickled my ears awake. What squirrel does not have a second

---

2. Roman unit of distance, about .7 of a mile.

or even a third hole around a house? Silent as I could be, I crept to the very eave of the roof, removing a loose stone beneath the roof beam so I could listen into the back yard. Even after all these years, I can remember what the women said.

Adah began her interrogation softly, having clearly sensed Mother's reluctance.

"I am sorry if I offended you, Yehudit, with all my questions. It has been some time since we last visited and talked, and much has happened to our families and our country since then. Jerusalem is a mess of confusion and rumor. Some say Jesus was a blasphemer, some say he was The Holy One's prophet, and many believe he was more than that! I know that his followers are in hiding from the religious authorities, and you say that you have been expelled from the Temple. Please know that I do not come from them!"

Mother murmured something that sounded positive to my ears, but still said nothing.

After a pause, Adah went on. "Many of our cousins gathered at the last Seder and they asked me to come here and find out what you know. Their families and those of my friends have been arguing and even fighting over what and who to believe—some blame Jesus for stirring up the Romans. Others blame the Elders for his death, while others believe he may be the long-awaited Messiah! Some even say that he died and rose again from the dead, but that has never happened before! No one can find his body to know if he is alive or dead. It is a kind of madness in the city! Please, please help me!"

"O Adah," my mother finally spoke. "You are asking me to step into the nest of vipers along with all the others!"

Adah gave a short gasp, and started to protest in some kind of urgent whisper I could barely hear. Mother cut her off quickly, however, ever fearful of offending.

"No, no, I am not saying *you* are a snake, Adah! Only that it seems to me in these troubled times that a small word dropped here and there can tumble into a flood—who knows the consequences?"

A silence came over them for a space, then my mother gave a kind of groaning whisper, "But in truth, if I do not tell someone what I have done, I shall truly burst. You are right, I do carry a secret, but it only started out as a kindness, you must believe me. . .."

My Mother, usually so quiet and small, seemed to shrink even further into the darkness of the night. In the filtered moonlight, I could just barely see Adah reach out a comforting hand on my mother's slumped shoulders.

"Yehudit," she said soothingly, "you know your Torah; you know how The Holy One and His prophets can pick even a lowly shepherd boy to do and speak great things. Why not you? Maybe you have had a part to play in all of this, but you must speak your lines. I promise not to judge you, whatever you say."

Mother took a deep breath, and slowly straightened her shoulders. "When the sentence was passed on Jesus, all I could think of was the pain he would feel up on that cross. It was too horrible to imagine, so I. . .I. . ."

Whatever courage she had seemed to fail her as suddenly as it had come.

Adah moved closer and wrapped her arms around Mother's shoulder. "Yes, yes, Yehudit, we all were in shock and pain. But you were the brave one, the one who did something. . ..So, what *did* you do?"

Mother again straightened herself, and looked deeper into the night, as if trying to summon the very images of that day. "I, I had a tincture with me brewed from a number of herbs and poppies, given me after my last baby nearly ripped me in two. I learned how to make this myself as needed, and carried some with me to Jerusalem. It helps, you know, with hip pain on long journeys."

In the darkness, I could hear Mother's voice shrink even smaller, as if she feared that Adah would shame her for being weak. Adah, though, was true to her word and said nothing, only cooing soft words of encouragement I could barely hear.

Mother continued, "Once he was condemned, all I could think of was to get him my whole supply, to dull his pain. But there were so many soldiers, priests, and other people crowded around Jesus that I had no way of getting it to him. '*Think, think, woman*,' I said to myself, but no answer came."

Adah was ready with her own story. "I was told they made him drag that cross over to that awful hill, where flies feasted and the stench of death was everywhere. I confess that I was too afraid and weak-stomached to watch further."

I could barely hear Mother saying something like, "There, there" to her cousin, and it sounded as if both were gasping or fighting back tears. I heard my mother say, "You must know, Adah, that it was only duty to my husband that gave me the courage to be there, but I could not even look up at Jesus or at the horrible faces of his tormentors. But then, what do I see on the ground just in front of me, but—miracle!—a jar of some sort of foul wine, left near the base of the cross. I learned later it was left by the caretaker of the dead, a drunk named Craephas or Cerbus or something. I managed to get to it and pull it under my robe. Then I poured the full measure of tincture into that cup and waited for further miracles.

"When Jesus called for something to drink, I saw my only chance. I pushed the cup at Joseph, who was allowed to approach his brother. How much Jesus drank I do not know, but soon his head seemed to wobble and he cried out a few words that were lost to me amid the angry muttering of the crowd and the caws of the carrion birds. Then all went slack in him . . . and . . . and . . . that was that."

Mother sobbed quietly with the memories, I guess, and Adah sighed along with her, murmuring soft words of forgiveness. "You did well, Yehudit, to care about his pain and to help. You were only human, yes? We should all have someone to care for us as we leave this life."

Eventually, Mother breathed a deep sigh, of relief, I suppose, at having a friend with her to share the jagged memories of that awful day.

Up in my sleeping loft, I was growing drowsy, and did not know what to make of Mother's secret. It seemed to me that she was just being dutiful, but also brave enough to be near the dying, the soldiers, and the angry crowd. I also knew from all my spying that secrets were usually as valuable as all the trouble people took to hide them, and others to dig them out. Adah had certainly traveled a great distance to hear Mother's account. Both women had done their best to avoid their husbands' company. They had sacrificed their sleep, had cried, and gone through many twisting emotions before arriving at the heart of the matter. Mother's tale must be worth a great deal, I thought at the time, but I did not know what use to make of it. It was only in later years that this memory of her simple act of kindness began to gnaw at me.

XI

Samuel's Tale

SINCE IT IS THE Day of Remembrance, my son, let me tell you a little more about your mother's father, your grandfather Cephas, but do not tell your grandmother! She has nothing but bad things to say about him, and he did have his faults, may The Holy One have mercy on his soul.

You were not even born when he died, but you should know something about the tree from which you have sprung. This is one of the main reasons we even celebrate this day, for if the names of our parents, grandparents, and older ancestors are forgotten, it will be as if they had never lived. And it will surprise you, I think, to realize that once everyone knew your grandfather's name.

But first, check to see if your mother is about, as she also may not want you to hear what I have to say. It is too beautiful a night to have her upset and wailing in my ears.

All clear? . . . Good.

To be fair to her, it could not have been easy for her to have him for a father. Drink will do that to you. It can give you a miserable life and an early and cruel death, so mark my words. Still, he had his part to play in all the events going on around us, and it is right for us to remember him.

Your grandfather was a difficult and hot-headed man, truth be told, but he had his reasons for his anger and his drinking. He had one of the worst jobs imaginable, as caretaker and gravedigger at the hill called Golgotha over in Jerusalem. That Golgotha was where the Romans would crucify people, nailing criminals and zealots to this post sort of thing, and leaving them out in the sun to die and rot.

Do not make such a face, son. It is time you learned how cruel the world can be. Your mother can teach you about soft and loving things, but fathers must prepare you for the rest.

Anyway, the Elders gave him that job as a kind of punishment for his frequent fights and outbursts. He had a wife and your mother to feed as well, so he took what he could get. Needless to say, this job made him unclean. It is a wonder your mother and grandmother even stayed on with him, but perhaps it was either him or starvation.

This is another lesson from your ancestors, son—you are often on your own in this world, and no man should judge you for what you have to do to survive. Well, perhaps there are limits, but not like the kohenim tell us. They would have us lose everything we own if even one piece of meat should touch cheese, or we should miss one payment to the Temple.

Now that I think of it, perhaps they are also doing what they must to survive. Ah, now I am tangling myself into knots, so it is better to return to your grandfather.

Not that his tale is any less twisted. He was often drunk when I first met him, but seemed to have stopped drinking after meeting this Jesus person you may have heard about. Some of what he said was a product of his drinking days, some of his sober ones, and the last whispered as a kind of deathbed confession. Maybe this is why your mother and grandmother never want to talk about him—he was a mess, a fabulist, a great teller of tales when drunk. Anyone who came near him soon stumbled over all the broken pieces of his life, not knowing what to believe.

And this is another lesson, son—Belief is the grandfather of truth, for without it, how could anyone build a certain path to what is true? One has to believe the facts, signs, and testimony of what and who comes before, but also keep steady on one's own feet on the winding path from confusion to truth. But back to your grandfather.

I first met him when I wooed his daughter, your mother, whom I had met at the market. It took months and much tenderness on my part to gain her trust and affection, as some deep hurt and shame seemed to close her off from the world. She finally consented to introduce me to her family.

Looking back, she surely thought I was her path out of misery. I certainly was one of the few who would venture near the family and that awful place, but I sensed something fragile and all too human in your mother that made me want to protect her. There was no pretense to her, no false walls or trap doors, if you know what I mean.

You do not? A lesson for another time then.

Her family hut at the base of Golgotha was dark and chaotic, with dirt, crusted food, and a rancid smell of bad wine everywhere. I was always on edge when coming to see her, not knowing if I would find her father's corpse inside. He did seem to enjoy my visits, as I was a new audience to his many stories of impossible deeds, resentment, and revenge. He would tell me all about the ghosts, walking bones, and shrieking voices he had heard and seen in his days as a caretaker of the dead.

Your grandmother, on the other hand, hardly spoke in those days, not like when she moved in with us later, if you can believe it. I rarely heard a kind word between them. They would take my small gifts and endearments with not a word of thanks, leaving me lost in uncertainty about my prospects with their daughter.

There came a time when events changed so rapidly that it was as if night had turned to day and then to night and back to day, all in a blink of an eye. I have told you about that Rebbe Jesus of Nazareth who the Romans put to death, and who some now claim was the very son of The Holy One Himself. What you do not know is that he was crucified on that very hill where your grandfather worked.

Yes, it is true. Your grandfather was in charge of keeping that hill cleaned and empty of bones, to make room for the next victims I suppose. He probably would have been the one to eventually take that Nazarene down from the cross if it had not been the Day of Preparation and if a rich man had not paid to have him entombed.

Your grandfather grumbled that this interference had cost him his usual cleaning fees, but all that was forgotten a few days later when your grandfather—yes, drunken, unclean, ill-tempered man though he was—claimed to be the first one to see this Jesus rise from the dead! Cephas told this to everyone who would listen, but at first no one believed him, knowing that he was a drunk and a liar.

Soon, however, more and more people started seeing this Jesus appear to them as well. Your grandfather was no longer shunned, but was given renown as the first to see this strange man who they said rose from the dead. Imagine that! Not a *golem*, not a Greek hero of myth, but a person we actually knew who had visited Sheol[1] and come back alive! I can scarce believe it myself.

Anyway, your grandfather now got invited to speak at all the inns and social gatherings of those eager to meet the man who had been that close to a Holy One. Suddenly, he had all these new friends and all the free drinks he wanted. I could almost see his head swell to bursting with pride in himself. His drinking was even worse, but at least he cleaned himself up a bit now that he had social engagements.

I myself heard him speak several times, often in the same words, how this Jesus had floated out of the tomb while Cephas was doing his caretaking of the area. Cephas would then fall on the floor, showing the audience how awe-struck, shocked, but humble he was, bowing before this apparent angel of The Almighty. Cephas would say: "Yea, truly, listen to me, you doubters and wonderful friends! It was after the Day of Rest, it was, and I was going about my regular duties, cleaning up and tending my little plot of vegetables. Well, I hear a great rumble, yes, like as the earth was shaking, and Lo and Behold! I see that the rock before his tomb has rolled back—and there he is, upright as ever before. This does not happen every day, so, just to be safe I throw myself on the ground and says, 'Do not smite me for my sins, Oh Great Angel of The Lord,' but you know? He just smiles at me and says, 'Rise, dear Cephas,' and can you believe it? He knows my name and I had never met him in my life! 'You are not such a bad man,' he says. 'True, true,' I say in return, 'but you may be the only one to think so.'

That got him his laughs and a fresh pour in his cup.

The crowd would then exhort him to speak on, which is like giving a waterfall permission to flow. "As I remember it, then Jesus says something like, 'I have seen death, and it is not so great. I came back to tell the living to, um, enjoy all the living they can while they still have time.'"

This simple-minded prophesy did not go over too well the first time he told it. His audience had started to grumble and turn away. Your grandfather could see his future drinking prospects start to dwindle, but he was never at a loss for words.

"Ah, this drink must have muddled my mind for a moment, but now I remember! Jesus looked me in the eyes and said, 'Cephas, I have come to offer forgiveness and eternal life to all. I can remove the rocks that weigh down your soul. I know the way through the door of death back to the land of the living. I am the door to all those who believe.'

"Well, I believed right then and there, I can tell you. If there is some kind of door, I want to be the first in line!"

---

1. Hebrew term for Hell, Hades, the underworld.

That usually brought the crowd back to him, and they would almost fall over each other trying to buy him his next drink.

Your grandmother, bless her soul, had had enough. With him gone so often to the inns of the city, he was neglecting his work, losing his fees, and failing to keep a tight grip on her whereabouts. One day of my visit, I found her and your mother packed, with their few household goods thrown onto a blanket in the middle of the floor.

"Samuel," she said, "it is now time for you and my daughter to marry, but all I can offer for a dowry is the rights to an olive grove in Galilee that has been in my family for generations. There is no one left to tend it, so it might as well be you. My husband, may he be cursed for a fool, must not know where we are going, or else he would bring his nonsense to our very door."

Well, that was the most I had heard her speak in the months of my courtship, and I was both stunned and excited by this swift turn of events. She clearly wanted me to take them away that very day, and was most insistent that it be done with urgency and stealth.

It was in our favor that they lived isolated from the rest of the city and had no neighbors to mark their passing. Needless to say, neither of them were known in the inns we passed, as your grandfather certainly had not brought them in to share his moments of glory and renown. We made it to my lodgings without notice. I gathered enough of my belongings to make the journey, leaving enough behind to allow me to tend to my city business while I entered marriage and the country life.

Maybe it was the loss of his girls that finally touched him, for I visited him four or five months after our elopement and found the place surprisingly clean. His small garden was well-tended, with new flowers planted out of the noonday sun. He was sober, I believe, although I had never seen him such and almost did not know this new man. He had set up a bench away from the cursed hill so he could look at the sun rising over the East wall, and there we sat and discussed further what he had seen and how it had changed his life.

He surprised me by asking first after his wife and daughter, and smiled when I assured him that they were well. He said he held no ill will about their abandoning him, saying he deserved all that he had suffered." He also confessed that he had hardly cared about their departure at the time, as his many new drinking companions had included a few of the looser women in the area.

"Something must have happened," I said, "to change your ways, as you were clearly drinking yourself to an early grave."

He smiled ruefully, and gave a sad sort of laugh, "You do not know how right you are—just look at me now."

It was then that I noticed that his right leg was bent and withered beside him as he sat, with a crutch in easy reach.

"This leg tells a tale. I had taken my 'show'—for that is what it was, no use denying it—out to the tomb where I had first seen Jesus. I was well into the wine when the whim came on me to preach from atop that very rock. With the help of my companions, I crawled to the top and started my oration. Maybe it was the exertion, or the stupefaction of the wine, but no great words came to me. I stumbled through my set speech, but the crowd had heard it all before. They began to boo, shout abuse, and walk away. A few threw rocks of their own, but their aim was as wobbly as their footsteps.

"I can only tell you some of what went through my mind—my old anger at being mistreated, fear of being hit with the rocks, panic over the wellspring of my words drying up. I was flinching from the rocks while reaching out to them to return when I lost my balance. I flailed in all directions before falling off my perch. My right leg caught in a cleft of rock and felt like it had been ripped from my body, while my head thumped solidly in the dirt. My few boon companions thought this was great fun, and waited a while to see my next act, but I was barely conscious. They must have tired of my poor performance, and wandered off. How long I lay there, I do not know, but in my delirium, I sensed dark shapes moving about me. I screamed, believing they were the damned dragging me into the underworld, but, instead, gentle hands lifted me up and brought me back to my hut. I passed out, and when I awoke, he was here."

I knew enough to be silent, and let your grandfather gather himself. He took a long drink of what I assume was water and continued his tale. "It was Jesus himself, come again to this awful place of his near-death."

I must have pulled back and made a face, as your grandfather then assured me, "I know how it sounds, after all my drunken tales, but I am telling you the truth now that there is no audience, and I myself have been to hell and back. Those gentle folks who had brought me home after my fall were undoubtedly some of his followers, and must have told him of my injuries.

"Jesus had filled out considerably, no longer gaunt and pale, but still with those beautiful, sad eyes. 'Why have you come,' I almost stammered, fearing that he surely would rebuke me for my boastful tales and for profiting from his story. Instead, he said, 'Cephas, you were the first to see me and yet you did not get the authorities. You freed me and clothed me with your own tunic when I emerged half-naked from the tomb. You gave me bread and wine, and ran to get help when my dear Mary was too stunned to move. I owe you my life, Cephas, and I have come to keep you from losing yours.'

"'Am I that close to death?' I wailed. 'My legs are a ruin, my head throbs and aches as if someone has pierced it with a spear. Am I to die tonight? I am no one special, I am not like you who can cheat death and rise from the grave.'

"Jesus calmly replied, 'I have come to tell you that you too can rise from the pit of pain in which your actions have placed you. It takes no one special to be worthy of new life. I was just a nobody from nowhere when I answered my calling. Partly in thanks to you, I get a second chance to speak what I believe Adonai wants me to say. My friends here can minister to your physical wounds and try to set your leg straight again, but I have come to set your twisted soul aright.'

"'Are you a magician, then?' I whined, for I was still not sure exactly who or what he was. 'Can you make my pain disappear, or my mind to forget all the harm I have done to myself and others? Can you reach inside my body and change who I am?'

"Jesus replied, 'Truth to say, Cephas, I do not know yet all of what I can do, or rather what My Father in Heaven can do through me and my followers. None of us has been down this road before. All we can offer you is a small thing which is yet larger than all the power in creation.'

"Jesus paused, and as the silence between us deepened, I began to fear that he was playing with me, giving me riddles that I was too weak and pained to solve. For once, I managed to control my temper and impatience, and asked, 'Please, new and mysterious friend, what is this small but huge thing that can cure the sickness inside me?'

"Jesus smiled that smile of his, and said simply, 'Love.'

"I was momentarily stunned, or maybe unimpressed—I had expected some special chant or arcane medicine that heals your bones and takes away evil thoughts and memories. When I said so, Jesus motioned to his followers who were tending me.

'See these new friends of yours? Love is the power that caused these strangers to leave the crowd and try to heal a fallen, unclean, and lost man like you. Love is what binds us to each other and even to you in true friendship—not the friendship as fickle as your drinking companions, nor the friendship of those who pay for the best seats in the Temple, for the one kind lasts only as long as the wine flows, while the latter depends on mutual flattery. Instead, we are a community who are committed to all that is good in you and our neighbors. You may not know it yet, but the love and friendship we offer you tastes sweeter than the best wine, lasts as long as your span of days, and opens your heart to all the beauty of Adonai's creation. If your heart lets us in, your soul will heal, Cephas.'

"I must tell you, Samuel, I cried like a baby then, cried like I had never cried when my mother died, or when my family left me. I cried until I thought I would die a second time!

"I must have passed out in exhaustion, for when I awoke, my whole hut had been cleaned. I was resting in a newly made and comfortable bed. There was a bit of soup on the fire, bread on the shelf, and an older woman there beside me mopping my head with a cool cloth. My leg had been set into a sort of wooden cage, and my headaches were gone. Each new thing was like a gift, undeserved and yet precious.

"I had never received anything but scorn from others before. I had given the world abuse and received twice back. My life had been a series of scrabbling attempts to grab what brief pleasures I could, and I could call no man a true friend. Yet, here was this Jesus and his followers who did not seem to count my sins against me. I asked the woman her name, and why all the effort to restore me and my house to health. 'You had need,' she said simply. She accepted no money for her time, and just asked me to remember the Master's words.

"For several weeks, different members of the fellowship would come by to tend to my needs while I slowly healed. When the craving for drink came on me, I would share my anguish with my new friends. They assured me that nothing earthly could move me if I had a firm foundation in love. It took me some time to realize that love was not something you just felt toward a woman, or your child, or only those who were first good to you, but it was like a love for all of creation.

"When I was strong enough to walk a few steps, they made this bench so I could rest outside my little room. I began to see the small beauties of the days as they passed, the regular songs of the night birds, the sound wind makes through warm palm trees, the laughter of children running in play.

"From my hut, however, I could still hear the march of soldiers, the noise of the crowd, and the cries of those crucified. I resolved to give the dying as much comfort as I had received myself, but I was not so foolish as to do it out in the open! Another man had been given my old job, but his house was on the other side of the hill and I was left alone. I have learned to sneak out at night and bring the condemned water and as many comforting words as I can recall from Jesus and my own well of gratitude. I only regret that I can not release them from their pain. I receive my share of curses, but also pleas to help the families they are soon to leave behind. I also pass along their requests to my new friends in the Fellowship, but with my mangled leg I can do little else.

"I get by with my little garden and help from the Fellowship; once the word got around town that I was no longer drinking, I even helped some of my old drinking companions to stop wasting their money at the inns.

"I am not a smart man, Samuel, and I suppose I needed to hit my head on rocks and break my ornery spirit before I would take this life seriously. Pain tells you that you are on the wrong path; so do all our feeble attempts to dull or avoid pain. This leg reminds me that I have paid for my sins, but it does not define me or make me bitter. I am not a young man anymore, but this new life of mine is something I could never have imagined. Once you get a taste of this love that Jesus talked about, you want to keep giving it, letting it flow to others in need. It is like the water needed for all growing things. It is like, like, aah, there are no words, really, to do justice to this feeling."

Your grandfather had said what he wanted to say, I guess, and seemed content to rest on his bench and watch the sunset. No longer was he grasping for the crowd's attention, or chasing that next drink. In a kind of stunned silence, I rose to leave. He gave me some bread and hard cheese for the road, and beckoned me closer. Imagine my surprise when he gave me a kiss on the cheek!

"That is what the Fellowship does, Samuel—the kiss of peace they call it. It shows that we trust and love each other enough to drop our guard and accept that the other offers no harm. Will you please give it to my wife and daughter for me? Tell them I am truly sorry for all the misery and pain I caused. Be good to them, Samuel—they deserve some joy and sunshine after having lived under my dark roof."

And with that, I returned to our olive grove. I told your mother and grandmother how your grandfather had changed, but they were doubtful, to say the least. Much bitterness flowed out of them, like a boil being lanced. It took some time for them to grudgingly admit that change was possible, even for one as wasted and neglectful as Cephas. They promised that we would all pay him a visit once the harvest was in and taken to market in Jerusalem.

So, the time came when we traveled to Jerusalem and finished our business at the market. We paid our taxes to the Romans and somehow evaded the ministrations of the Temple pursers and the other fleecers and hawkers who linger at the edge of all places where money is exchanged. We went to visit your grandfather, but to our dismay we found him in a very sorry state. Some kind of infection had traveled from his leg to the rest of his body; a sour, rotting kind of smell hovered over him as he lay limp in his bed.

A young couple—country-bred, by the looks of them—were tending to him as best they could, but they shook their heads when I asked what could be done to help. "He has been preparing himself for Heaven," said the one; "Perhaps The Father has need of him." I was too upset to probe his meaning, but thanked them for their help. "We will be outside if you need us," he added, and then they both took their leave to give us time alone.

An awkward silence followed, as you might imagine. Your grandmother just stared at her husband, as if not recognizing the man. He had shrunk even in the little time I had been apart from him, but a strange warmth and glow seemed to shine from his smiling face. "I have never seen him smile in all these years," she whispered, "Especially when events go against him." I believe she was more suspicious than anything else, as if he would suddenly leap from his bed or ask her for money.

I roused myself from my distress and gently urged her and my wife closer to the bed.

My wife was the first to speak. "Hello, Father, it is your daughter and wife come to visit," she said simply.

No use asking how he was, as it was plain he was dying. He fluttered his eyes a few times, and an even bigger smile seemed to light the room when he finally brought her into focus. In a weak voice, tremulous with long-suppressed emotion, your grandfather stammered, "My hearts have returned, oh, the blessings I receive."

Your grandmother harrumphed at that. "Yes, a fine blessing it is to be dying and to have to rely on strangers to care for you!"

Cephas looked around for his friends and said, "They are part of The Fellowship of Jesus, come to ease my journey to Heaven. Without them, I would not have lived long enough to see you, my hearts."

Cephas then looked at me, giving another of his rueful laughs, which in his dry throat sounded like the creaking of trees in the wind. "I once said, Samuel, that I wanted to be first through Jesus' door to Heaven, and it looks like I will be. Be careful what you say, my son!"

I could see that he tired easily after each declaration, so I got him some water and propped him up as best I could. Cephas thanked me and turned again to his daughter.

"Deborah, you have been a dutiful daughter who gave much more than she received from me. I am sorry truly for all my selfish, neglectful ways, and ask your forgiveness."

Your mother was crying by then, son, and could only give him an awkward hug, perhaps the first of her life. She nodded her head and smiled; her father let out a kind of mournful but happy sigh, as if freeing himself from a lifetime of shame and guilt.

"You have set my heart at ease, my dearest. I would be clean of the sins and hurts I have caused when I go to see The Father. I only regret that you have not met this Jesus who has saved me from myself."

Cephas then looked at your grandmother, who stood still as a rock and just as emotional. They stared at each other for a time, your grandfather smiling despite the sternness in the woman facing him.

"What have you got to smile about, you fool?" she finally said, though not unkindly.

Your grandfather nodded almost meekly, saying, "Well, you have me there, wife. I was a total fool for most of my good years, but hope to have been a good soul in these lame and broken days." He asked for some water then, and seemed to gather himself again. "I smile because that is the only gift I have left to give you, the only sign I have of my new life. It is too late for regrets and recriminations, as I have little or no future left in which to prove or redeem myself in your eyes. I am only sorry to leave you before really knowing you with my own new eyes."

He looked down out of habit, I believe, but then reached for a smile and raised his face to meet her gaze. "Bless you for coming, Leah. Soon I shall pray for you before The Lord Almighty, if what the Fellowship says is true about Heaven."

"And what is that?" your grandmother replied, relaxing her stiff silence a bit. Cephas now held your grandmother with his eyes.

"They say that, just as Jesus was raised from the dead, so we who die will come alive again before The Lord Almighty. Alive again! No broken bones, no drunkenness, no hateful soul, only the joy of being with Adonai!"

I could see that he believed deeply, and that his faith had taken away any fear. He was fading even as he spoke, however, and I knew that he would take his memories to the grave if I did not ask him all that he could remember of his time with Jesus.

"Please, father;" I said, "You have more than just smiles to give, you have memories of this Jesus to give us, the living."

Your grandfather disappeared into himself for a time, no doubt gathering the shreds of his memory into one place. "Please forgive my old brain. Even now I have trouble separating what really happened from what I imagined or what I embellished to get those free drinks at the inns. This I know: I was hungover that early morning near dawn when I went out to do my business behind the hut. I heard some kind of moaning from inside the tomb where he lay. I must have thought some animal was trapped in there, and, fearing that I would be blamed for any desecration, I went to investigate. I pushed the rock aside as best I could, and was startled near to death to see this shrouded form writhing on the ground. I really put my shoulder to that rock then, and squeezed inside.

"He was flailing at the linen wrap, and not getting very far with it. I remember asking something like, 'Are you still Jesus?' as I could not be sure what manner of creature it was, a *golem*, a devil, or what. He muffled what I took as a 'yes,' and I screwed up enough courage to first free his head and mouth. He gasped for air, and said, 'I am still Jesus.' Recognizing the face, gaunt and sickly pale though it was, I grabbed a shard of rock or pottery, and cut away the remaining shroud until all that was left was his loincloth.

I helped him stand as best he could, and somehow, we both squeezed back through the cave opening. I then sat him out in the gathering sunlight, away from the stench and darkness of the tomb."

"So, no floating apparition?" I asked.

Cephas just shook his head. "I always knew how to tell a good story, Samuel, and for that I ask forgiveness. But who would want to know the dirty parts of truth? People want truth to be shiny and heroic, and how I yearned to be heroic too, if only for a moment.'"

He paused and a heavy silence followed for a time, until I asked him to go on.

"I could see that Jesus was in a bad way, so I ran back to my hut to get what I could, a wine jar along with some bread and my work tunic to clothe him against the dawn chill. He was a weak mess as you can imagine, with ribs showing and scabs forming on his bloodied wrists and side from the indignities of the cross. I helped ease the wine down his parched throat. After a time, he was able to hold the bread in his two damaged hands, and so he gathered some strength.

"Even in my muddled state, I knew enough that the Romans would not take kindly to a failed crucifixion, as that is what I thought it was at the time. I asked him where his family or followers were staying so I could alert them and get them to spirit him away. He named an inn that I knew from my drinking, and off I went. After a short while, I ran into some of his women coming up to sit by his tomb, I guess. I must have babbled something, for off they took. I confess that I was so shaken by the whole experience that I continued on to the inn and had some drink. Eventually one of his followers came down for an early breakfast. I told him my story, but by then I was slurring and nearly incoherent with a mix of fear, exhaustion, excitement, and perhaps a jar or two. He just looked at me in confusion and disbelief, and backed away.

"I do not know what he did or what happened next with his friends, but in the days that followed, more people reported seeing Jesus and hearing about his having returned from the dead. I started getting many new friends and drinking companions, but lost you and Deborah, wife, due to all my foolishness."

We sat in stunned silence for a time, and Cephas was understandably spent from the exertion required for his tale. He nodded off to sleep, leaving so many questions unanswered that I almost thought to rouse him from his rest. Did he believe Jesus had really died and been restored to life? Who could prove that this so-called resurrection was not the messy business Cephas described? Out of respect for him and all that he had been through, however, I controlled myself, as did his women. *"There will be time to learn more,"* I thought.

We sought out his caretakers, told them where we were staying, and took our leave after imploring them to alert us if his condition worsened. Not a day later, however, the husband came to our lodging and told us that your grandfather had taken a turn for the worse. We rushed to his side, to find him feverish and even more limp, as if melting into the bed. He still had that smile on his face, though, and briefly opened his eyes when we held a water-soaked sponge to his dried and cracked lips.

"Good-bye, my hearts," he whispered, "Love . . ."

And that was all.

Your mother wept, and even your grandmother seemed shaken by his passing.

In the months and years that followed, son, we half-expected to see your grandfather again, as Jesus himself had reappeared to his believers. Your grandfather had certainly played a special part in all the events surrounding Jesus, and we all had hoped he would be rewarded somehow. We wondered if your grandfather had somehow displeased The Almighty and thus been denied life again on this earth, or if he was alive but in some other world separate from ours. We did not want him to just be dead.

It is almost impossible to know the unknowable, son. Some things do become clearer over time, but so far Jesus is the only one I know who came back from the dead. You will no doubt hear many people speculate about the events of Jesus' resurrection and what it all means, but your grandfather was actually there.

For myself, I can only say that Jesus cured your grandfather of his drinking, and changed his very soul through the power of love and fellowship. As you know, your mother and I have joined the Fellowship ourselves, and it has seemed to us that small miracles occur every day. You might have even noticed that we do not beat you as other parents do to their children— see, that is a small gift to you from your grandfather and this Jesus!

Yes, yes, there is still much pain and death in the world, son, but we have found that believing in Jesus and love makes it all easier to bear. As to whether or not there really is a Heaven, I am afraid we will not know what is true until we die. Even then, we may not be able to tell you ahead of your time so you can be prepared. Heaven and death are indeed shrouded in mystery, my son, but this feeling of love seems real. I suppose we all should hold onto what we know, and leave the rest aside until we know more. No reason to let our imaginations run wild in areas where it does not belong.

XII

Resurrection Road—The Steward's Tale

I WRITE THIS EPISTLE of my own now that my lord and master Joseph has died. My name is Jason, Greek by birth, heritage, predilection, and training. I was *epitropos*[1] to his estate here in Arimathea, and now live out my remaining days on retainer in a pleasant corner of his property. His death, though sad in many ways, has freed me from my vows and my service to him and his family. I now have time both to contemplate my life's work and to prepare myself for whatever shall come after this life.

My master had always urged me to consider Heaven my reward, and to repent of any sins prior to facing my own final judgment. Of the many subtle and at times not so subtle transgressions inherent in being his *epitropos*, I have no regrets. Business is business, as normal and essential to life as breathing and eating. I spilt no blood, nor was anyone killed or even maimed by my direct actions or on my account. If more wealth came to my master as the result of my cleverness, I would much rather take credit

---

1. Greek term for 'steward" or house/estate manager.

than shame. Let shame be the clothes of the sorrowful and meek, neither of which suit me. The God that I learned about from Jesus of Nazareth will surely understand and admire a man of my skills and achievements. What was it that Jesus said about the Talents? Ah yes, let them multiply, so that their increase can glorify God. Well, I have certainly added to God's glory, and so what if I kept a bit for myself? He has plenty to spare.

Besides, I had a not-insignificant role to play in Jesus' later life, from his alleged resurrection to his disappearance afterwards. No one has found my name in the accounts of Jesus' ministry or life, and it is time to set the record straight. I shall not keep my light under a bushel, especially as I have no other legacy to mark the meaning of my days on this earth. Surely my actions are already forgiven by this all-knowing God and count for something in my favor.

No, I do not write this for God, but for future generations. I believe that Jesus spoke to me in unguarded and totally honest moments, away from his adoring disciples and those who exalted him for their own purposes and dreams. The small realities of our time together hopefully will prove a kind of leaven for the mix of belief, faith, mystery, and myth that is already enveloping him.

Out of respect for Jesus, however, I will bury this account in my tomb so that no one learns from me where the living Jesus currently resides or what he does. Let the years go by until this generation is good and dead, and Jesus safely gone. Let it be up to God whether these future generations discover my testimony. I can only hope that this wasting disease gives me the time to tell the tale.

Let me start with the Passover when the Sanhedrin accused and eventually had the Romans do their killing of Jesus. Ah, the Sanhedrin. By and large, a most imposing collection of self-important, judgmental, and entirely pedantic sourpusses with not an ounce of joy to them. I knew that my master had joined their council to promote his business interests, and because it was a great honor in itself. He was not beyond ambition in those days, although he gradually weaned himself from that heady drug.

I do not know exactly when he first started following the exploits of this Rebbe Jesus, as I dealt with the business and not the social or religious side of his estate. It could be that Joseph kept these matters secret from me, as well as from the Sanhedrin. He knew how to present different faces to people of different backgrounds. That was partly why he had me, a Greek, in charge of his estate to begin with. I could deal with Judeans and *goyim* alike, and could continue his business dealings even on the Sabbath, when he himself was enjoined from work. Joseph had a keen nose for business, and was most anxious to extend his trade with all the nearby nations and peoples outside the reach of Jerusalem. Perhaps this is why he favored this Jesus to begin with—he saw a man comfortable with all races and religious persuasions.

Joseph rightly feared the Sanhedrin knowing about his contacts with the Nazarenes. He did have to do some fancy footwork to explain why he had paid to have the body wrapped and entombed, but his protestations did not last long. He was imprisoned for a time for his apparent involvement, but if the Sanhedrin had really known all that he had done through me, they surely would have put him to a cruel and shameful death. Upon his release from prison he had the welts and bruises to show the disciples what he had suffered for their cause. He was a true friend of Jesus', a trusted confidant, a man who should be basking in God's favor even now.

I myself walked very carefully in those tense days surrounding Jesus' crucifixion and resurrection. However, any good *epitropos* knows discretion and I was better than most at my chosen trade. Joseph had asked me to choose a trusted servant to discretely watch over the tomb, and alert him if any damage was done to it or to Jesus' body. The tomb was to be his and his family's final resting place, and he wanted it protected.

I chose an older Greek servant named Ezekias for the task. He had been through war as a Roman conscript and had no fear of evil spirits. Ezekias knew how to camp rough and avoid detection. He must have found a somewhat comfortable spot for himself outside the tomb, and there he crouched. He reported later that he did see a Roman patrol the day of Jesus' death and Temple guards at the tomb the day after. These guards were replaced the next day by a single one, but he eventually disappeared, perhaps grown bored or thirsty.

On the morning of the third day, Ezekias awoke to some sort of commotion just before dawn. In the dim light, he thought he saw a figure enter the tomb. As instructed, he ran to my chamber to alert me to possible trouble. I sent him along to wake Joseph and then return to the tomb as quickly as possible, to help me as needed. I hurriedly dressed in my robes of office, but had enough sense to take my knife, staff, and purse, not knowing which might be required.

In much haste I arrived to find Jesus sitting alone by the tomb, gnawing on some bread and cheese and smelling of a foul mixture of sweat, putrescence, and, was it wine? He was in an awful state, as one can imagine, both emaciated and weak from a loss of blood. I quickly introduced myself as the *epitropos* of Joseph of Arimathea, to which Jesus gave no sign of recognition. He was too weak to challenge me or even stand. I knew it would be up to me to take the next steps, whatever they might be. I asked quickly where the other fellow was that Ezekias had seen, and Jesus nodded vaguely back towards the city while croaking, "To seek my friends." Relieved that help might soon be on its way, I nevertheless knew that he must be hidden in the meantime.

Although I was somewhat afraid that my spotless linen cloak would be soiled, I urged him to reach up and grasp my shoulders. I helped him to his feet, and we both rather stumbled away from the tomb and towards what looked like a filthy hovel at the base of Golgotha. It was the nearest shelter and I was most relieved to find it empty. I sat Jesus in the one chair that looked strong enough to hold him. Grabbing a ratty broom by the door, I started back towards the tomb, sweeping away our telltale footprints and looking for any signs of trouble or help.

Ezekias was back first, and warned me that he had seen some women coming this way with baskets in their arms. Not knowing if they were friend or foe, I arranged myself and Ezekias at the tomb as if we were there on official business. I straightened my elegant white cloak and drew myself up to my full height; Ezekias stood at attention, like the soldier he once was. As ill luck would have it, the women came directly to the tomb, and started to scream once they saw the rock dislodged, the tomb empty, and two stern men guarding the entrance.

"Silence, women!" I commanded in my best *epitropian* voice. It would not do to alert the Roman patrols that a great deal was amiss. "The man you seek is not here. It has been foretold, it is ordained," I said, hoping they would accept that all was as it should be. "Be gone with you," I added, hoping to buy some time so that I could effect Jesus' escape.

Two of the women were clearly disconcerted, and had started to walk away when the third one, a rather comely woman, boldly asked who I was and what had happened to her dear friend Jesus.

"And who are you to ask me?" I said in my most imperious tone. "What if I am sent from God?" I had learned from my many business dealings to always wrap myself in the authority of the highest-ranking person in the situation. Better to apologize for misunderstanding than to lose the deal due to cowardice.

The comely maiden paused a moment and then introduced herself as Mary, and the others as the mother and sister of Jesus. There was a tense pause while I weighed the truth of what she said. Hoping to put myself in a position where they had to answer to me, I asked them what their business was at this early hour in this deserted and deathly place. This Mary stated that they were bringing spices and ointments for Jesus' body, but I snorted at this.

"Hah, I know that a man from Arimathea has already paid to have the body prepared. You lie!"

This Mary looked me right in the eye, and calmly replied, "You may know this, but the Roman patrols might not."

I realized then that I was dealing with a clever woman who had carefully planned this excuse should they be questioned by the authorities. Here was a woman not to be dismissed or taken lightly.

With the sun having risen just above the horizon, cocks crowing, and daylight beginning to stream across the hills, I knew we must resolve matters quickly. I looked deeply into their eyes, and, besides a bit of defiance from this Mary, I saw only the expected sorrow of grieving women, mixed with fear and confusion over Jesus' disappearance.

"Follow me," I said, still in my most imperious tone. Perhaps I was enjoying being an agent of God after all.

I took them down to the hovel, and there they screamed again, in delight over the risen Jesus. They nearly broke his arms again with the force of their joyous hugs, but to this assault Jesus could only smile weakly. I felt somewhat rude interrupting their reunion, but we were all badly exposed to witnesses, with little between us and ruin. I asked them where the safest place would be outside Jerusalem for Jesus to hide while he recovered from his ordeal. They conferred with each other and with Jesus, and came up with a sympathizer's house south of Jericho, along the road to the Galilee. This house was near some hot springs, a place where Jesus could soak his battered bones and regain his strength. It was certainly too far for him to walk, but I thought if I could get him one of my master's city donkeys, he might get far enough away from Jerusalem to avoid being re-arrested. I sensed that this safe house could not be that far from Joseph's estate in Arimathea, so my master could provide additional help as needed.

I quickly decided that our little party should split up, as the women were known associates of Jesus and should not be seen with him. Ezekias, even more strategic than I in such matters, urged the women not to tell their friends they had actually seen Jesus, only that the tomb was empty. We needed to get Jesus well away from Jerusalem before anyone could celebrate and draw attention to his resurrection, however joyful. Ezekias also urged them to tell the disciples to leave for the designated meeting house by ones and twos over a few days so as not to attract suspicion.

Mary again asked who we were, and by what authority we were directing them. I looked up to the heavens, rather theatrically I must say, and replied, "Jesus knows." Although I was known in Jerusalem as Joseph's man, these country folks of his did not know us, and the fewer excited spreaders of news and names, the better.

I do rather wish I had given my name to that lovely Mary, and perhaps been offered her gracious thanks, but that would have to wait for safer times.

We then had a quick discussion how to spirit Jesus past any guards and out of the city. We noticed what looked like women's clothing in the hovel, but with his beard and height, we all knew that he could not pass. There was no razor knife in sight and no time to shave him.

The simplest, most realistic plans are the best in a crisis, I thought, so I decided to play an *epitropos* and he a servant. I asked Jesus if he thought he was strong enough to walk, and he answered, "I must be." I gave him my staff and asked the women for one of their baskets. Turning to Jesus, I said, "If questioned, we three will say we are walking back from the market with spices. If questioned about your truly shabby appearance, I will state that I am merely giving a beggar a chance to earn a few leptons."

Looking around the hovel for the props needed for our escape, I dressed Jesus in a threadbare cloak that lay in a dusty corner. Off we all went in our several directions, with Jesus trailing the required distance behind me, who naturally was playing his better. Loyal and true Ezekias flanked us as scout and protector. I had given Ezekias my knife in case we had to fight our way out of trouble, but Jesus had roused himself to give a simple, "No blood."

There indeed were times, even back then, when I sensed the presence of a higher power, one that we do well to appreciate, honor, and acknowledge. It was as if some invisible cloak descended on us as we glided like spirits back through the Gennath gate towards Joseph's city abode. Or maybe it was the imperious airs that I had already taken on, and that came to me naturally in any case. We passed through the early morning crowds as if we were just three drops in a gentle stream, flowing to join the rivers beyond.

There is always something peaceful and hopeful in a Jerusalem morning, before the heat of the day and the fight for business brings tension and subtle warfare to the streets. I could see that Jesus himself was looking all around him, drinking it all in, perhaps with new eyes. Thankfully, he did take care to lower his eyes, shuffle his feet, and act the beggar's part when passing any soldiers or Temple authorities. No one expected to see him and no one did.

We eventually got to Joseph's residence, fairly collapsing in the shade of the stable. Joseph had been waiting anxiously; he greeted us with tears of joy and great hugs, heedless of Jesus' sharp odor of spices and putrescence. I explained our situation as quickly as I could, and Joseph immediately set his servants to preparing food for the journey. He ordered another to bring warm water, cloth, and cleansing ashes so that Jesus could refresh himself further before departure.

Ezekias had gone to the stable, where he selected and brought forward the shabbiest of donkeys, meant to match Jesus' low estate. It occurred to me then how fitting but almost painfully ironic it was that Jesus should leave on a beast so similar to the one he had ridden in triumph mere weeks before. In his diminished state, he gave no indication that he noticed or cared, but he did seem most grateful to all of us for our help. He said lovely blessings upon us, which my master took with great solemnity.

Other than that, Jesus took in all the commotion around him with a sense of great peacefulness. Perhaps he was just harboring his remaining strength for the effort needed to play his part and endure the physical demands of his escape. I found him hard to read, but having come this far, I was determined to see our plan through.

Ezekias readily accepted the danger of taking Jesus back through the gates and towards sanctuary. He dutifully returned my knife, knowing that it would not do to be found in possession of such a fine blade. He had his own eating knife and a staff for support and protection while he walked next to Jesus. These would have to suffice for any bandits encountered on the road. They talked briefly with us about what they would tell any curious fellow traveler or more confrontative authority. We decided that the simplest truth again would serve—he was a sick relative going to the hot springs near Emmaus for a cure. Jesus certainly looked the part and his true destination would indeed take him quite close to the Emmaus waters.

Joseph asked Jesus if he needed any money for food, medicines, lodging, or other necessities, but Jesus just smiled.

"My Father in Heaven and my friends will supply my needs, as I would do for them as needed," he said. I thought this too idealistic, as my experience as an *epitropos* had proven to me that money solved many of the world's most vexing problems. I was in no position to gainsay a man of God, however, so I said nothing of my own beliefs.

With that, we bade each other farewell. Joseph and I returned to our quarters, and the two of them departed through the servants' gate and alley.

I was to learn later from Ezekias that the journey had been uneventful until Jesus met up with a follower of his and this disciple's companion. Although Jesus had wanted to announce himself to this Cleopas, he did not know the other man. Ezekias had cautioned Jesus to remain in his present guise as a sick traveler. He himself then fell back some paces as if going about his own business. He kept an eye on the two men to see if they startled or recognized Jesus, and was entirely ready to eliminate them as witnesses if they suddenly make excuses to veer from their destination.

When the party reached an inn for a midday meal and rest, Ezekias sat between the three of them and the door, again ready to block any unexpected move. Cleopas finally must have recognized something in this gaunt, friendly fellow, exclaiming, "My Lord, it is you!" His traveling companion merely looked confused while Cleopas and Jesus kept hugging and giving each other a kind of kiss.

Ezekias did not like the looks of the companion or the others at the inn, who seemed to be taking too much notice of this strange outburst of affection. He coughed three times and went to the door, both being a signal to Jesus that it was time to leave, and leave quickly. Jesus managed to extract himself from the warm welcome, but not before he was asked to give his blessing. He did so and promised to see Cleopas again soon. Ezekias remarked to me later that Jesus now seemed to hold his head higher and step with renewed energy, just from the encounter.

Ezekias was all for changing their route in hopes they would not be followed, but Jesus admitted he had told Cleopas he was traveling to the hot springs, when in reality their route branched off up the Jericho Road.

"I thought you men of God always had to tell the truth," said Ezekias, not unkindly.

"Ah yes, in a perfect world perhaps, but we are a fallen race, we are, we are. My subterfuge will do no harm to Cleopas, and hopefully our chance meeting will do him much good. On balance, I believed it was better to be safe than fully truthful." *A practical man for all his vaunted godly powers,* thought Ezekias.

Their journey continued uninterrupted and they arrived late at night to their destination. Jesus was exhausted by then, and the caretaker deferred any of the many questions he must have had so that Jesus could get much needed sleep. By the time he awoke the next day at mid-morning, he was exuberantly greeted by those of his disciples who had managed to arrive. Again, there was much hugging and kissing, with the disciples shouting their questions and hosannas over each other. Jesus was almost unable to make himself heard over the celebration. Ezekias felt that his mission was complete, and took his leave silently before he was drawn into the commotion.

There was another encounter with Jesus that bears some mention, as it proved momentous for all of us. It was perhaps two or three months after this journey when Jesus presented himself quite alone at our door in Arimathea. Joseph happened to be in residence and welcomed him in; he invited me as well and asked for Ezekias to be with us as servant.

"I am returning your lovely beast," he said. "She has done me excellent service, taking me from one fellowship to the next while allowing me to heal." He had gained some needed weight, but did not refuse any of the meats, cheese, fruit, and wine that Joseph gladly offered him. We made small talk during this meal, with Jesus beaming with a sort of blithe pride when listing some of the cities and towns he had visited and found disciples.

He seemed almost surprised at his preaching success, and I was again struck by his lack of guile and simple humility.

He, of course, gave glory and credit to his god, whom he called "My Father." I knew that his own father had died some years earlier when he was still in his teen years, but it occurred to me then that he had developed some sort of intimate, ongoing, and even hourly communion with this god figure. This "father" seemed to give him the strength, purpose, and resolve to continue his preaching even in the face of hostile authorities and dubious listeners.

His continued deference to and mention of this father made me think of my own, a distant and distracted man who had worked so hard at his trade that he died right at his work bench. As a middle son, I had been left to fend for myself, with only my wits and sharp eyes to guide me. I was generally pleased with how far I had come in the world. I had grasped early on the art and calculus of advantage. I could measure, weigh options, predict costs and gains, probe weakness, and ally with strength. All these skills involved a kind of hunting acumen; I was a lone wolf lusting after prey, proud of my stamina, sharp claws, and teeth. The struggle for advantage—for myself, for my master—had fully occupied my days and guided me with confidence through countless complexities.

But even I knew how lonely I was in my deepest heart. I had never married, but had followed unknowingly in the very dogged work path that had killed my father so young. Was I a dog or a wolf, then, or some dull oxen plowing the same ruts so that my master could reap the benefits? Had I forgotten or never even known how to be fully human?

Something like an ache and an emptiness started to devour me from within. I could feel myself become hollow and insubstantial; I felt as if I was floating above the conversation into some dark void. My mind frantically searched for something to hold onto, something to anchor me back to this life, something to believe in. As a Greek in a Hebrew world, I had always had a bemused detachment from the hundreds of rituals and obligations that had occupied most observant Hebrews I had met. Their god had always seemed too remote and stern for my taste, more a judge to be appeased than a father, or a mother for that matter. My skeptical, rational Greek mind had found plenty of human follies to doubt and even ridicule; indeed, I had feasted on these follies looking for advantage. I knew what I was not, but now I wondered if I knew who I was.

It was not my own vaunted knowledge and thinking that found answers or tethered me to something solid—It was the gentle touch of Jesus' hand on my shoulder and a kind voice asking me what was going on. I found I could not talk for fear of dissolving into tears, tears I had never shed for my father, any other human being, or even myself. I just stared at his face, so close to mine but seeming to be on a far distant shore that was receding into mist even as he spoke.

"Come back, Jason. You belong with us," he said simply. He waited to see if I could respond, and when I just blinked, he said again, "You are our friend and helpmate. We will wait until you are ready to return."

And I did return after a time, with some of my well-earned dignity intact I suppose. No tears, no cry for help, no loss of face before those I esteemed. Only later did I realize that Jesus had reminded me of my valued place in the scheme of things, of the presence of friends for comfort and understanding, and of the honored space they provided for me to make my own choices.

Yet, more than anything else, it was his gentle hand on my shoulder that stayed with me. We are so much more than just our thoughts and the images of ourselves we believe others hold in their minds; we are living, breathing bodies. I needed that reassuring touch that did not presume to intrude farther than I would allow, but rested in peace until such time as I was ready to acknowledge it. His hand was also solid and real, as was the affection and care behind it; I could not rationalize it away. In my position as *epitropos*, no one had dared touch, hug, cajole, or trespass on my body. I had been like some demi-king alone and isolated in a stout fortress no one could breach. Now I realized it was time to come down from my stark throne and mingle with people.

A kind of light must have come back into my eyes, so Jesus drew his hand back but kept his gaze firmly fixed on me.

"How did you know to reach out to me?" I finally asked.

"Oh, I know that far-away, even lost look," he said. "When my dear father died, I wept for days and could not be consoled. Then I went into a kind of numb, half-dead state where no food had taste, no words had meaning, and no sleep brought rest."

I nodded in sympathy for his loss and to keep him talking, so that I would not have to.

He continued, "My father had been my guide, my playmate, my fount of love. I must have thought of love as something almost physical back then, as if his death actually took something away from me that could never be replaced. In truth, love is like water—it flows in and out and around all the terrain of this world, but it is always love no matter where it is found. It can be scarce or ample, it can upend the boat of your life or bring the crops of your field leaping onto your table. It keeps us alive, and its absence starts us on the way to death."

Here he looked at me even deeper, "That is what I saw in your eyes, Jason, the pull of death in the midst of life. Believe me, I have been there more than once."

Perhaps it was the wine after a long ride that loosened his tongue, or just the intimate setting, so different from the usual large crowds that hung onto and drained him of every carefully crafted word. He told us of his early years as a doctor, of seeing the spirits of life and death wrestle over the souls of his patients. Of the importance of faith, hope, and God in tipping the balance to life.

"My followers are most enamored of those times when my cures seemed to win life from the brink of death, but of course I cannot tell them of those battles I lost. They need hope, and at times that can be as difficult and seemingly impossible as wringing water from the hardest rock. Moses did it for our ancestors, but only after they nearly died of thirst in the desert. Perhaps many of them did die, but were not mentioned in order that the tale prove hopeful. I must be that water of love for my followers. I cannot get salty or filled with bitter alkali. There can be no room in my heart for hatred, envy, or jealousy, even though these are feelings that God has seen fit to give us human beings. By the grace of God, My Father, I have somehow tapped into a deep spring of fresh, sweet, life-giving love that just keeps on flowing."

I had never known until now that I was so thirsty for this same water of love. Wine was a delight to the senses, and of that I had had my fill. Power and success were like some heady brew that fed an appetite that could not be sated. It had driven some men mad, while me it had left nearly friendless and alone. My pride would not let me show this thirst outright, but thankfully I simply had to keep the spigot of Jesus' life story open.

"You are indeed a blessed and god-given gift to those who heed your words," I said. "A rebbe of the highest order, even a prophet. But what of these claims that you are actually the very Son of God? I saw you nearly broken and left for dead at Golgotha, and surely no heir of God's kingdom should be made to suffer such shabby treatment."

This created quite a pause in his narrative, and Joseph gave me a sharp look, as if I had just accused a king of being a pig in disguise. For a moment, I feared that I had stoppered this spring of love, for I saw a look of some pain and even bewilderment cross his face.

He gathered himself and almost whispered, "You must know that it is not easy to be called by God, as the prophets have well understood before me. Yes, I believe that He supplies me with this spring of life, for love just comes to me and through me, not of my own volition. Where else could it come from but through The Lord's efforts to sustain life in this parched land? When I faced and then suffered crucifixion, I knew that I was facing a great evil, a hatred against all that I felt My Father stood for. I would be that soldier who fought to the end, only wishing to be worthy enough to take on My Lord's greatest adversary. Only once did my resolve weaken, when I feared that He had abandoned me. I *am* human after all, the Son of Man, as I have said many times."

Here he paused and took another sip of wine while we sat rapt and a bit awestruck to be invited into the very mystery of his existence.

"I fell into something like a deep sleep on that cross, with the screaming pain from those nails and my splayed limbs receding from me like a bitter memory. I remember nothing of that sleep, not even a light or singing angels or the fires of Sheol. I awoke after what seemed an eternity into the cocoon of my burial shroud, not knowing who or where or what I was. I struggled for hours to free myself, but could not.

"I again fell asleep, only to awake with somewhat more strength. I made enough noise that a man named Cephas finally freed me and returned me to the land of the living. He was as lowly a creature as God has ever used for His purposes. He restored me some with wine and bread; then I met you, Jason, a bit of a savior yourself.

"Did I die and resurrect? Did I linger in some half-world between Heaven and Hell, only to return to this world? It has been a nagging mystery to myself ever since, as it is only with my human mind that I can comprehend such matters. Truly, that mind has found no answers. That mind was blank while whatever happened to me happened. God is my only answer to mystery, and it must be God's will that I feel so alive. Resurrection has long been foretold in Torah, Jason, and now it seems to have happened to me. Above and beyond all my reported miracles, this is what has given my followers the most hope and joy. We humans fear death above all else, but perhaps no longer, no longer . . . "

After a polite pause, Joseph persisted, asking, "But does not the resurrection prove that you are truly the Son of God?" Knowing Joseph, he doubtless was eager to be told that he had played a role in saving God's own soul, flesh, and blood from death. Perhaps he imagined some great reward in Heaven for his good deeds.

Jesus smiled ruefully, and said, "Some of my disciples have begun calling me that, and I must confess that I have let them. It gives my words added authority and seems to explain much of the mystery surrounding my healing powers and my coming back from the dead. I hope it is not vanity that is speaking through them and thus through me. Perhaps it is beyond my human mind to grasp, that I indeed could be a Son of the Most High. Who is to gainsay what The Lord can and cannot do? He humbled Job, He brought whole cities to rubble—He could certainly have made me go through the doors of death just to test my faith, or the faith of His people, Israel.

"There are times when I am praying to God that I seem to hear his voice, reassuring me that all will be well and that He is well-pleased with my work. Like a son to his father, I can only hope to be worthy enough that He continues to answer me when I call. But. . .and this I beg you to say to no one else." He paused to look us each straight in the eye until we nodded our vow. "I have never heard My Father call me Son, not in so many words anyway. Who is to say He always uses words anyway? Often, I just feel a presence beside and around me, and that is enough."

He helped himself to some more wine, and it began to dawn on me that something more was bothering him, something that required wine to unearth from the dark reaches of his soul.

It was Ezekias, of all people, who named it first. "The night before battle, and sometimes in the morning as well, we soldiers would get good and drunk. We each had our own reasons, I suppose, but if I may guess, Master Jesus, it would seem that you are facing such an ordeal."

Jesus bowed his head; his shoulders slumped and his hands came together in prayer. He began to rock back and forth, as some believers do when communing with The Almighty. Joseph began to speak, but I caught him with a sharp cough, trying to give Jesus an honorable space as he had done for me.

Back and forth Jesus rocked on his stool; side-to-side went his head, as if his thoughts were tugging at some impenetrable knot. After a time, he stopped his rocking, released his breath in a gust, stamped his feet, straightened his shoulders, and put down his cup of wine. "Take this cup from me, Ezekias, for you have named my dilemma aright. It is good to be able to talk freely with friends like you who are outside my disciples, for they only reflect the best, most powerful images of me. The truth is that the Sanhedrin's soldiers and Roman spies are coming ever closer to re-arresting me. The more people report my resurrection and reappearance, the sooner they will be able to torture my secret location out of some unfortunate.

"No, I came here alone, hopefully without being followed, with the full intention of disappearing from this land, for their sake and my own. This is a most grievous decision for me, one that rips me from the very soil that gave me birth and purpose. But I would not tempt My Father to save me twice, and it would crush my believers to see me beaten and crucified again. Better that they think me gone, or ascended to Heaven and with them in spirit; better that they last remember me alive and vibrant, a true Son of God saved from death for their salvation. I must beg of you to help me escape once again."

My master and I were both stunned into a momentary silence, as we both felt the enormity of his peril and what it took for him to ask for help. I believe we had been so thrilled to see him alive that we never realized what added dangers this resurrection brought to his entire movement.

Joseph roused himself to ask the obvious question of where Jesus thought he should go.

"This whole world is ripe for a harvest of reborn souls," he finally said, "but I need to go to a land outside the reach of both Roman and religious authorities. There are Roman outposts in all the corners of this Earth, and many scattered Hebrew settlements as far as the Parthian Empire, North Africa, and Ethiopia. Just as I must leave my followers, I cannot risk even a passing caravan discovering where I am."

A silence again fell over us, as we realized that he did not even know where he was headed, only why.

My Greek mind was already calculating the geometry of his problems. "So, not on a trade route, and thus in an area with nothing to trade with either Rome or Jerusalem. Perhaps in a city where you could be lost in the crowd, but not one with a Roman or Judean presence. In an area where your message will find fertile soil, where the people are open to new ideas about God. In an area relatively free from warfare and strife, as you will have no kin for protection. And perhaps in an area where you can find work to support yourself while you gather your flock." It was not my task to solve his particular problem, but at least I could spur his thinking.

Ezekias shuffled his feet with evident hesitation before speaking, "Masters, if I may offer some small suggestion?" He waited a modest time. "Every soldier knows not to go into a strange land alone, so I wonder, Master Jesus, if you have distant kin or others who might receive and shelter you? Also, many a time I have disguised my true identity when scouting a new territory, whether for the Romans or my master here," nodding towards Joseph. "Would it harm your purpose to seem to be someone else for a time?"

Joseph nodded vigorously to this last suggestion, "Yes, please consider that, my Lord. You should know that your name is on every lip, and is passed from friend to friend like a precious blessing. Sad as it is to say, but your very name could become a curse for you if you keep it."

In his slightly inebriated state, Jesus showed every thought, doubt, and worry on his face. It was clear that these suggestions were all new and strange to him, and furthermore, that he had no experience in such matters. His head jerked up and down, and his eyes fairly jumped between the three of us. I had the uncomfortable image of a rooster pecking away at the ground looking for the one good morsel.

Then he shook his head, collected himself, and again went into prayer, but without the rocking. His head now tilted slightly from side to side, as he literally seemed to be weighing his choices. Now I had an image of him as alert as a heron stalking a fish; he seemed to be waiting for his God to send him what he needed, and I could tell that he was ready to strike immediately when he saw the path forward. It was marvelous to see his transformation and focus. I knew that with he would soon find his way.

Again, a sigh, but this was of pressure leaving him. "I thank you, friends, for your wise counsel. It seems that I am being pushed by circumstance and also called by My Father to resume the work of my kinsman, John, whom they call the Baptist. Rumor has it that there are a group of his followers who have fled to the land beyond and east of Damascus. I have heard John preach many times, and can easily pass as one of his disciples. They have not been hunted down like my followers, perhaps because their numbers are small and their leader dead."

Here he paused and said a brief prayer for his kinsman—so disrespectfully slain for no good purpose—and disappeared within himself for a time. When he returned to us, he seemed to have worked out the path of his personal salvation. "These Baptists are now led by those they call the presbyters, elders of the group who are seasoned in the ways of man and God. I hope to be accepted merely as one of them, and not as myself. It may take me some seven or eight days to reach their territory, if I am fortunate enough to have the use of one of your blessed beasts," he said to Joseph. "I would be most grateful for any supplies you could lend me for the journey, knowing that I could never return to repay your kindness."

Joseph for once did not gush or feign his humble thanks to be so useful. Even he could grasp what it took for Jesus to ask for help and to acknowledge the end of an entire chapter, nay, the entire first book of his life. He solemnly nodded to Ezekias, who left us then to make the arrangements.

Impelled by something unexpected and new within me, I heard myself saying, "You will need a companion on your journey, one outside your fellowship who will not betray your destination. I offer my heartfelt service to you; I can be that clever snake you preach about, and I only hope that you can bring out the nascent dove within me. I feel I am ready to love this world and your God."

At these last words, I began to cry for some reason, and I heard Jesus mutter, "Yea, water shall flow from a rock." I had to laugh at that, and then laugh at all the walls, pretense, self-denial, and obduracy that had defined my days. Oh, the tears and laughter had a merry dance within me; how unseemly, I thought, how odd but well met were these partners. As strange as these feelings were, I knew that I wanted to make room for them in my soul,

I who had scorned such emotions as womanly. I was teetering on the brink of some great expansion in my vision of life when the practical necessities of the situation finally settled me down.

Jesus gratefully accepted my offer, and gave me the first of many subsequent embraces, as warmly as if I were an old comrade. I took my leave, then, and went to my chambers to pack, still in some disbelief at myself for such a rash and sudden change of heart.

After a brief time, Joseph appeared at my door, saying "Is that you whistling, Jason? By all the heavens, I did not know you had it in you!" He then started to grumble about how much it would cost him to equip us and hire my replacement. I was momentarily taken aback until I saw a large grin crease his weathered face.

"Of course, you must accompany Jesus! He is such a babe in the woods, but he surely has been touched by The Almighty. You will be his common sense, and he will fix your soul so that you are fit for Heaven!"

We embraced a goodly time, having been through much earthly and perhaps even heavenly business together. As I wiped a tear or two from my eyes, I said, "You have been as close to a father to me as I could have wished, master, and I have been proud to be your *epitropos.*" We went on like that for some time, trading blessings, thanks, and lists of things that he now would have to attend to in my absence.

While we spoke, I went through my goods deciding what to take and what to leave. All my most precious life achievements and gains would have to fit into two saddle bags, but it was suddenly easy to tell the gold from the dross. There was some adventurous but discerning spirit taking hold of me, as I felt more and more sure of my decision and no longer tied to all those material signs of my past success. I was as excited as a new lamb in pasture, and it took almost no time to wrap up my affairs.

I took a last look at my rather nicely appointed chambers, and a quiet voice within me at last awoke. "Master," I said, "I would take it as a great blessing if you would preserve my remaining property in some space of yours, in the unlikely event that circumstances impel me to return. It is said that where your goods are, so shall your heart be, but I hope to have a big enough heart to manage both. I may be like some homing pigeon that yearns to both fly and return to his coop at the setting of sun."

Joseph laughed at this naked admission, and said that I was more like a gambler who hedges his bets and preserves a stake, and less like some flighty bird. He readily agreed to my request, however, and at last all preparations were completed. With final goodbyes, and yet more heartfelt blessings from Jesus, he and I saddled up and headed off into the uncertain future.

Jesus was his usual quiet self as we set out on the road, and out of respect I did not intrude on his thoughts. The slow plodding rhythm of our donkeys and the bathing hot sun lulled us into a kind of swaddled near-sleep. A cocoon of warm collegiality enveloped us, with neither feeling compelled to make small talk. I was in some kind of suspended state between who I used to be and what I wanted to become, and perhaps Jesus felt the same. He had shaved his beard prior to leaving, hoping the disguise would ease our departure from Roman territory. He absently stroked his chin as he rode, as if reassuring himself of his new identity. Often his head tilted back and forth, whether from pushing heavy thoughts up and down like some Sisyphus, or simply from the gentle motion of his beast.

Perhaps it was both, as I was to learn over the next weeks and months. He was quite adept at fitting himself into the limitations and requirements of almost any situation in which he found himself. He could sleep whenever he so chose, and spring to alertness at a moment's notice. He seemed to have some unerring poise that carried him through the full gamut of human experience, from the wildest celebrations to the most dire confrontations and dangers. He could sense traps and ambushes without giving away this knowledge, and also join in with spontaneous joy when a party came alive enough to warrant it. He could make me laugh at the silliest things, as if we were both well drunk and loose. I could imagine him doing the same at weddings, feasts, and other celebratory occasions. Indeed, he seemed to have done so at a wedding in Cana, a tale that was making the rounds of gossip.

He required many of these skills on that long and fretful road to the Baptists. On the downward slope of Mt. Herman, he saw a few rough characters loitering at a crossroad inn. He alerted me to hold my knife close while praying that no blood would be shed. He greeted the fellows before they could accost us, then he asked after both the weather and the condition of the road ahead. They mumbled some reply, for which he thanked them most heartily. As thanks, he invited them to take a meal with us, but they demurred, claiming they had no money.

This was when they probably would have pressed us for alms or some payment for safe passage, but Jesus disarmed them by sympathizing with their penury in words most respectful and kindly. He shared that we were on our way to study Midrash in Damascus, but would they accept some bread and cheese from us? They warily accepted seats at the table, being clearly ill at ease to be invited into such an inn, one that no doubt had their measure and had refused them service in the past. Jesus proceeded to talk to them as if they were fine fellows well met, and they gradually warmed to this rise in status.

When the apparent leader of the ruffians winced while eating a crust of bread, Jesus asked if he had a rotten tooth. He smoothly talked the man into letting him pull it by telling them he had pulled my tooth just days before. I duly showed them one of the gaps in my teeth—of which there were more than I cared to admit—and the man reluctantly agreed. Jesus took a thin thread out of his pouch, wrapped the offending tooth, and with just a flick of his wrist pulled the tooth out before the man could complain. He bought the man a cup of rough wine to cleanse the wound, and toasted the fellow's good health using one of his heartfelt blessings. Whatever mischief the man may have intended vanished in a kind of country gratitude; he merely grunted his thanks and wished us well on our journey.

Our luck held for the next few days, but just before entering Damascus, we encountered a drunken Roman patrol. Jesus' beard had only just started to fill in, so he still looked quite different from the crucified Messiah. They demanded that we dismount, and I braced for trouble. I was taken aback, however, when Jesus tripped and fell off his beast, making sure to get his hands good and muddy from the road. It took me but a second to realize that he was trying to cover the lingering scabs and scars on his wrists and hands. I pretended to upbraid him for being so stupid and clumsy, and he dutifully acted the fool, a guise the Romans all too readily accepted, given their low opinion of all the conquered and benighted people living outside Roman citizenship. His face and eyes turned slack with dullness, and his speech lost all of its native wit and eloquence.

The patrol pushed us around a bit and made a show of going through our goods, looking no doubt for something worth stealing, or, barring that, something seditious enough to give them an excuse to arrest us. Jesus always travelled with just enough to get by, while I had the usual trappings of my past life as scribe and *epitropos*. When they found my writing kit, I duly explained that I was on my Master's business in Damascus, and gave a name of a market known to me from my previous visits. I said that Jesus was my Master's nephew sent along to keep him out of trouble and to learn the business, adding "Though goodness knows I could teach him all my remaining days and still not make a dent!"

The patrol had a laugh at Jesus' expense, adding a few comments of their own about his general unsuitability for any trade. They let us go and we set off at a slow pace that belied our beating hearts and bated breath.

When we had gone some leagues away from our peril, I asked Jesus where and how he had learned to shift his persona so rapidly and accurately. "One minute you are a doctor, another a rogue's friend, and then a dimwitted fool. I, on the other hand, am always and seem evermore to be an *epitropos*."

He considered a while and said, "I have always had an imagination and no certain role to play in my family. I was my father's son, yes, but he did not constrain me. Rather, he seemed to love me without compunction or expectation. He taught me marvelous games and encouraged me to use my imagination. My mother died at birth, and my lovely step-mother therefore did not feel entitled to shape me according to her own desires. My older siblings already had their parts to play in the family business and village life, while the younger ones did receive Mary's tutelage."

I nodded gravely at this glimpse into his childhood, and encouraged him to go on.   "With this freedom, of course, came some loneliness and uncertainty, as I met no one else with my same open room to play. I invented friends and playmates to act out the various parts in my imaginary games. My father built me toys and a temple playhouse that gave me room for my dramas. If I had not found my present calling, who knows? I might have become an actor or dramatist myself, perhaps like one of your Greek notables!"

Well, this gave me an opening for which I had been waiting for a considerable time. "If it is not too rude or presumptuous to ask, how *did* you receive this calling? I had heard you were a great rebbe and teacher, but nowhere did I learn where and from whom you studied. Frankly, I had never heard of this Nazareth of your childhood, and certainly had not heard of any famous school or rebbe there. As your ministry grew, some started calling you a prophet and then even the Son of God."

Jesus gave out a sigh weighted with an emotion I could not name. "Oh, how I have been conflicted over that innocuous word "the." Certainly, I believe myself to be like *a* son of the Most High, for I have felt His loving presence throughout my days, as a caring father for a favored son. I have tried with all my soul to heed His direction and I have been given extraordinary wisdom beyond my own understanding. If the infinite, wonderful, loving Creator can be said to even have human sons, I can only hope to be one. Even you, Jason, have been called by The Lord to play a part in His creation, but perhaps as more of a step-nephew!"

Here his eyes twinkled in delight, as though to tweak my pride. "I want all my followers to consider themselves children of God, and for that I have taught them to pray 'Our Father, who art in Heaven.' But to be considered *the* Son of God—and the only one so called in all these generations—well, that finitude and exactness speaks more to the human need to be the first and best than to Godly purpose. What is 'the only' to Adonai, He who has created the universe in all its splendor and diversity? In all creation, has there ever been a singular, 'only' creature unlike any other? I hopefully have never presumed to call myself that, even in the full transport of ecstasy and imagination."

"And yet," I reminded him, "you have been called that by others."

Jesus smiled ruefully once again, but continued in the same, thoughtful manner. "Perhaps I have been too gentle with those of my followers who seek to elevate me to the godhead, in hopes that I can redeem and liberate Israel, raise the dead, or save them personally from all human evil. Now that I appear to have risen from the dead, they expect even more from me!

"Certainly, I have done what I can to heal this sinful generation. I have been more than willing to play the part they would have me play, for belief is a strong part of all cures. I learned that from my mentor and friend, Rebbe Nathan of Nazareth, a good and saintly man who suffered for his beliefs, but never lost his love of humankind."

"And he must have taught you well, for you are a most exemplary fellow," I said. "To have cured a leper, driven evil spirits out of a madman, fed the multitudes, survived a crucifixion, and *still* to have kept your humor, love, and equanimity. It is no wonder that people believe you to have divine powers."

He paused once again, as if carefully sorting through his thoughts lest he give the wrong impression. It occurred to me that, almost irrespective of his intentions, his every word was freighted with meaning well beyond that of the rest of us mere mortals. It was not just that he had had to strike such a delicate balance with the religious authorities who had tried to trap him into giving seditious or blasphemous utterances. More importantly, he carried the burden of never misleading or giving false hope to his worshipful followers. He could not share his self-doubts, equivocations, or pettier emotions with them lest they turn on him or against each other. I had had pressure in my life to strike the best bargains for my master and be a good steward of his possessions, but never had I the responsibility for so many hungry souls. I wondered if he had even known the weight of responsibility and expectation he would have to shoulder when he first took up his calling. The mere physical load of that cross on Golgotha was as nothing by comparison.

Jesus may have sensed some of my thinking, for he said, "I am most pleased to share my inner thoughts with you, Jason, for it has been years since I have been able to speak freely. As a Greek and a skeptical man, you are well outside my circle of avid followers who hang on my every word. You seem to accept that I am human like any other, with doubts, missteps, fears, and dreams. At first, I tried to convey these limitations to my followers, but with each small miracle they were less and less able to hear me. It was as if the steady breeze of their faith and need were building behind me, forcing me to sail in one general direction. I could tack and try to lower my sail, but never turn around or drop anchor. Like the wind to the sail, I too was filled

with their hopes and belief in me, and that carried me through some difficult days. It is a marvelous thing to be carried along in such a warm, loving
embrace, and I thanked My Father in Heaven every day to be so blessed.
That is, until I hit the rocks of Jerusalem."

He was silent again, and again I watched him retreat into his inner
territory, where his memories, thoughts, and feelings wrestled and spoke
to one another. I knew Jesus well enough by now to let him return to our
discussion when the time was right. As it was, we were approaching Damascus, and needed to shift our attention to our own personal survival and the
mission that had sent us there.

All through these first days of our journey, Jesus had kept a keen eye
out for any Hebrew or *goyim* who seemed unusually clean, circumspect,
and at peace with themselves. When I had questioned this, he stated that
those free from sin and the fear of Hell carried themselves differently, perhaps with head held higher and eye contact more direct. He also had heard
that they ritually bathed themselves out of respect for John's practice, even
though water was a most precious commodity. Again out of respect, some
had taken to wearing a woven band or necklace of camel hair under their
tunics, but hidden away from prying, suspicious eyes. They were still considered a heretical sect and had learned from the deaths of both John and,
supposedly, Jesus to keep their beliefs to themselves.

It was not much to go on, but we blessedly made contact with a trades-
man that night who was staying at our same inn at the far eastern gate of
Damascus. He had the requisite camel-hair necklace and a quietly bemused
look upon his face, as if the affairs of men were of no matter to him apart
from entertainment. Jesus gave me a nod, and I casually approached the
man, saying that he reminded me of an elderly friend of mine. When the
man protested that he was not old, I pointed to Jesus and said, "No, he is
the elder I mean," for of course, I had used the Greek *presbyter* and not the
usual Aramaic.

We waited with held breath to see if the man would give us any sign
of recognition, and sure enough, he slowly nodded his head and said, "Ah,
I see that he resembles my friend John." We shook hands all around, with
the man saying his name was Pincas and Jesus introducing himself as "Yet
another John, what a coincidence." He had taken on his kinsman's name, out
of respect, I believe, and not some presumption to once again be glorified.

I introduced myself as myself, a former *epitropos* thrown onto the road
of life upon my master's death. "I have a new master now," I added, "a man
from Nazareth who has need of men to work the field and sell the harvest." Jesus only rolled his eyes at this poor rendition of one of his favorite
parables, but Pincas brightened once more. "Yes, of course I have heard of

Jesus, bless his name, for he was a kinsman of my friend John. You are well met and I would be pleased to speak more with you if we can do so quietly. These are troubled times and we must be circumspect."

The three of us found a corner table, broke bread, and had some wine. Jesus again said a heartfelt blessing over the food, as was his habit. Pincas raised his eyebrows and said, "You have a fine way with words, John, with a voice that shows considerable learning. Have you studied in Yeshiva or been student to someone I may have heard about?"

Jesus said fluently, with no pause or apparent guile, "Thank you for your kind words. Yes, I studied for a time with a Rebbe Nathan of the *Beit HaMikdash*, but had to withdraw for family reasons. Now I am but a carpenter, my family trade, although I did pick up some medical learning from my mentor along with bits of Torah and Mishnah."

Pincas was most pleased to hear that Jesus could build as well as heal, and immediately inquired about his future plans and whether he had ever considered settling down with John's followers.

Jesus seemed to pause in his thinking, as if weighing this option for the first time; he was as fine an actor as I had ever seen. He "conferred" with me, asking if I was prepared to accept the risks, rewards, and theological practices of staying with the Baptists.

"I had rather preferred to find a community of Nazarenes," I demurred, "but have found none in our journey so far. More than anything, I would like to feel safe from condemnation by the religious authorities and investigation by the Romans. Truth to say, I know little of your fellowship beyond ritual bathing and avoidance of anyone who would covet my head."

Pincas made a kind of pained face at that last remark, and I wondered how long it would be before my own speech and sense of humor would be cleansed of its double-edged sharpness. The only care I had given my words while Joseph's *epitropos,* was whether or not they would secure advantage; now I had to consider my listeners' soul and what harm might come to it from the jest, pain, or outright poison hidden in my words. This realization ran through me like a cold rain, so I hastened to add, "I have been trained in the reading and writing of several languages, as well as account keeping, all from my former employment. I would gladly share these skills with you and your assembly should they be wanted."

Pincas smiled broadly at our seeming acceptance of his offer, and then spent some time describing the Baptist community. It was a thriving little collection of newly built houses mostly connected to each other and arrayed in a circle around a common plaza, in the center of which was a communal well and a baptizing pool. Towers two-stories tall were placed in the four cardinal directions with an ample gate beside each. Pincas explained that the unusual layout allowed for a stout defense should they be attacked, while encouraging families to remain open and accessible to each other in the plaza. Farmed plots and grazing land radiated out from the houses surrounding this central plaza, placing open ground between the village and any approaching force.

Baptists were not pacifists, but had done enough good works with their neighbors to be on peaceful terms with them. Roman soldiers generally left them alone, and some even attended services. These services were held in the common plaza area as well as in one of the larger buildings. Baptisms of new converts and those believing themselves sinful were done in a kind of communal pool, which was off-limits otherwise.

Both religious and community decisions were led by a group of presbyters, or elders, who were chosen from among those who had personally met and been baptized by John. Pincas was one such, and was generally trusted with conducting business with those from all nations. He was charged with taking the community's trade and farm goods to market, bargaining in good faith, and returning with items needed by the village. The assembly tried not to have money, as they feared its power over weaker souls, but instead bartered and traded directly with sympathetic merchants. Pincas travelled with two stout helpers who loaded and watched over their wagon. He indicated with a slight nod a plain, almost non-descript man who sat across the room from us, but kept the entire room in his view. We assumed the other fellow was with the wagon, readying it for the return journey.

Jesus did flinch slightly at the mention of Roman soldiers attending some services, but did not explore this further, perhaps assuming that these soldiers would be sympathetic. He did ask whether the village was ever visited by passing caravans on their way to Judea and Jerusalem, saying that he had relations there with whom he wished to communicate as needed. Pincas said that the village was a small way off the main trade routes, but did not have enough water or sleeping space for large groups. They did host pilgrims searching for Baptist contact, services, and learning; even now, there were four or five scholars there studying with some of the elders. However, Pincas offered to pass along whatever Jesus needed whenever he, Pincas, was in Damascus on business.

Pincas went on to say that most farm and manufacturing implements were held in common, for the benefit of all who needed them or were skilled in their use and application. He admitted that this got awkward at times when planting, harvesting, shearing, and other seasonal activities came due at the same time. He added that he was glad not to be in charge of arbitrating need, as he tended only to supplies and trade. However they worked it, the village seemed able to meet all its needs and had enough left over for charity. This was a most prized virtue, with Baptists showing no partiality in helping those even outside their faith. They held a charity afternoon after Sabbath worship, and the surrounding villages were encouraged to partake. The Baptists awaited a messiah for themselves, and offered the chance for salvation to any and all who were so inclined.

"The Lord above can sort out His sheep from the goats, so far be it for us to close the door to any in search of redemption," he said. Many believed that Jesus was this Messiah; nightly vigils were assigned to each family in turn so that they would be awake as Watchmen should the Messiah come in the night. No, Pincas said to my inquiry, no one had ever met or seen this Jesus, as they had fled Judea soon after John's death, when Jesus was just beginning his ministry. Pincas admitted that there was some anxiety in the community over whether the village would know him when he came, but then added calmly, "The Good Lord will let us know what we need to know."

I had to bite my tongue throughout this discourse, and stole several glances at Jesus to see how he would handle this obvious temptation. On the one hand, his announcing himself would send Pincas and his village into paroxysms of joy, but, on the other, it might bring the Roman and Sanhedrin authorities screaming down upon them. It occurred to me that Jesus probably never intended to be the Messiah, at least not in the military sense of liberating Judea from the Romans. He abhorred bloodshed, and instead sought to change his followers from the inside out, with ripples of love, charity, and mercy radiating out from their hearts. Yes, he had talked about granting eternal life to those who truly repented and loved God with all their heart, but he did not mean immortality, as some believed who wanted to rise from the dead as he had. Rather, he offered an image of living after death as some kind of spirit in Heaven with God and His angels. I could see nothing but dashed expectations and even bloodshed if his true identity were discovered.

Jesus affected a pleased and even eager demeanor throughout Pincas' recital. He was fascinated by the design of the village as a kind of wheel, having only lived in places that splayed out haphazardly in all directions like most villages, or in tightly boxed walled cities like Jerusalem.

"You indeed seem guided by Adonai to make all your dwellings houses of The Lord, open and welcoming, yet prepared for any evil," he said. "I would be most pleased to meet whoever conceived of such a thing."

Pincas smiled broadly, and said, "It was my own daughter, of all people. She had a dream in which she saw Ezekiel and his wheels descending to earth, where they turned into houses. She was so excited and struck by the image that she begged me to gather the people for discussion. We had been living in our shepherd tents, and I believe the assembly was more than ready for new prospects. So, the seed idea from my daughter found ready and fertile soil to take root, and we have grown, all testaments to The Most High's power at work among all of us."

This satisfied all our questions, and to smiles, embraces, and agreement to conjoin our parties at dawn, we separated to our sleeping quarters.

"Well, this is a godsend," I said. "I used to say it was luck, good fortune, or my own skills that brought me to some desired outcome, but since travelling with you, I have sensed the presence of your Father. He is indeed generous beyond expectation."

To this Jesus smiled broadly, as he would with any mention of his Father. "I see that gratitude is growing in your heart, Jason. I only caution that we not expect Our Father to answer *all* our prayers, for then we become His master instead of His grateful subjects. It is a fine line, of course; we cannot be arrogant enough to demand answers, but we also cannot sit idly waiting for the heavens to open.

"I was rather struck with Pincas' imagery: Seed, soil, water, and tending—each is needed to allow good works to come to fruition. We have to be open and willing to see where God is pointing or hear what He is saying. However, His is often but a whisper among many. So, I give thanks to My Father, but I also do my part to ready myself and discern seed from tare "

I replied, "Something tells me that you will have more than enough opportunity in the village and even beyond to continue your teaching. There are scholars and teachers in the village who may prove very open to your ideas, but, if I may add a word of caution, please determine beforehand where each has come from. You need to be sure none will recognize you, else our charade is ended and Messianic fever break out in the village." This was another fine line for Jesus to walk, although this one was more of a knife-edge.

Our journey to Pincas' village—a name we always used instead of the more proper Chadash ha'Yarden, or New Jordan—was uneventful. We were welcomed in with a kind of solemn and careful kindness, but the residents warmed up to us when they learned that Jesus was a carpenter as well as a doctor of sorts. As might be expected, they were a motley and varied assembly, having come from many walks of life drawn by the Baptist's message. They had not had a proper doctor in all their time together, and many of their buildings had a slapdash, amateurish quality about them. The village was filled with enthusiasm and vision, but was sadly lacking in practical skills. Jesus would have more than enough carpentry work to keep him busy and fed.

Their reliance on bartering meant that many needs were not being met, for not all Damascene merchants would trade with them. With my business background, I was sure I could increase their resources and ensure a more balanced economy. I knew money and had enough of my own not to be tempted by its glitter. I was certain that Jesus and I would fit in and contribute.

And so we did. Jesus urged me to submit to a full community baptism, which I did with an open mind and heart. There was something primeval in being in that baptismal pool and being dunked half to drowning. Each emergence into blessed air indeed felt like new birth. I wondered later if that was part of the conversion into gratitude away from smug self-sufficiency— I arose from the water cleansed in mind and body, and just glad to be alive.

Jesus also submitted to baptism, rather than betray his previous encounter with John to any who might have been there that day. Thankfully, no dove came down from the heavens to mark his true identity. He whispered to me as an aside, "I just want to be 'reborn' as simply John, another son of My Father."

Jesus renewed his teaching ministry by meeting with the visiting scholars and anyone else who wanted instruction. The "scholars" were as motley as the other villagers, and none had been near Jerusalem or at any of Jesus' many appearances. The villagers had all heard of Jesus, certainly, but the estimates of his looks and whereabouts varied with the personality of the speaker. The short ones felt that he must be short, the tall ones thought him tall, the meek thought him shy, and the more aggressive thought him a zealot and messiah come back to overthrow the Romans. The more observant among them thought him Elijah, returned from the beyond. The *goyim* and less observant ones believed him to be who he said he was, but even they varied in whether he was human or some God-made spirit come down in the shape of a man. None could confirm his whereabouts, and all seemed to accept the rumors that he had died, risen from the dead, and then ascended to Heaven. He was spoken of quite reverently, although the village made sure that their own John received much praise.

Jesus thus felt free to be his new self with little fear that his past would catch up with him. He developed a following of sorts both within the village and from those who would come for charity, services, or other purposes. He was soon elevated to the leadership council of elders, having described enough about his kinsman John to be taken as legitimate. He began to lead services with the other elders, helped settle disputes, and participated in baptisms. In addition to his religious duties, he could barely rest from the many house repairs required in the village, as well as illnesses and accidents that required his healing. He was spared birthing duties, as the village had its own midwives; these were kept busy by the requirement for the assembly to be fruitful and multiply. He was as gifted a healer as the people had ever seen. As no one expected him to have divine powers, however, they merely thought him a skilled physician. If his fame or prowess reached beyond the village, it was as a man, on a simple human scale. This suited both of us, and I often wondered if Jesus was secretly relieved not to have messianic expectations placed upon him.

I had somewhat more difficulty getting accepted and established. At first, I was called in as scribe for legal disputes and settlements, and my fine handwriting and clear explanations soon were enough to verify my former employment. I worked on removing venom and superiority from my speech and attitudes, and gradually opened my heart to the simple humanity of others. Like Jesus, perhaps, I found that I liked being on an equal footing with my neighbors. I had not realized how my aloofness and sense of superior status cut me off from friendships, laughter, and the broader, spiritual dimensions of life. With no slaves or underlings to order around and do my work, I found a joy in what I could accomplish myself, with the freely-offered help of others.

With a new and more peaceful soul, I was able to bide my time. Gradually, I made suggestions as to how Pincas and his trading practices might improve. He thankfully was open to new ideas, both out of a desire to increase the villages' security and wealth, but also because he had no fear for his own status or title. Something in the Baptist's teachings must have freed him from many of the prideful defenses and posturing seen in men of lesser character but greater wealth. Although a bit too sober and serious for my taste, he nevertheless proved a good business partner, and we soon developed a fine working relationship that benefited the entire community.

I need to report one particular conversation with Jesus that has stuck with me to this day. Each household in the village—of which Jesus and I made an odd, bachelor one—was required to perform farm services of various kinds, both to support ourselves but also to increase the food available to all those in need. The terrain was even more arid than Galilee; it was nearly desert, and required both irrigation and constant tending to crops. This was both of our most direct exposure to the rigors and rhythms of agriculture, and we took to it fairly well, if I must say. We learned about local superstitions meant to bring the rain, grow the crops, and manage pestilence. We learned how to irrigate and prepare the fields, and how to root the plants carefully so that the most tender shoots could find Mother Earth. We learned the marvelous power of water to bring out life, but this time it was more than metaphorical.

As was his habit for prayer and alone time, Jesus often walked out into the desert that lay just beyond the limits of the village. There he experienced the desperate calculus of survival and the utter silence of the nights. He once came back from his desert walk and remained silent for a time before speaking.

"It is hard, Jason, to find My Father's handiwork in the desert. There are poisonous creatures, sharp thorns, and a total lack of welcome; the barren land seems a rebuke to all the love and abundance He values. The desert seems to be a kind of grim battle line between the forces of life and death, Heaven and Sheol. Although it has been easy to talk to my father in all that silence and apparent emptiness, it still does not seem part of His domain."

I could see that this thought troubled him, he who believed in a merciful Father who ruled over all creation.

"Perhaps Our Father can only do so much, despite all His powers," I said. "If we are truly His children, perhaps these deserts are part of our inheritance, meant for us to redeem and make fertile. As your Torah claims that Adam and Eve got us thrown out of the Garden, perhaps it is up to us, their descendants, to bring Eden back into the world."

"That has been one of my main missions," Jesus said with some resolution, "To bring life out of death, the water of love to the earth and peace to all. My only regret is that I have not yet learned how to tame the lions and vipers of this world, so that we can all live in peace. This will fully occupy my remaining days, and is a bequest I will lay upon all who follow me after I am gone."[2]

"Amen to that," I added with as much conviction as I could muster.

And so, our days progressed with a steady rhythm, good purpose, and rising contentment. It might have been a year or two after our arrival, however, when I began to lose weight. At first, I thought merely that something in my meals, wine, or water did not agree with me, for I could only nibble at food. I was not a young man by any means, but outside work had built up muscles I did not know I possessed. I had thought myself in the best of health, certainly more so than in my more effete days as *epitropos*. Jesus was the first to notice my thinning frame and face, and began to ask after my recent habits, aches, and fatigues. He patiently waited while I made my denials that anything was wrong or needed examining.

"You should know me by now, Jason, that I do not trespass into another's personal domain unless there is some urgency. You would not have me sit idly by if thick smoke was billowing from your window; nor can I ignore your sudden change of health. I have witnessed nothing untoward in your habits these many months, nor has a contagion come into the village.

---

2. Some believe that Jesus was the model or perhaps even the actual person behind the Prester John legend, Prester being derived from "Presbyter."

No, my dear friend, there is something amiss particular to you, and if you let me, I will try to determine its nature."

Well, of course I had to trust him, after all we had been through and what I knew of his God-given talents. He had me lie down on my sleeping cot after stripping to my loincloth. He began with my eating problems, exploring with questions and probing with fingers from my tongue, to teeth, to throat, to stomach, and to my elimination canal. He smelled my breath after asking what and when I had last eaten or drunk, and how much of each item. He encouraged me to give voice to any pain he elicited in his probing, to the degree of its intensity.

"This is no time to practice your fabled Greek stoicism, Jason, but you must let your body speak to me through your reactions. Pain has its own language and reveals much about what we cannot see or grasp by any other means."

And so, I did, with mild pain in an area just under my jaws and next to my throat, and the most pain from some kind of small, tightly knotted *thing* buried deep in my stomach area. "Ah," he said, "this lump does not belong here, if you Greeks are built the same way as all other of Adonai's human creatures." He had me roll over so he could probe the area from the back, and then had me sit up. In a very casual and even nonchalant way, he asked me to make water in one of our jars, and, to provide him with my stool as soon as I could.

I was not really surprised by these intimate requests, as I had heard that a skilled doctor could almost tell a patient's future by what passed through his body, as if one's ingested food picked up evidence of health or illness as it made its journey. I voided my urine, which he took to swirling in his glass while he peered intently and then smelled. "Hmm, there is a faint pink tinge to your urine, Jason, which I take to be blood. The smell is also off, perhaps a bit sweeter than normal."

I did not want to know how many other men's urine he had smelled to make such a comparison, and in any case thought such a procedure was unbecoming for a Son of God. At the same time, I did not like my blood being where it did not belong.

Jesus had me get dressed, and said he had to meet with a few students but would come back as soon as I voided my bowels. He reassured me that he would explain his findings fully once he had completed this final examination.

I was certain by now that something indeed was quite wrong with me, and decided therefore to take the rest of the afternoon off from my labors. A score of fearful and dire thoughts raced through me as I paced our small two-room house. Perhaps it was this tension that added difficulty to my attempts to void my bowels, although I also had eaten and drunk too little recently to make much of a show. The whole process was mildly humiliating and painful, but I soldiered on as best I could. He had advised me to take no wine until my stool was passed, and I heeded this until the very next moment after I voided. I took a long draught or two before setting out to find him, after first covering up my stool so as not to attract flies or other insects.

Jesus must have seen me coming across the common area, for he soon met me not even halfway across. We returned apace to my dwelling, having discussed in brief the level of pain experienced in voiding the sample. He proceeded to smell my stool and probe it with various thin metal blades, some of which slightly changed color when withdrawn. At any other time, I might have found it fascinating to learn what he was doing, but this time belonged to me and my future. I waited as best I could before saying, "Well?"

He looked at me with deep thoughtfulness and warmth, with his head tilted slightly and his hands held in prayer before his lips. "Your stool tells me you lack water; traces of blood on its outside could have come from the effort of voiding. However, there was more blood within the sample and that blood color is off. You also have blood in your urine, throat tenderness, and a small lump in your stomach that is quite painful to the touch.

"I can see by your eyes, Jason, that you are prepared for the worst, and indeed I think you wise to be so. I believe you have the wasting disease, one that gradually eats you from the inside but does not let you eat."

I hung my head for a minute to collect myself, then gave a kind of smile before asking him, "Do you think it in your power, my friend, to stop or reverse this disease?"

Jesus paused a moment before saying, "I have said prayers to My Father to spare others with this disease, but until now have not had my prayers answered. Nor have I learned from other doctors or healers what has proven efficacious for them. No one knows where this disease comes from, why its victims are chosen, or how long a person has before they succumb. I have heard some preachers claim that the disease is a punishment for sin, else why would an all-powerful God allow it to flourish? Others claim that it is a loving Father's way of calling His chosen people home to Heaven. As you know, I have been as close to My Father as any one; I have had His guidance throughout my ministry, but I have not heard an answer to this question.

"I know that there is evil in this world, and it has been my deepest desire and purpose to do all I can to fight this evil so that people can have abundant, loving, and long lives. Evil tried to kill me, but by the grace of My Father I survived. I am afraid, Jason, that you will be a casualty in this war. You are a dear companion, help, and even a counselor to me, and all my blessings go with you as you face this disease and prepare yourself for Heaven."

Here, he held my very face in his hands and kissed me on the forehead, tears forming in those deep eyes that had seen and known so much. His tears mingled with those of my own, and for a long moment neither of us could speak.

And that was that.

My rational mind must have already begun to arrange my affairs and plan my exit from this life, for I neither raged nor mourned my fate. The equanimity that had entered my life since I met Jesus, the love that I had tasted for the first time in my life, the joy I felt at having been allied with one of God's own messengers—all these were a permanent part of my soul now and could not be eaten away by whatever evil was inside my body.

I did ask Jesus if he knew what usually happened to people as the disease progressed, as I wanted guidance on what to expect and plan for. Jesus then calmly and carefully described the mounting pain and weakness, occasional fevers, and growing incapacity to function. Looking around me, I believed that my new friends would try to stand by me as long as they could, but my heart knew that this was not home and not where I wanted to be buried. I also did not want to be a burden and distraction to all that was so newly conceived and fragile. The Baptist community was trying to give birth to a new way of living, and they needed all the vigorous and energetic souls they could muster.

I shared with Jesus my intention to return to Joseph's estate; he nodded immediately, as if he knew ahead of time what I would do. He said he would ask around the village for ingredients to make a tincture to dull the pain when it struck; he also told me the recipe for making it myself when I reached Arimathea. I duly wrote the ingredients and process down, and have benefited from its use ever since.

I asked Jesus how I should announce my leaving to the village. Again, I did not want to cast a pall over their hearts and souls, but no longer wanted to lie or dissimulate, especially to those I considered friends. Jesus thought and prayed for a time, and then simply said, "Tell them that you are sick and wish to go home before you die. All of us understand that we usually seek our kin and the place of our birth when we cycle back around to our death. Some in the village, like myself, do not have a home they dare return to; perhaps they will envy you the choice, but they will certainly understand."

Thus it was that I said my goodbyes to Pincas and my new friends, shed tears that were still new to me, and gathered myself for a final farewell to Jesus. He stood at the western gate to the road that led to Damascus and Judea, a gate appropriately enough open to the setting sun. My whole being was filled with a kind of marvelous sadness, a mix of joy at the gifts of love and freedom he had brought to me, and grief that I would never see him again. He was a most humble hero, a wise babe in arms, a life-giving teacher, preacher and healer who had never gone to school. Mostly, he radiated a love that showed no partiality, like the very sun itself. Thousands had grown into a new life thanks to him; his words and deeds were the very seeds of hope, light, and gratitude in a dark world. His God was now my God and Father, a figure no longer distant and punishing, but forgiving, intimate, loving, guiding. I would never feel alone again in this world.

All this I wanted to say to him as we stood there at the gate, with one of our donkeys and one of Pincas' market helpers waiting a respectful distance away. These words buzzed in my head, but one look at Jesus' deep brown eyes told me that he already knew what he meant to me, and I to him. It was as if he somehow held the full memory of all our time together in his heart and needed no additional words to explain their worth or consequence. Words would be like the chaff, light and insubstantial, while love was the grain that fed the soul.

Certainly Jesus and his Father in Heaven did not need to hear my thanks and praise, whether in prayer or psalm, because they were already and always with me throughout my days. Rather, it was I who needed to remember lessons learned and show forth both gratitude and love in my actions. So, I filled my being with as much love as I could muster, said a simple "Thank you, dearest friend, for everything," and gave him my warmest embrace. I knew he could feel the strength of my affection for him, a love beyond words. It was as if I had crossed over the rocky desert that usually divides one soul from another and made full contact with his living, pulsing heart.

Strangely enough, a terrible pain is ripping through me as I write these words. Is God or his enemy reaching out to me somehow? Is my buried grief over leaving Jesus rising up from the dead like some moldy *golem*? Or has the tincture simply worn off? I pause and collect myself as I have seen Jesus do on numerous occasions, large and small. I go to the well of prayer and communion with my God, and I hear a soft voice or presence that seems to say, "*It is nearly time.*"

As much as one can prepare for this, it is still a shock. Time for my human time to cease, and eternity begin. My human mind is comforted by images of angels, clouds, heavenly choruses, and a bearded God presiding over creation on His throne; but my Greek mind still suspects that these oh-so identifiable and human images are only meant to comfort the dying as we enter the unknown, like scared children.

Thanks to Jesus, I believe in something deeper and more indefinable. I am ready to go into The Divine Presence that is God, where I shall lose all speech and thought and only feel love.

XIII

Diary of Salome the Younger

MAY THE HOLY ONE of my ancestors, and The Almighty Father of my brother Jesus of Nazareth strike me dead if these words are not the truth.

I write this as a record of truth, for I have been a witness to momentous and sacred times. I write this in hopes that the written word will outlive me, who is old and surrounded by enemies.

There doubtless are many who cannot believe that a mere woman can even write, but I assure you that James, Bishop of Jerusalem and my brother, can testify to my learned skills. It was he who taught me, in secret to be sure, hoping that I could quietly record for him all relevant conversations, promises, and complaints I hear when attending to all who come to see him. Who among those esteemed men would notice that their serving woman has unusually keen eyes and ears? Who among them has even asked my name or place in this church? True, they call me "sister," out of respect, but they do not know my lineage or my loyalties. What they see is a somewhat stooped and grey-haired maiden of modest and minimal speech and manner, for

James insists that I blend into the very stones. For my brother I do this, but it is not my true nature, as the reader will soon discover.

As to my lineage and my loyalties, the first carries the most importance, as it is the very roots and branches of the family tree from which my loyalty comes. How we Hebrews have delighted in tracing our ancestry back to someone famous and proper, hoping, perhaps, that some dusty ancestor's name was mentioned in the Torah, and that our present generation would gain some of The Holy One's favor as a result. In many ways, however, the birth and exalted ascension of Jesus has freed my family from such an excavation of the past, for his bright presence has given us all we can handle of The Lord's favor. At any rate, it is just as well not to excavate, as ours is a tangled and thorny tree. I must stop for now, as the light is fading and duties await on the morrow. Tracing the family tree also requires more time than I have at the present. Lord willing, I will get a break when the Bishop leaves to tend his flock.

God be praised, I have some time to myself, as the Bishop has gone off with Brother Simon Peter to settle a dispute in a nearby community of brethren. To continue where I left off: As the branches of any tree go in all directions, I will start with my father Joseph, my own dear departed mother Salome, and then Mary, the blessed in all ways, but not the mother of Jesus. There has been some growing appreciation for Mary's role in Jesus' glorious ministry and ascension, and she has certainly witnessed and contributed to many wonderful deeds. It is right and even perhaps overdue that a woman should find her place among the most favored of The Holy One's children. Truth is truth, however, and Bishop James and I both spent our tender years with Mary and know the real story.

But let me first get to my father's heritage and offspring. Father was always a bit vague on how and why his clan had settled in Nazareth, and I had a sense that they were herdsmen who had just found a place where no one else bothered to live. Although some in the village claimed to have been mentioned in the Torah as "not least among the cities of Israel," I would not want to visit any lower ranked town. There was almost no trade with larger towns and villages, as we grew just enough for our own needs and mined nothing special in the surrounding hills.

In short, there was not much to the place, and this was a blessing, it turns out. We were too small to attract the attention of warring armies or other aggressive factions. The 400 or so souls in the village all knew each other, if they were not direct kinsmen. With few other options available, a kind of peaceful balance was always present. Some with more imagination claimed that we were protected and guarded from danger by The Holy One, for that was how Nazareth derived its name. Surrounded mostly by kins-men, we never starved or truly suffered, except perhaps from boredom.

My father Joseph was a carpenter and what might be called a handy-man, for his father Jakob had bequeathed him tools that were most precious and valued in the village. He found enough work in Nazareth and in the surrounding villages to make a living and to meet those outside our clan. Whenever you are useful, you gain some esteem and what passes for wealth, and so it was that my father was able to make a good match with Salome and convince her family to let them marry. He eventually accumulated enough land on which to build a small compound for his family and his brothers. Uncles Clopas and Benjamin, both younger than my father, had their own adjacent houses and small plots of vegetables and various fruit trees. They helped my father with any heavy tasks and, when they married, their wives became like second mothers to us.

My father was a busy man in all ways, and, soon after she had had a bloody and painful miscarriage, my mother got pregnant again. I was about five then, and even I could tell that something was not right. She could not get comfortable, could not sleep, could not keep food down, and could not even work around the house. Aunt Mariah had to assume some of those duties, but also had her own pregnancy to attend to. Mother was not one to complain and did the best she could, I suppose, but finally one night she pleaded with my father for help around the house.

While I pretended to sleep, I heard them arguing over cost, with Father wanting a younger person who would not tax our resources. Mother wanted an older kinswoman who could be both midwife and helpmate, but, as he was adamant on cost, they then argued over who would be best suited to join the household. Apparently, they both wanted someone from their own lineage, and names flew back and forth of people both known and unknown to me. Father did not want his business and personal doings known to all our neighbors, as gossiping was one of the few entertainments available to everyone in the village. He wanted someone from outside, and both wanted someone of fine, devout (if possible), and obedient character.

As the debate wore on, Mother was clearly tiring of the effort to reach a solution; her voice got weak and I thought I heard her crying. My father was moved by this, as he often was by the suffering of his beloved wife and, indeed, any living creature. He offered to speak to her kinsman Zechariah, a priest and a Levite who lived not too many stadiae[1] away, in a much big-ger Gallilean town (as were almost all places!). Both agreed to abide by the

---

1. Roman units of distance, about 660 feet.

choice that Zechariah made, believing him both righteous and knowledge-able of who best to serve them.

After some further discussion, it was agreed that my oldest brother, Simon, seven years older than me, would travel to Zechariah, remind him who we were, and explain our dire situation to him. It was clear that mother was nearing the end of her endurance, while our kin had their own burdens. Father did agree on hiring an experienced midwife to help ease the coming childbirth, which we all sensed would be difficult.

Father gave Simon his best pair of (old) sandals, which were only slightly too big for him, and prepared him with a rough map, a stout walking stick, and enough food for a long journey.

"You are a man today," said Father, "The first test of adulthood is to believe you have the strength to face all obstacles, and that there is always a way out of danger. Belief and faith in yourself must come before you have actual experience; belief and faith allow you to face the unknown. Our love and the grace of The Holy One will protect you as well, so never fear."

I could see that my brother was both excited and scared about this responsibility. He would take several steps out to the gate, then pretend to have forgotten to kiss Mother, hug Father, or say goodbye to his dog. As for me, I had been struck by my father's words. As only a child might, I also believed firmly that if I believed hard enough, Simon would return safely. This thought kept my eyes from exploding into tears. Even after all these years, I know that this was my first test of faith.

Enough for today, or should I say, "Sufficient unto the day are the words therein."

As the Bishop seems to have been detained again by the authorities, I write these words with some trepidation, although he has been through many such trials before. I shall pray for his swift release, and also give thanks to synagogue in Heaven for the extra time granted to further this witness. I say "My Father," as I must believe that such a loving God will not allow his faithful, pious, and gentle servant James to be harmed or attacked by His chosen representatives on Earth. Perhaps the sins of humankind are so many that more martyrs are required for sacrifice, but our Lord Jesus seemed to speak against sacrifice. And yet he also was attacked and later killed. Is this generation a brood of vipers indeed, beyond the reach of the God of Love? It is very confusing to me.

Let me stick to what I know, then. About a week or so later, Simon did return safely shortly after midday. With him was a small retinue of Zecha-riah's household and a comely girl of about Simon's age named Mary. She apparently was some sort of kinswoman to Zechariah's wife, so not a blood relation to us, though from the same ancestral line. She was appropriately modest, with eyes cast down, hair bound and covered, and clothing of an un-bleached wool of somewhat coarse weave. The steward of Zechariah's house-hold led the retinue, and explained that Mary had been raised mostly in the synagogue that Zechariah served as priest. She was a kind of maidservant there, and thus well-versed in both Kosher practices and general service.

The steward and my father spoke at some length about the terms of her employment, moneys owed now and in the future, and how she was only a year away from being of marriageable age. This rather haughty steward looked around our poor village and seemed to shake his head sadly, per-haps not finding the kinds of prospects he wished for Mary. Father quickly reached terms before the steward could change his mind, adding only that "The Holy One will provide, but if He is busy elsewhere, I am sure we can work something out."

Simon stifled a laugh just in time to avoid a stern look from the stew-ard, who seemed even more anxious then to get on the road back to his civilized world. Money and promises were exchanged, and water and bread were given to the retinue for their long journey home.

Father had scarcely allowed this Mary to wash the dust off her feet when he took her to meet our mother, so eager was he to ease Mother's wor-ries and burdens. Simon and I tagged along, curious about this outsider and new member of the household. If mother was grateful or impressed I cannot say, as she seemed absorbed in her pains and weak from enduring them.

Mary surprised us all by quietly, firmly, and immediately taking charge, telling my father and Simon to fetch cold water from the well and to find a pillow to take weight off Mother's swollen stomach. She enlisted me to fan Mother's feverish face, and even felt familiar enough to gather Mother's damp hair into a sort of bun above her head, to allow whatever faint breeze there was to cool her neck. Once Simon had brought in a bucket of well water, she set to washing the sweat off Mother's face and limbs, cooing some lilting song into her ear. You could almost hear the sigh of relief that came over all of us—this woman-girl was indeed a godsend.

I was to learn later that Mary could see problems and solutions before others could even articulate them, having grown up to serve kohenim who demanded faithful adherence to seemingly thousands of shifting and even contradictory Kosher rules and laws. As we got older and our age difference lessened in importance, she confided that in her first years at her synagogue, the priests would scorn and beat her if she made even the slightest mistake. She had been made to feel small and stupid, but had gradually learned to an-ticipate what others wanted by somehow weighing mood, facial expression, situation, time, and precedent all in an instant. She learned the quirks of each kohen and rebbe, their likes and dislikes, their own particular beliefs, strengths, and fallibilities.

Mary once told me, "I learned to shrink myself like a mouse, sneaking in and around all those big sandals without being stepped on." Although she was largely confined to the synagogue grounds and never allowed to venture out on her own, she had few regrets. "There was an entire world to explore in between what people said and what they did, between what they said they wanted and what they truly needed. When you are small like a mouse, you see what others are too big and self-important to see."

She did lament that pain and guilt had seemed to play such major roles in her education, but thanked The Holy One for having learned such gifts of prescience and service. "I can teach these to you too, Salome, but without the beatings!"

I was glad of that, I must say, and indeed I owe much of my present joy and skill in life to her love and teaching.

Oh, my Lord, could not you let my joy linger a while? I was so full of warm memories when last I picked up my stylus, but these feelings have been trampled by the Temple zealots who have ransacked our humble Bishop's abode.

It was only by Your grace, O God, that I was awake early and neatening up the residence when I heard dogs barking furiously up the lane. Why did I know that men were coming for us? Perhaps because the Bishop had not sent word of his condition in the last week, most unlike him to leave me in the dark. I quickly hid the chalices and Fellowship correspondence that were the only outward signs of our new covenant. I hid them where even the Bishop does not suspect, as he has been too kindly and even innocent to plan for such attacks. I, however, have observed and noted the evil that men can do, and had prepared for this day. The death of Jesus—his murder, really—had only confirmed what I had known of the Romans. I had not been prepared for my own Temple's behaviors. All men—even pious and supposedly godly ones— are capable of destroying that which they do not understand.

I knew to remove any sign that we were different from our country-men. I also knew to shrink myself into a house mouse, douse the light and fire in my eyes, and play the part of a doddering old woman, which is what I soon may be if harm should come to the Bishop and our followers.

The zealots questioned me rudely with such animus as they would a Samaritan thief. I could have claimed my right to respect as a Levite, but some wisdom kept me still and bowed. I answered all questions as meekly and obediently as possible.

"Yes, I know James, for he is my brother."

"Yes, I clean and cook his meals."

"No, I do not meet or know whomever he sees. They are not from my village."

"No, I do not know where he goes when he leaves the house, but it may be to see a woman who lives over by the southern gate of the city" —far from us, so let the zealots go chasing her!

The men did confer for a minute, and two were sent off in pursuit of James' phantom mistress. My interrogation continued, however.

"Yes, of course I knew Jesus, he was my little brother."

"No, I will not believe he was sent by Adonai until the wise men of the Temple tell me so."

I thought it prudent to add, "I saw him pee and poop, so how can he be a god?" (May The Lord forgive me for saying this, but He knows what is in my heart and that is a great comfort. A God of love allows more room for us to be human, I must say.)

I did all this with many signs of deafness and poor eyesight, as if I could not be a witness even to what they were all doing by rummaging through the Bishop's baskets and shelves. I never once asked why they were there, who had sent them, and on what authority, for I had learned early on that it was not a woman's place to question men. Men, in their turn, have little or no interest in what women have to tell them anyway, so these men soon tired of their interrogation. As the Bishop lives simply and keeps all the Kosher proscriptions, there was little for them to discover and nothing to distinguish our house from those around us. Just as one brown mouse looks like another, we in the Fellowship easily blend with those of the old covenant.

If this gave the zealots pause, they did not show it, but they simply stormed off as suddenly as they had come, offering no explanation or apology.

It was some time before I could stop my shaking, and even now this stylus seems to be as nervous and jumpy as my thoughts. Should I flee? Should I try to find the Bishop? Simon Peter? The others? On my knees, I ask my Lord for strength, for endurance, for direction. I know that my brother has been asking the same and that our Heavenly Father will mete out what is needed for each of us. As is often the case, no immediate answer has come to me, so I will continue with my duties until such time as I am needed and directed elsewhere. This silence from The Lord is a comfort, truly, for it gives me time to quiet my own fears and tend to my own garden, as it were, while He prepares the future. I have learned that one cannot hear the voice of The Father if one's ears are filled with panic.

As Jesus said, be awake for signs, for no one knows when the master of the house shall come. So, I shall be awake, with all eyes and ears tuned for the next disturbance or miracle. In particular, I have been studying the faces and movements of my neighbors, for someone may have alerted the authorities to all the comings and goings in our house. I have learned from Mary how to mingle with neighbors, shopkeepers, and authorities, and to know which of them to avoid, which to tell a convenient fiction, and which to invite into your heart. When I am done with this day's writing, I shall go again to the well and the market, and see if a Judas walks among us.

I am reminded of what Jesus once said during a dinner with his disciples, that they should go out into the world as cunning as snakes but as innocent as doves. I could hear Mary's voice in this, for she herself had learned to effortlessly slide between the obstacles and travails of this life while maintaining her inner joy in all that life offered. She was more a mouse than a snake, however, but we must allow Jesus his Genesis reference. He knew his Torah frontwards and back, and was not afraid to give the old words and images new meanings. Torah came alive in his speech, and was not the fusty cudgel used by our priests. How I miss you, Jesus!

Enough! The recent house invasion has quickened my pace, and I now write close to my hiding place in case we are visited again. I have marked my spot with what hopefully looks like a scratch to the authorities, but a fish to our Fellowship. Oh, how I wish we could hold our light out in the open and not hide it under a bushel! (And this is not a clue, faithful ones!)

Back to Mary and how she entered our life.

Mary was a great comfort to my mother and indeed to all of us. She was both a nursemaid and a playmate, being in that age between childhood and adulthood. In the little time she had to herself apart from her household duties, she would play dolls with me, and of course we both played House. We invented handsome husbands, loving children, pesky neighbors, dangerous beasts, and wonderful futures for ourselves.

Mary would ask me who in the village I thought the most suitable as a husband, but there I drew a blank. I only knew my own kin as Uncle This or Cousin That; I could not imagine them otherwise. Of other men outside our line, I knew scarcely a thing, only what they did. She accepted my limitations as kindly as she accepted all the life she saw around her.

But mostly she worked. My mother's time was coming, but by now she could no longer get out of bed, and needed to be helped in all things. The old midwife from the village seemed confused and muddled, and Mary had to step in several times to make sure that the herbs and ointments meant to ease pregnancy and delivery were mixed properly and applied to the correct place. The pain did not cease, however, and my mother started turning a color not seen in plants or animals. Her stomach became hard as iron, her breath came in fits and starts, and there was moaning all through the days and nights. It was finally too much for my father, and he begged the midwife to do something.

"I will have to induce," she said, and with my father's silent nod, she began brewing a foul mixture of god-knows-what. She shooed the men out of the room, and my Aunt Mariah and Mary took hold of my mother's head as the old hag (Lord forgive me) forced the drink down her throat. We children—including some of the cousins—looked on with not a whisper between us for once, and the women were too preoccupied to notice or shoo us away.

The scene is still etched in my mind all these years later: The awful gagging, vomiting, and screaming of my mother, the old midwife and Aunt Mariah pushing my mother's belly in hopes of forcing the baby out, blood everywhere, Mary dropping down between my mother's trembling legs and wheedling, pulling, cooing, almost enticing the baby to come out. With a final push and scream, my mother let go of the baby, and all of her pain, suffering, and future hopes went with him.

None of us noted this at the time, so intent were we on this bloody, squalling, tiny creature, so unlike the dolls of my childhood. The midwife had nearly fainted with the effort and went to sit down, leaving Mary and Aunt Mariah to clean the baby off, cut and tie off the umbilicus, and wait for the sac to void. Only it never came.

Aunt Mariah began talking to my mother to push some more, and got only silence in return. It was then that we all noticed Mother was not breathing. Aunt Mariah slapped her a few times as she had done with the baby, but this time no cry of life was heard. My dear Mother, bless her soul forever, had passed on without having held or seen her new son.

The women and we children all began a wail that brought my father and uncle running into the room. Father nearly broke his neck looking all around the room while trying to understand what was happening. He saw a passed-out older woman, a new baby, a clump of children who should not have been there, and, finally, almost tucked away and forgotten in the corner, his silent and listless wife. Although my eyes were too tear-filled to see, I could hear his voice stutter between confusion, joy, and finally heart-rending grief when it finally dawned on him that his wife had died. Something must have snapped inside his soul that day, for it seems his mind could not encompass all he had seen. It was as if he fallen from the heavens into hell in an instant and was broken by the journey.

He was never the same again, and became like an over-grown child in many ways. It was Mary who cared for the baby, Mary who roused the Aunts to prepare Mother for burial, Mary who kept us children busy preparing for Shiva,[2] Mary who made sure our father ate something, changed his clothes, and kept up with his work duties so the family would not starve. He did what she commanded, but more like a disembodied spirit or a sleepwalker from one of those bedtime stories told to us by our mother in better days. Mary asked Aunt Mariah to find a nurse maid for baby Jesus, for that is the name that Mary had to give him, as Father was incapable of choice. She held us together when we wanted to fall apart in our grief.

It was beyond a cruelty that soon after sitting Shiva, we and the entire village were summoned to nearby Sepphoris for the Roman Census. (Later on, there were rumors that we had gone to Bethlehem of Judea to register, but that was some 120 mils away and far from the local Roman post in Sepphoris.)

We were among the last families to go, as there were still burial duties to attend to. Despite Mary's best efforts, there was an understandable pall and lassitude hanging over the house, and preparations for the journey moved at an agonizing pace. Our kin could wait no longer; they went ahead but promised to find us lodging if and when we finally arrived. In his newly descended confusion and haze, Father was unconcerned about soldiers harrying us for our tardiness. He did much staring about and kept calling Mary by our mother's name, when he was not crying outright. He only began to stir when Mary had us and the baby all bundled up. She had decided to tell him we were going to visit her parents' grave for a religious day of observance, and would he be so kind as to help her with our baggage? Obedient as ever, he roused himself and situated Mary, the baby, and our travel belongings on the family donkey. There would be no singing and very little conversation on this journey.

There was also no room when we eventually arrived, just as dusk was falling. Our kin had done their best, but all of them were crowded into what looked like a storage room at the back of a roadside inn. There was a rough kind of shed across the stable yard, and, although it smelled strongly of the various beasts that did the Inn's work, the roof and walls were good and its proximity to our clan meant that we would be protected. Mary said that the animals would keep us warm, and asked only for some new hay to spread our blankets on. However, I soon began to sneeze when I lay down to sleep off the fatigue of the road. Aunt Mariah heard me and took me into her already crowded bed. My brother Simon found some village playmates in another part of the inn and stayed with them.

---

2. In Judaism, the traditional 7 day period of mourning the newly deceased.

In the morning, there was excitement as old friends and relatives gathered, but also something unsettling in the air that my childish brain could not quite place. Our relatives gathered around Mary to see the new baby, who seemed relatively healthy and happy despite all that had befallen at birth. His nursemaid had also travelled with us for her own Census appearance, but left to find her own people once she had fed Jesus. The little shed soon got crowded with our relatives, the old family donkey, and a few of the inn's animals too interested in us to go out to pasture. Mary looked as proud and loving as any new mother, and indeed some of the more distant relatives thought that my father had taken a younger wife. This added even more to his general confusion, as he was expecting Mary's relatives and a graveside ritual, not his own jovial kin.

Father was still befuddled when we reluctantly left the friendly confines of the inn and went to the town square to be sorted, named, counted, and taxed according to the Roman law. With all the commotion, Mary had not informed him of the true purpose of the journey, and she now hurriedly tried to ease him into the truth, no longer an easy thing after the shock of his wife's death. In too short a time it was our family's turn to face the stern aedile,[3] his soldiers, and a representative from a local synagogue, there to ensure adherence to the Law.

Father readily named us older children, but stumbled when asked to name Jesus. I remember him saying, "This is our baby," and Mary had to whisper "Jesus" under her breath. The aedile was immediately suspicious, and asked Father how he could not recall his own son's name. In his own defense, for once, Father blurted out, "He has just been born. . .sir."

When asked about Mary, Father said simply, "This is Mary, the mother;" then, to the aedile's next question, "No, we are not married." There was an audible gasp, with the kohen suddenly rousing himself from his boredom. A baby born out of wedlock was a shameful, unsanctioned, and even leprous thing, unprotected by the Law. Father was slow to understand what all the fuss was about, as he must have felt he was just telling the simple truth.

Mary, however, having grown up in a synagogue, instantly knew what trouble she and Jesus were in. With her tender heart, she would not tell the whole story of Salome's death, fearing what further damage might befall Father's fragile soul. She somehow collected her wits and calmly said the first thing that came to her: "It was by miracle that Jesus was conceived."

This bought her a little time, as the authorities were momentarily stunned. She must have sensed that she needed a strong ally against the Law,

3. Roman bureaucrat or official.

someone even the kohen could not gainsay. She added words that would follow her to the end of her days, "Elohim sent him."

Looking back at this incident, I have not been as surprised as most people. During our childhood play, we would cuddle and coo to Jesus for hours. I often heard Mary tell him, "You are a gift from the Lord above," but she had only meant how dear he was to her, she who had always dreamt of motherhood. It must have seemed to her but a short leap under the glaring eyes of the kohen and Roman authorities to go the next step.

The kohen was momentarily flummoxed, his fiery condemnation speech now stuck in his throat. Ever the helpful and intuitive soul, Mary meekly offered to go into a nearby tent and prove her virginity to him. She knew from the married maidservants from her synagogue days how each prospective bride had had to undergo similar examinations before being allowed to legally marry. If they could do it, so could she; once she had a plan, she was not one to shrink or quaver.

Besides, she told me later, she needed time to flesh out her story so that it would not all fall apart or create more doubts than belief. "I forced myself to focus on how miraculous it was for him to emerge alive from a dying woman. I went into a kind of trance or dream. These words and images just came to me, including the names of angels I had heard mention in our services, may the Lord above forgive me."

I did not think one so clever and loving should need much forgiving, but then I was only five. At any rate, a soldier duly escorted Mary, Jesus and the kohen to a tent, while Father, Simon, and I were pulled roughly out of line.

My little heart was pounding with fear and also hope, fear that harm might come to us all, including blameless Jesus, but hope that Mary would once again prevail in keeping our fractured family together. My heart was pulled between the two extremes. If I had been older, I might have had the further fear that I would snap and become like Father, who at that moment was becoming more and more agitated.

Simon did his best to reassure Father that Mary knew what she was doing and that all would be well. It was a great blessing that Simon had learned somehow to put authority into his voice. He was indeed becoming a man, even the man of the household due to Father's diminished state. He had to put hands on Father in front of all those in line, but if anyone saw this disrespect, they did not comment upon it.

After what felt like an eternity, the tent party emerged. The kohen still looked perplexed, but all steam and condemnation seemed to have left him. Mary walked obediently behind him, her eyes downcast, her manner meek, but a slight smile was just visible to those of us who knew her well. She joined us, and Father roused himself enough to ask, "Are we done here?" The kohen and aedile conferred, then the aedile seemed to get angry at the kohen. He puffed himself up and said that the whole matter was of too little importance in this backwater town to warrant any further discussion or concern. The crowd also had grown tired of waiting in the hot sun, so with a grumble, the aedile entered our names in some roster. Father paid some coin (or rather, Mary did, as she was now the keeper of our money, such as it was), and the soldiers hurried us on our way with a clout to Father's backside.

Thankfully, Father merely kept on walking, as if nothing untoward had happened. In truth, we had all grown used to clouts from the Romans from our few interactions with them. Simon and I wanted to run as far and fast away as we could, but Mary hissed a warning. We forced ourselves to slowly follow our shambling father as he more or less drifted back to the Inn.

Not a word was spoken as Mary and Simon gathered our belongings. It was as if we were under a kind of protective spell that any word might shatter, bringing the authorities down upon us all. Father loaded the donkey, we filled our waterskins, and then said our goodbyes to our kin. Many of them just stared at us, speechless and stunned. Perhaps they were afraid of being associated with us, or perhaps they too had heard Mary's fabulous story and did not know what to say or think. Those who had attended Mother's funeral knew that Mary had lied to the authorities, and that this put our family and perhaps all of them in danger. They held our fate in their hands, but thankfully none of them seemed to have any ill will towards her or Father. On the contrary, they seemed to have joined Mary in swaddling Father with as much solace and distraction as they could manage. He had been a good provider, kinsman, and worker for all in the village. I was to learn later in life that there was nothing like a common threat or enemy to bring folks together, protecting their own.

And now to the market, if there is any time left in the day.

Well, now I know the Judas—it is our neighbor across the alley. He could not wait to crow and tell me of his betrayal, which he did in a long-winded speech that seemed more designed for others in the market than for myself.

"I knew something was not right with James and his friends—in the midst of our nation's occupation, bondage, and misery, they were still light-hearted and even gay. I knew them not to be Roman sympathizers, for they were silent whenever centurions did their rounds, so at last it came to me: They must belong to those perverse *koferim* who rejoice at the death of that Jesus, whom they proclaim some kind of messiah! What kind of king allows himself to be so easily slain? Where was his army, his fortress, his armor, his defiant speeches? Our nation cannot put its faith in such a weak man and such a feckless movement.

"I was only too glad to share my insights with the Temple authorities, for in them I see the salvation of our nation. We must rid ourselves of anyone who weakens our resolve, who preaches love when we must gird for war. Turn the other cheek, indeed—shall we bless those who thrust their spears in our side, and who take our women and our wealth?"

He went on for some time like that, attracting some in the crowd, while others hung their heads and went about their business. I knew that I must become doddering again, and sank once more into a grey cover. He soon forgot about me, as his audience was giving him more attention. I did note those who nodded along or added their own hosannas. My spirit began to sink even lower than my bent back and averted eyes, until I remembered that my people had gone through idolatrous years throughout our history. Now they seemed to be worshipping some kind of war god instead of our God of Love, although, truth be told, I often wonder how love will allow us to overcome the principalities and powers of this world.

I need the Bishop or some stalwart brethren now to strengthen my faith, as I am starting to fear that he may be sacrificed to the blood-lust of the crowd. It is hard to rejoice in the world's condemnation and scorn, as Jesus preached, when the price of that scorn may be losing someone you dearly love. Then again, I have to remember that our Lord Jesus knew his hour had come, knew he was to be sacrificed, and yet he still rejoiced, fed his disciples, and forgave those who had him crucified.

I can only hope to be made of such stern stuff. I return once again to the knowledge that even though I understand many of the fickle and even evil ways of men, I do not know God's ways. I do not really know how or why he chose Jesus as his messenger and prophet, but I do know that I must cling to Jesus' vision of a land bathed in love, peace, and justice.

Dark, turbulent, and dangerous waters surround us, and we must hold onto something buoyant else we drown. God of love, I beg you to keep me afloat until I reach the other shore, in this life or the next. Though I love this life, I also love the promise of Heaven, of reuniting with those who have gone before. It is this love which calms my spirit . . .

So soon?

I hear the boots marching once more to my house. Apparently my Judas is not done with just James.

Into Your hands, O God, I commend my soul, and into this hole I commend this witness, may it live on . . .

XIV

The Life of Jesus, By Miriam, Daughter of Clopas

I AM MIRIAM, DAUGHTER of Clopas, who was brother to Joseph of Nazareth and uncle to this Jesus of whom much has been spoken. My father it was who out of duty, love, and charity took in Joseph's family upon his death. Joseph had children of his own before marrying his Mary, with whom he had a few more. All of those cousins entered our household, although in truth they spent much of their time in the house that Joseph had built for them.

I was some years older than Jesus, but of an age with Salome the Younger, who was more sister than cousin to me. She it was in her adult life who taught me how to read and write, not that I can make a trade of it given women's low estate in this world. I at first questioned why she bothered to equip me with a tool I was almost forbidden to use, but she seemed to see possibilities in the future that I could not see at the time.

I see that that time is now, for she has been taken away by the San-hedrin authorities. This leaves me heart-broken but also charged with her most recent duty, that Jesus' life history be told truly before the wolves and fawning sheep have their way with it.

She has left me enough parchment, ink, styli, and money to do some honor to Jesus, and for that I am both grateful and resentful. I have never had to order my memories, and do not know the rules and requirements for diary writing. In our faith, there seem to be rules for everything, but in this diary I will grant myself freedom to just write until I can no longer do so.

Wolves and sheep are my words, not Salome's. Poor soul, she could not bear to criticize another person, those she called the "Children of The Lord Most High." (She also wants me to spell G-d right out; she claims that He is more like a benevolent Father than a fearsome creature, and that He would take no offense. Well, plenty of His chosen people seem to take offense on His behalf, so I will not take the chance.)

At any rate, I am not so bold, nor can I call a thing by any other than its actual nature. When I see how that sweet Jesus was treated, he who did no one harm and only wanted to heal, I see that there are mad wolves, vipers, rats, and worse all around us. And those poor followers of his who could not see the danger for love of him, what is to become of those gentle sheep? Scattered by the wolves and smiling stupidly as their blood is spilled. Jesus had warned them to be as cunning as snakes and gentle as doves, but not a one of them had the sense that G-d gave those snakes. No, they listened to another of his sayings, they turned the other cheek, gave away their cloaks, took the hits, and got martyred for their troubles. And now the wolves have my Salome and I am mad with grief.

It may be that all this tale I am about to tell will be colored red with my anger, then blue with my tears and yellow with the fears I carry for my Salome and indeed for all of Jesus' family who are associated with his cause. Perhaps by the time I am done with this diary, I shall be clear-eyed once again.

I shall not begin at the beginning, as Salome has already done that. There is not much to tell of Jesus' infancy, as he was like all other babies—he spit up, shat, cried, and gurgled with happiness when tickled, just like the rest of us. Mary had arranged for a wet-nurse to carry him past the death of his mother, and he took immediately to a breast not of his own flesh. Per-haps this was the earliest sign that he was indeed attached to this life even in the midst of death. He was weaned in good time, and seemed to accept that his nurse came less and less frequently to the house. She of course lived in our village, so he was to see her throughout his childhood. He loved her and she him for all their days; indeed, he seemed to love easily, from the village idiot to the meanest cur. Of course, this may have been simple habit, as he was surrounded by love from the start.

Even as young as I was at the time, it seemed a miracle that he was not blamed for his mother's death. His father perhaps was too befuddled to properly trace the cause of his wife's death, while Mary for her part was completely taken with him. She had known only the cold, formal, judgmental world of her kin Elizabeth and Kohen Zechariah, but here she was thrust immediately into a kind of motherhood she had only dreamed of. She was like that wonderful desert flower that just needs rain to blossom, and blossom she did. I do not believe Jesus ever had to cry for more than a few seconds before she would rush to hold and calm him. They had a kind of inner communication between them from the start, one that made me envious. At times, I was even resentful of my own mother's harried and distracted care. Of course, it did not enter my childish heart that Mother had so many duties that she barely had a thought for herself. I just wanted what Jesus seemed to have.

Not only did Mary have Jesus to lavish her pent-up love on, but also a ready-made extended family of bumptious, excitable, free-spirited children. She was almost always modest in front of my parents and adult kinsmen, but with us children she would take a quick look around for any adult witnesses, and then release herself to the joys of a childhood she had never had. At first, she was remarkably unschooled in childhood games, and needed even us younger children to instruct her on the rules and purpose. It amazed me that a child would even be allowed to tell an adult what to do, for at 12 or 13 years old, she seemed adult to me. She would cinch up her shift and run with full abandon in all our contests and games. She was as tall as Simon and almost as fast; her presence as the girls' champion kept the boys from lording it over us too much and gave us girls someone of our own to admire and emulate. Mary did not scold or patronize us, although she would appeal to our better natures when we were cruel and selfish, as children can be.

I believe it may have been Mary's innate treatment of us girls as equals that gave Salome the courage to eventually read, write, spy, and do other brave deeds. I am less brave by nature, and it did take me some time to trust that Mary really did care for us and would not betray us to our parents. She was a kind of child-woman who somehow bridged that great divide between the generations.

The adults in our world were considerably more reserved, occupied or perhaps just tired as they were with our families' survival. I do not recall if Uncle Joseph ever even talked to me before his wife's death; I never heard him mention my name. After that blow to his spirit, however, the stern patriarch in him shattered and was replaced by a soul that found pleasure in all the small, simple things of daily life. It may be that he no longer took life for granted, but held onto anything or anyone who was alive and new. Perhaps there was no such conscious change in his attitudes, but rather a break in his link to adulthood, leaving him stranded in childhood.

In any case, he was clearly delighted by the growing Jesus. Evenings would find him carrying the toddler around the compound on his shoulders, or letting Jesus ride him like a horse. As Jesus got older, Uncle would fashion little stick horses, carve farm animals, and build little playhouses out of scrap wood. At one point, he made him a mock Temple complete with Ark and altar. While Jesus would intone some prayer or imitate our Rebbe Nathan, Uncle—with his long beard now growing white—would loom over the little hut and play Adonai.

Some of us younger cousins would be allowed to participate, at least until we could no longer squeeze ourselves into the make-shift Temple. My father at first thought this play-acting might be blasphemous in some way, but Uncle had a way of laughing off any such restriction on play. "You are only young once," he would say to Father, "unless you are me and get to do it twice!"

Now that I write this, I see that Uncle and Mary were two kindred spirits despite their age difference. Aunt Salome had been a very proper wife in all ways, as she was intent on following all the many rules and regulations set down by our forefathers. Perhaps she feared what others would say in the village if she expressed her own opinions or did something outside the customary. I was married for a time myself, and knew how it felt to be an outsider in my husband's village. I had tried to fit in by being twice as good as any woman who had lived there all her life. Aunt Salome may have carried a similar desire, while Mary held no such ambition.

"I had no childhood," she once said to me, "and Joseph has given me permission to play how I want, at least as long as the house is in some order and the children fed."

Between the two of them, they created a tiny world where laughter, invention, surprise, and whimsy were ever present. This rubbed off on my parents and Uncle Benjamin's household as well. Joseph was still the patriarch, and his light-hearted, good-natured moods set the tone for the whole family. Uncle Benjamin, as the youngest, was quick to adapt to this changed atmosphere. He had been a bit more spoiled than his brothers, and, if I must say so, often looked for excuses not to work. He was a fairly good singer, and delighted us children by popping into our games while singing invented songs using our names for the characters in his little stories.

My father's efforts at play were tentative at first, as if he had had no childhood himself and did not know the territory. Up to this point, he had rarely laughed and always seemed to have a sour expression on his face, as if life were a bitter fruit he was forced to eat. He had some resentments over Benjamin's somewhat careless attitudes about the family business, and this may have kept him worried and overly dutiful for longer than the others. Eventually, however, he must have realized he was outnumbered, and even he began to loosen up.

The rest of the clan and village were not as amused by our antics and carefree ways, however. The sympathy they had extended Uncle after the death of his wife soon evaporated. I heard from some of the other village children that their parents had gone to Rebbe Nathan to complain that Uncle and Mary did not keep the Sabbath properly. Their house was not as clean as it should have been at High Holy Days and that they committed other crimes against our Faith and traditions. A gentle soul, Rebbe Nathan reportedly said something like, "But they seem happy."

My Uncles and Father continued to attend synagogue, and if they took any notice of the stares and tense silence around them, they never showed it. Village life requires a certain kind of surface peace whatever else might be brewing below ground; clan feuds are frowned upon, both in Torah and by common consent. It takes too much effort to remain angry with people you see every day, and whom you must rely on for many of the essentials of life. It could be that Nazareth was far enough removed from the pressure of Jerusalem—with its Temple authorities, Roman occupation, and scramble for survival—that there was room for us to simply live as we saw fit. It was only in my adult years that I realized how wonderful those early years were, how much breathing room life could give you if you were allowed to explore its limits.

So, this was the little world that Jesus grew up in. He had an immediate family who loved him, cousins and siblings for playing with, toys for make-believe, and, once his father and Mary married, younger siblings Joseph and Mary as well. He witnessed the miracles of birth and growth, and had the pride of being their "big" brother. He would play with them, assigning them parts in his stories even if they could barely sit up. As toddlers, they followed him around the compound like little ducklings, while he was both mother and father to them. He showed them the love and care he had received from so many, yet was protective and instructive as well. He would barely have learned something from his older kin before turning around and teaching it to the little ones, sometimes with unintended results. At family meals, he would see his father carefully wash his hands before saying the blessings and serving the food. His father told him this was to wash away impurities of the heart and soul, but Jesus must have taken this literally. Once, when playing house with the younger ones, he doused them completely—head to foot, heart down to their soles—before letting them eat. They did not appreciate the ritual and screamed for their mother. Mary came to their rescue, but then laughed too hard to scold Jesus properly.

Outside the family, the person who had the biggest influence on Jesus was Rebbe Nathan. He was both the teacher in our little Midrash, but also served as kohen for services, although he never called himself such. He had taken an early interest in Jesus, perhaps due to sympathy over the death of his mother. The Rebbe may have been expecting to find a damaged soul in need of his healing touch and wisdom, but instead he found a boisterous boy at ease with himself and the world. I suspect that the Rebbe had to sift through his own voluminous knowledge of Torah and Talmud to find just the right sort of approach to take with such a carefree spirit. It would not do to laden him with hundreds of shoulds and should nots, proscriptions appropriate for the more barbaric generations past. This was not a boy to trim down to a slim cog, one that could fit snugly into the machinery of a large urban mass, nor was he a boy to scare into meek obedience.

The Rebbe himself had known such shaping, having trained and then worked at the *Beit HaMikdash* in his early years. I was later to find out that he had been expelled for helping a wounded Maccabean[1] rebel heal right under the very noses of the Roman occupiers. He had studied the healing arts and was simply extending his skills to one in need. He was no rebel except in the eyes of his superiors. He had dutifully told them, and they in turn had banished him to the wilderness, lest his actions bring the Romans storming through the Temple Complex. They stripped him of his Kohen title, and removed any reference to him from their documents. Of the wounded rebel, even Rebbe Nathan would not say, whether out of respect for the High Priests or shame at their craven betrayal.

Rebbe Nathan brought considerable learning and sophistication to our little forgotten town, having been well taught at Temple. However, he had been humbled and had his career sacrificed for simply being merciful to a stranger in need. A lesser man could have become bitter and unforgiving, but the Rebbe instead studied everything he could in Torah about mercy and loving the strangers in our midst, no matter their background. He must have read enough to heal and sustain his own bruised spirit, and he shared this vision with our village.

He found a receptive soul in Jesus, who had been raised in love within a sharing, even open-minded clan. Jesus often travelled with his father, uncles, and older brothers to work in nearby villages, and so had mingled with peoples from many backgrounds. There was a Roman town called

---

1. A zealot soldier committed to ridding Judea of Roman invaders.

Sepphoris not too many mils away that had been damaged in one of our rebellions. They often required workmen such as Joseph and his brothers, and it was there that Jesus was exposed to the wonders of Roman mosaics, dramas, and marble works, wonders unknown in our backwater village. As the youngest, he had little real work to do, and spent many of those visits playing with and getting to know the local children.

When Rebbe Nathan talked about the pilgrims from distant lands whom he had met during feast days at *Beit HaMikdash*, Jesus would listen intently, adding those exotic stories to his own experiences. He would ask Rebbe Nathan any number of questions, with no fear of rebuke for speaking out of turn to his elders. For a small-town boy, he was exposed through experience and imagination to social castes, races, religions, and regions far from his own.

The Rebbe clearly saw Jesus as an inquisitive, attentive student. He began teaching Torah to him and a few others in the village. Reading came somewhat easily to Jesus, but he never could master writing. In all his brief life, I do not believe he ever wrote an epistle or a letter home; at that time, none in our clan could have read such a letter anyway.

Jesus was quick with languages, however, having picked up enough to play with the children from surrounding villages. He once told me that he learned how to shape his thoughts so they could fit into the language of his listener. He compared this to woodworking, where he had to fashion new parts to repair any variety of broken objects, each one different from the last. He would listen to how his audience spoke, thought, felt, and feared, and would adjust his words to repair what was broken or missing within them. In all the sermons he gave, I could imagine him shaping his words, building his foundation, then erecting his stairs and ladders so that his listeners could begin to approach Adonai Himself.

Of course, it also helped that Rebbe Nathan was such a good preacher. He had a way of taking obscure texts and extracting everyday meaning from them, something that our little village could relate to and use in our daily life. The previous kohen Zebadiah seemed to have his ambition set on Jerusalem, and delighted in being as scholarly and pedantic as possible. My father would marvel at the big words, claiming that the kohen was "so smart the rest of us do not understand him." The kohen could be seen walking through our village with his head held high, or else buried in some parchment. There was never any eye contact or casual talk with his assembly. Uncle Joseph would snort, and claim that the only good thing to come from the Kohen Zebadiah's sermons was a good nap.

Rebbe Nathan, on the other hand, seemed genuinely pleased to be among us, as if we were the most interesting village in all of Israel. Jesus clearly loved the man and seemed to absorb everything about him, from the rhythm of his voice to the intricacies of Torah interpretation. Such adoration must have been a great blessing to the Rebbe, who after his exile from *Beit HaMikdash* needed someone to believe in him.

Let me add one more thought about how the Rebbe influenced Jesus. The Rebbe had learned the healing arts while in Jerusalem, which of course attracted the best doctors and teachers from all the surrounding territory. His store of knowledge and his skills far surpassed those in our village, and he soon was in great demand. He freely shared his knowledge of herbs, ointments, and cures both mundane and obscure. He improved the skills of our local midwives without shaming them or threatening their practice.

However, the Rebbe was already somewhat old when he got to Nazareth, and he needed help carrying his medicines and other equipment on home visits. Who should he pick but young Jesus, his acolyte! No doubt the Rebbe used the travel time and the visits themselves to pass along his lore to the ever-attentive boy, perhaps hoping that Jesus would want to be a doctor himself when of age.

I remember one case in particular that caused a great commotion in our household. The Rebbe came to our compound one spring day asking after Jesus as well as his parents. I happened to be spinning some wool with Salome beside me when I heard the Rebbe inquire whether Joseph and Mary would allow Jesus to accompany him some distance away to treat a man suspected of leprosy. This was a dread disease and even the word itself sent shudders through us. Uncle Joseph merely looked befuddled, as he often did with difficult situations, but Mary simply asked the Rebbe to tell her more.

The Rebbe claimed to have stumbled on a possible cure for the disease when examining a rather boring passage of Genesis 14 relating to the War of the Nine Kings. Certain tribal kings or chieftains in the areas surrounding the Dead Sea had gone to war, with the armies of Sodom and Gomorrah being defeated after they were driven into the tar pits in the Valley of Siddim. One of their soldiers had escaped the destruction and capture, however, and run to the patriarch Abraham with the news. Abraham's kinsman Lot and many others had been captured and enslaved by the other side, and all their goods forfeited, so Abraham dutifully gathered his troops to seek revenge and freedom for his kinsmen. He defeated Ched-or-lao'mer and his allies, freed his kinsmen, and returned them and their stolen goods to Sodom.

The Rebbe told Mary that he was curious how Abraham had rewarded this soldier, as Abraham himself had taken little or no reward from the King of Sodom for freeing the prisoners. It was one thing for a man of wealth like Abraham to decline reward, but should this proscription also apply to an underling, a man whose name is not even noted? Does Adonai expect all

His servants, even the humblest, to merely do their duty? Are the rich, like Abraham, allowed to keep their blessings and thanks to themselves?

Rebbe Nathan had found an old parchment in the deep archives of the Temple where a long-deceased rebbe had mused on the subject. In thanks for being so alerted, Abraham had indeed wanted to give the soldier a portion of wealth taken from the defeated kings. The soldier surprisingly declined, saying that he had received reward enough from Elohim, who had miraculously saved him from the enemy when he had fallen into the pits. The Lord had also cured him of his "scales," which even in those days Rebbe Nathan knew to be a reference to leprosy.

The Rebbe had wondered whether there was something in those tar pits near the Dead Sea that indeed could cure or at least soften the impact of the disease. He knew that salt from the Sea had many medicinal uses, and was also used to "cure" meats and fish. Same word, same meaning, he wondered? Could there also be something in that oily, sticky tar that could calm the skin and help it heal? He had gone searching for any other references to the curative powers of the tar pits, even another word that might link the tar to something beneficial to man; however, he had found none.

The Rebbe, persisted, however, and even journeyed from Jerusalem to the Dead Sea. He collected many samples of tar, salts, alkali, sea water, and, for good measure, the strange algae that grew along the shore. He then played with these materials some, using an unfortunate slave boy as test subject. Finding a few compounds that did not immediately cause welts or pain, he traveled back to the area to build up a modest supply. His subsequent exile to Nazareth had put him far from the Sea, however, and this had pushed the entire subject far from his thoughts.

Now, however, he had a case which gave him a chance—even an obligation—to try this new treatment. Would Jesus be willing to accompany him on a great experiment to test The Lord's miraculous cure? The Rebbe would make sure that Jesus did not come in close contact with the affected one, but would only help carry the supplies and prepare the mixtures.

Mary could tell by the expectant and eager look on Jesus' face that he was all for this daring re-enactment of one of Adonai's almost unknown miracles. Even the very idea that mere mortals could channel godly power must have appealed to him. He begged Mary, but she seemed not at all sure if the Rebbe and Jesus should tempt fate, or worse, the wrath of G-d. She knew, of course, the story of Adam and Eve, and how The Almighty had banished them from Eden for eating of the Tree of Knowledge.

She raised this concern to the Rebbe, who paused a while in thought before answering.

"Many of my colleagues argue the same thing, that Torah tells us all Adonai wants us to know about His creation. To seek more knowledge is to have *hubris*, I think the Greeks call it. I take a different view. Once Adam and Eve ate of that tree, Adonai did force them out of Eden, from this land where all things had simply come to them without their thought or effort. From then on, we mortals have had to toil for what we gain. Our nation, though favored among all nations by The Lord, has had to toil even harder than most. The Lord has mostly rewarded our toil, at least when we deserve it. He will let me know if my cure is for the good of His creation; it would almost be a sin *not* to try to help one of his suffering creatures."

The Rebbe continued, "I dare not speak for Adonai, but it seems from my reading of Genesis, that all of creation was concentrated in that one spot, lush and bursting with life. Upon our transgression and fall, all that perfectly harmonious life was broken, strewn, and scattered across the whole face of the earth, awaiting man's toil to gather it back. Among many other tasks The Lord has set for us, we must seek to reassemble that Tree of Knowledge. This will be an homage to Him and repentance for what our sin did to scatter His creation. Knowledge is not for us to own, covet, or use against His creation, but it is meant for healing and harmony, as it was in the beginning of time."

Mary and even Joseph had been nodding silently throughout this discourse. They must have had their fears relieved, at least enough to give Jesus their blessing. He quickly assembled his traveling kit, one that he kept close at hand due to his many trips with his father, uncles, and the Rebbe. After kisses and good-byes, off the two of them went, the Rebbe now lecturing Jesus as soon as they left the door. I overheard Mary say to her husband, "I pray this is not the last we see of our boy. My heart and faith would die if he were to get sick." She began to cry silently, something she rarely did and for which Joseph seemed helpless to stop.

I do not believe either of them slept much the whole week that Jesus was gone. The house was unnaturally still, as if all its members were holding their breath. Even when he returned, Mary kept a slight distance, perhaps afraid of coming too close to him or seeing telltale scales creeping up his legs or arms.

Jesus gently rebuked her for the lack of welcome, exclaiming, "O ye of little faith! It worked, Rebbe's ointment worked!" He related how the Rebbe had had to talk to the man and his family for a considerable time before they even allowed him to proceed. The man evidently had given himself up for exile to a leper colony and an early death, and needed much reassurance that a treatment was even possible. The Rebbe had had to stretch the truth considerably, saying that the treatment had been newly established in Jerusalem, or had the man not heard? The mention of that fabled city and Rebbe Nathan's training there seemed to calm his fears and kindle his hopes enough to submit to the treatment, which consisted of a stinking, oily mixture of tar, sea salt, and alkali, all gently warmed and thinned to a kind of paste.

Nothing had happened for a time, but at least the man had not collapsed in pain or thrown the Rebbe and Jesus out of the house. By then, Jesus said, the man had been as obedient as an old dog, meekly lying there awaiting his fate. Nathan had continued his encouraging words and gentle prayers, while Jesus had assumed the stance of a serious, competent assistant. Tall for his age, and with the hint of a beard now that he had had his Bar Mitzvah, he had been instructed by the Rebbe how to hold and present himself, especially in front of nervous and fearful patients.

After two days of treatment, the Rebbe washed off the mixture, and found to his utter surprise that the man's scales had started to fall off. The good doctor had to control his joy and pretend that this was totally to be expected. A sharp glance at Jesus told him to do the same. Before taking his leave for other business, the Rebbe applied a second treatment and told the family to wash it off in three days, with instructions to call for him if the situation worsened. He accepted the profound thanks of the family, who saw a future for themselves now that their breadwinner seemed to be healed enough to continue providing for them. After receiving some small gifts, food and water for the journey, they had returned home. With release from their solemnity, they were as excited as schoolboys about what had occurred.

Even in their joy, however, Jesus had dared to ask the Rebbe why he had basically lied. The Rebbe said, "The man was already so resigned that he was almost looking for a reason to quit this life. If he had known he was the first, he surely would have balked completely. To another man with more fight in him, I might have done the opposite, telling him how brave he was to be the first, a pioneer whose name would resound through the ages as the man who beat leprosy. You must fit the cure to the heart and soul of the one who receives it."

Jesus also noted that the Rebbe's voice had changed while talking to the man, going lower and slower. The Rebbe was evidently pleased with Jesus' keen observation, saying "Yes, I had to show *gravitas*, as the Romans call it, as if I was solidly convinced of my own words. You can show no doubt or uncertainty when dealing with those at the end of their hopes. Your faith in your own abilities must be rooted like the tallest oak, or like one fully braced when hauling a lost calf up from a pit. Your faith must supply what they lack; if they have faith already, you supply permission to believe. Sometimes, your mere your presence is enough, so that they do not feel alone."

It was in many such cases that the Rebbe passed on his knowledge of human nature and the healing arts to Jesus. He taught Jesus from parchments and illustrations written by the Greeks generations ago, material he had smuggled out of the archives of the *Beit HaMikdash*. He reasoned with Jesus that the stolen medical books were payment for his lost career as a Temple Kohen.

"Knowledge belongs wherever there are eager minds to learn," he once said, "It is not to be hoarded and hidden away." He taught Jesus how to identify, find, and grow wild ginger for the treatment of various kinds of upset and nausea; anise to cool high fevers and settle the stomach; henbane and hemp seeds to induce sleep; gentian and other bitter herbs for kidney stones; and basam for making the famous Balm of Gilead admixture. Jesus learned how to lance and drain boils, close wounds, keep a clean work area, and use all of the Rebbe's tools for probing, cutting, and sewing. He learned relatively painless ways of removing infected and rotten teeth, and even how to work bronze wire into weak teeth to strengthen them and prolong their effectiveness.

He was aided in all these studies by having so many older brothers and cousins available for carrying on the family business. He spent his teen years as an apprentice to Rebbe Nathan and then became our village doctor when our Rebbe got too old to work. At first, Jesus was considered too young and familiar to be taken seriously by his fellow Nazarenes. They would talk only to Rebbe Nathan, who would then turn to Jesus and ask him what to do. This went on for some time before Jesus was accepted for his own skills. He had learned from this how to appear older than his years, and the surrounding villages had no such problems with him.

Jesus did report two main frustrations that daunted him in some ways. He was unable to travel all the way to the Valley of Siddim to refresh the Rebbe's stock of ingredients to treat leprosy. The time and money required for such a long journey were beyond his means, and over time the Rebbe's supply was used up. Rebbe Nathan and Jesus had been successful with two other cases, but had used up the remaining ingredients in a fruitless effort to heal a fisherman from nearby Gabae. This man lived alone near a fetid swamp, and his leprosy had spread too far to be treated by the time that the Rebbe and Jesus could respond to his kin's frantic request for help. In any event, these three were the only cases in the immediate area, so the infected families and their kin were the only ones to know such a treatment even existed.

I often imagined what would have happened to Jesus if news of this leprosy treatment had reached the bigger cities. Would he have moved there and left us all behind? Would he have become a respected, even wealthy doctor for the rest of a long life? Or could he have died of leprosy himself before reaching a normal span of days? Many talk now of how he was fated to be sacrificed at Golgotha for the redemption of our sins, and it is easy to look backwards at a person's life and see what appears to be the straight line that brought them to their end.

I am only a woman writing a story no one may ever read, but as I sit here I can imagine what might have been if just one traveler, having heard of a miraculous cure, had sought out Rebbe Nathan and confirmed the existence of a treatment for that dread disease. Jesus surely would have been swept up in all the excitement, hope, and desperation; the tide would have carried him far afield from where he ultimately landed.

Or perhaps not. As it was, Jesus' other frustration was that he was not a rebbe or a kohen. The latter was out of the question, as he was from the tribe of Judas, not Levi. Yet he yearned to be taken for a kohen, for he saw how people responded to Nathan's prayers, encouragement, recitation of scripture, and promises to intercede with The Almighty on their loved ones' behalf. He could sense how much calm and hope would come into a sick room when the Rebbe appeared, with his low, authoritative voice, his shawls, cloak, and other signs of exalted office.

"Oh, you come from Jerusalem! Oh, from the *Beit HaMikdash*! You grace us poor villagers," they would cry, never mind that he was in exile in Nazareth and had been stripped of his title.

Jesus himself must have wanted that same *gravitas*, if only so that people would open themselves to his healing. He had always been an advanced student of Torah and Talmud, and he continually engaged Rebbe Nathan in argument, explication, clarification, and even some good-natured competition as to who could come up with the most obscure reference to a particular problem. Rebbe Nathan was in no position to sponsor or proclaim him a rebbe, however, and Jesus had met no other rebbe in his travels that he wanted to emulate and follow. Had he learned too much already to submit to another's limitations, or had he simply wandered in the wilderness around Nazareth without meeting or impressing the right teacher?

There is another story being told among his current followers about how he preached at the *Beit HaMikdash* at age 12. No doubt Mary's panic over almost losing him made the episode stand out in her memory far longer than his other adventures. Anyone who subsequently talked to her about Jesus' life would have heard that tale of his early independence, budding promise, and divine gifts.

I take another view, as I often do. Had he been seen as the truly talented and precocious orator, scholar, and student that he wanted to be, surely someone at the *Beit HaMikdash* would have taken him under their wing.

And he would have gone. He was a middle son in a large, stable family, and thus not essential to Joseph's patrimony. His parents would have been honored to have him called to the *Talmidim*.[2] Again, was it fate or something like scorn for a presumptuous country nobody that prevented the Temple rebbes from taking Jesus for the *Talmidim* road? What would have happened to his vision of Adonai and himself if he had been called to join that very center, epitome, and stronghold of our faith? Would he have become an ambitious scholar and teacher, pleased to have the brightest minds in the land to shape and mold? Or would he have followed the path of Rebbe Nathan, eventually being expelled, exiled, and discredited?

I must confess to the reader (if any) that I can only raise these questions and not answer them. It may be that I am like some lowly creature who cannot see anything clearly when looking up at the heavens and the sun, but sees many things when they are right at her ground level. The heavenly shine around Jesus enthralls but also blinds many of those who worship him. They keep their faces so turned towards the sun that they forget their earthly cares.

I see but the practical necessities, the everyday choices we all have to make, the many small victories and defeats that make up a careful life. I can imagine the roads not taken by Jesus, but that is the extent of my imagination. I remember the merely human choices he made, the off-hand things he said that his followers now never repeat or discuss, but that revealed to me his everyday thoughts and feelings. I see him in his particulars, including his gradual assumption of the mantle of the rebbe he always wanted to be. He worked hard at his studies; he was kind, gentle, and loving, perhaps a bit more so than the rest of us, but still on a human scale. He developed followers of a kind, although of a dirty, disorganized sort if you ask me. He amazed some people with his healing skills, but I already knew that he was well-trained in those arts. The more people wanted him to be great, perhaps the more he thought so of himself. He tragically pushed his luck with the Elders and the Romans and got himself killed for his temerity.

This path, this series of life events I have described makes sense to me; it is something human I can grasp.

Or maybe I am just so tired of this life that I cannot dream or imagine like others do. My dark, deep sleep gives me just enough rest to face another day, but there are many in my clan who report wonderful dreams during the night. They awake excited about the adventures they see in their mind's eye, and perhaps it is such as them who have made a dream of Jesus and

---

2. Officially sanctioned and supported students of the Talmud, the Holy book of the Hebrews.

his Father in Heaven. Oh, to believe that love is everywhere, that He knows their names, that death is not the end but merely a three-day hiatus before the great heavenly pleasures that await!

I know from Torah that Adonai knows how to talk to His prophets through dreams, but never have we heard of Him inhabiting a human or giving birth to a son. The Greeks have all kinds of stories about their gods taking human (and animal) forms and having congress with humans, but we do not believe as they do. I suppose it is possible that our Lord has defeated all the Greek ones, and has absorbed some of their powers and proclivities. Perhaps I should rejoice over such a victory, but I have not heard any kohen, rebbe, prophet, or follower of Jesus confirm or even suggest that such a battle and victory occurred.

Am I the one to be pitied because I lack imagination and do not dream? I bite my tongue when I hear Jesus' followers rhapsodize about a loving Father in Heaven, Jesus' sacrifice, and all the rest. I know that just as dreams come in the night, so too do nightmares. I have heard my own children awake screaming in the night, as if some evil is trying to drag them into a painful, awful place. I cannot explain why some can dream, others have nightmares, or still others have none at all. If Jesus' G-d only comes to the dreamers, is there a different G-d for the rest of us? Or no G-d at all? I cannot explain how a man I grew up with, a man who seemed so normal in many ways, how he could be a Son of The Almighty without me knowing it! His followers always have an answer to my doubts, but it is almost always the same—The Almighty does what and how He wants. How can a mere mortal, a woman, a mother from a small country village compete with that?

But perhaps my memories are poisoned, for I have just learned that the Sanhedrin has put Salome to death.

I am filled with bile and loathing for this life, and am even more confused than ever about why the Holy Father—whom Jesus declared so loving—would allow such things. Is the evil in this world the match for His powers? If this G-d wants to "call His children home" to Heaven, like some say, could He at least do so in a more loving and painless way? Especially for all the blameless, beautiful, harmless creatures like Salome, James, Jesus, and how many others. The pain of their deaths, and the pain of the grief I feel are all too real to me, but all those promises of Heaven are just so many words of things beyond my sight and knowledge. Maybe I am indeed a lowly creature, a mouse who can only see directly in front but cannot see the whole firmament of angels, gods, and saints above.

I can feel myself getting angry that Salome entrusted this task to me, although truth to say I did not know that all these thoughts and words were even in me. Surely Adonai would have told her to pick a worthier scribe, one who can dream properly, one filled with hope and faith.

A part of me wonders if my bitterness now is like the herbs used at Passover, some kind of remembrance or warning to us mortals not to be captured or enslaved by false gods and false hopes.

Perhaps all I have written is some kind of manure meant to fertilize and nurture some new growth. Maybe it is just manure.

It is all too much for me to comprehend. I feel like Salome would want me to go on, but I cannot go on.

XV

The Search For Salome's Diary

THERE IS MADNESS STILL everywhere around us, and it was surely madness that had me preparing to reenter the ruins of Jerusalem. My mother, bless her soul forever, had charged her sister Miriam and then me with recovering the diary she had begun, detailing the true-life story of my uncle Jesus, who is now called the Christ.

There had been nothing but turmoil, siege, and war ever since my Uncle James' death and the Roman suppression of our many ill-conceived and poorly organized revolts. Legionnaires had battered Jerusalem's walls in their siege, leaving only piles of rubble where once stood the *Beit HaMikdash* and many homes in the surrounding neighborhood, including my mother's and Uncle James'. All of Jerusalem's inhabitants had been routed or killed by the Legionnaires, leaving only desolation and death where once had stood our shining city. It was some time before open warfare ceased, and in this lull I dared venture to Mother's ruined house.

Before I left the compound in Beth'el where we now lived, I had asked Miriam for help locating both the house and the hiding place. Mother had

left Nazareth and moved in with James as the Church—as they called it—
tried to get established, and I had visited her there but once or twice when
young. Miriam had moved in there hoping to finish the diary, but soon left
to save herself from Mother's fate. Though old and feeble now, Miriam grew
animated as she warned me not to go. When I persisted, she lowered her
head and spoke in a voice nearly choked with anguish.

"Gideon, I was so bitter over your mother's death that I marked the
doorway with ashes and my own blood. I bashed my head against the floor,
for I wanted to bleed as my sister had bled. I burnt my stylus, inks, and skins
so that I would have no more contact with them—I blamed them for the
diary that tied her too long to that cursed house.

"Yet I could not bring myself to burn the diary itself, as it held her very
words, hopes, and dreams. To sanctify her and James' sacrifice, I smeared
the blood and ashes on the doorway lest anyone else think to enter and
desecrate their memory."

She thus urged me to look for such a doorway, but also pointed out
landmarks to guide my search. These would not prove useful, however, as I
would find whole streets buried beneath rubble and most trees cut down by
one side or the other in the rebellion.

Mother had taught us to be as cunning as snakes, but gentle as doves.
I was not the gentle kind, however, and had, in fact, been part of the revolt.
As an adolescent, I had heard Brother James bar Zebedee speak, he with the
ready sword arm and zeal for the poor. It was only natural that I later joined
with some of his followers when this latest revolt began, although, truth be
told, we mainly crouched in the dark hoping to ambush Roman patrols.
They were not so foolish as to march in unfamiliar countryside at night,
however, so our group saw little action.

Although I am relatively old now, being up in my forties, I remembered
much of the swordcraft and stealthy tactics learned in my warring days. I
still possessed a badly nicked Roman gladius that I had found abandoned in
the revolt. Night travel did not daunt me, and I believed I could find many
places to hide from any roving soldiers if I could just breach Jerusalem's
walls. Of ghosts and demons lurking in unholy places I had little fear, as I
counted myself skeptical of any such superstition. Our village kohen had
conjured many a frightening creature to silence us rowdy children during
services, but I never listened. I had grown up in a family that believed in love
and mercy, so fear held little sway over my emotions. If the God of Jesus still
held favor for his family, I felt I had some chance. My own skills would have
to suffice for the rest.

I took enough food and water in my traveling bag for a week's sojourn,
knowing that I would find no aid or succor in and around Jerusalem. I

strapped my sheathed sword beneath my black traveling cloak, for defense against the Romans and the many desperate bandits who are spawned in the wake of any war. I brought my stout walking staff, my eating knife, and a length of rope that might prove useful for scaling Jerusalem's many walls. I hoped to avoid all patrols, but if challenged, I could fight or act the part of a grieving son intent on finding his mother in the rubble. The fates would decide.

With such plans and faith in my mission, I made my way along the Northern Road. It was grimly decorated with many a crucified rebel rotting on their crosses, with only carrion birds for company. *There but for God's grace,* I thought, as I kept my eyes cast down on the road and even affected a kind of slumped resignation. It would not do to show any pride or purposefulness, but rather I must act the part of a defeated, older man who was no threat to anyone. I walked slowly, letting those ahead of me encounter whatever dangers there were in store.

As dusk was falling, I saw what I dreaded, a Roman roadblock and a queue of travelers petitioning fruitlessly to enter the city. I could just make out its battered walls in the near distance. I knew I could not be found in possession of the sword, so sat down awkwardly on the verge of the road, leaning heavily on my staff and looking all the world like a lame beggar. I stretched out my hands for alms, all the while scanning the walls for some break or unguarded entry point. I eventually saw a battered, v-shaped gap in the near distance, and tried to fix it in my mind's eye as best I could. With luck and a good moon, I hoped that gap would reveal itself to me again in the night. But as yet, I had no way to get there undetected.

I knew that Mother's house was somewhere in a small neighborhood squeezed between the Pool of Bethesda, the Sheep Gate, and the junction of the Northern and Jericho roads. The gate and crossroads would be heavily guarded, and whole legions were reported to be camped down in the nearby Kidron Valley to the east. Something about the gate nagged at me as I sat in the dust, praying for a way forward. I knew the gate had been the entry for those driving *korban* rams and lambs to the Temple for sacrifice. After a time, it finally came to me: Where there were drovers of animals, there must be paths and shortcuts off the main road, or from before there even was a road. Such paths hopefully could take me close to the outer wall without being seen.

Thinking fast while there was still light, I hobbled to my feet, and limped slowly across the road and out some ways off into the rocks and scrub at its edge. Looking around, I spied a promising path just off to my left whose trailhead was hidden from the road by a large boulder. I let my staff and travel bag fall at my feet, and gathered up my cloak and under tunic.

Squatting down, I made as if defecating, taking long enough that any observer would grow tired of the spectacle. I looked up at the sky, I grimaced, I looked around as if embarrassed, but, in reality, I watched and waited for my chance. When I saw no eyes on me, I gathered my goods and crawled off behind the boulder, listening for signs of pursuit.

None came despite the sound of my heart beating frantically in my chest. I steadied my breathing as best I could, and, crouching down beneath my dark cloak, I scuttled down the path on all four limbs like some giant beetle. My eyes were but a cubit[1] off the path, which I could both feel and dimly see in the fading light. I looked up periodically to keep the v-shaped gap in the city walls in my sight, and kept branching off onto those trails that seemed pointed in the right direction. With aching old joints, various scrapes to knees and hands, and many near-misses of the dried scat strewn along the paths, I made it close to the base of the v-shaped gap as night fell properly and fully.

I collapsed for a time, and as I gathered strength, I allowed myself a small satisfaction that my stratagem had worked. While not exactly a Trojan Horse, my dung beetle impersonation had helped me avoid detection. My old commander would have approved, but he was not there to help with the next leg of my journey.

I knew that I needed my dark cloak for cover and both hands for scaling the wall, but my sword, staff, and bag would hinder me. I needed each of them for survival and certainly could not leave them behind to be found by a patrol. After a moment's thought, I tied one end of the rope to the bag and staff, and the other end to the middle of the sheathed sword, thus making a crude grappling hook. I forced some twigs and sticks between the sheath and the sword blade until the sword was firmly wedged in; it would not do to have that sword come flying out, announcing my unwelcome presence with a loud clang.

It took several throws for my sword to find purchase in the gap in the wall, with each thump of sword and wall causing my heart to skip. With my last strength, I managed to ascend. No sound or light came from within the dark and doomed city, which stretched out before me like some vast necropolis. I had planned to simply reverse the procedure on my descent, but then it occurred to me that I would not be able to unhook my sword from the notch. And what if the drop was longer than my rope? What jagged rocks might be waiting for me if I fell, old and spent as I was?

I pondered these dangers while some of the stillness of the empty city seeped into my tired bones. It finally dawned on me that the dead night was

---

1. Roughly the length of a man's arm, from elbow to fingertip, about 2 feet.

telling me what to do, and that was nothing. '*Nothing could be done, and nothing should be done. There is a time for nothing,*' it seemed to say. '*Amen,*' I replied in surrender. I wrapped myself in my cloak, used my bag as pillow, and blissfully surrendered to sleep as best I could on the broken stones.

It was the dawn's early dew that woke me, with almost a tickle to my face. I startled a bit with the unfamiliar surroundings, and nearly fell off the ledge. The scramble for safety woke me fully. The morning birds greeted me as we both began our day, but it was the harsh rasping of the carrion birds I heard, and not the sweeter tunes of the lark. Piles of rubble and broken, burnt wood stretched out beneath my feet and out into the bleak morning light. The sky was a bruised and glowering thing that the rising sun could do little to dispel. All of nature seemed to confirm the defeat of what my people had held to be most beautiful and God-given.

I could not afford to linger on the wall. From my perch, it was still some seven or eight cubits to the rough ground. Looking around me, I saw where two protruding stones jutted from the wall like teeth on a ravaged jaw. I could place my grappling sword on the city-facing side of the stones, thread the rope back out between them, then loop the rope back towards the ground. My own weight would wedge the sword against the face of the stones. Once on the ground, I could slacken the rope and the sword's weight would hopefully bring the whole assembly back to me.

And my plan worked, although I did have to drop the last few cubits. An old knee sprain duly complained, reminding me that I would not be able to run from any patrol. I would need a small hiding place from which to observe patrols, learn their habits, and plot my next move. All remaining intact houses would be the first ones searched by any patrol, but there seemed to be any number of dark holes amidst the jumble of fallen walls. With my cloak over me, I thought I might find a spot to wait out the day. I would just need to think and bury myself like my new friend the dung beetle.

I was not sure if the Romans patrolled either the north or eastern wall, but knew they would be on the roads that ran to the Temple complex. I feared watchmen up on the walls the most, for they could spot movement for several stadiae in all directions, as there were few tall buildings remaining that could block their view. Once I knew the walls were no threat to me, I could deal with the other dangers.

I cautiously ventured out into the tumbled and ruined landscape in the general direction of the Temple, all the while checking the walls behind me and to my left. The first promising hole smelled badly of death, while the second one proved too small. I wasted time crawling in and out of this hole before deciding that it would not do. My time out in the open was fast disappearing, however, like the proverbial sand in an hourglass—the rising sunlight had finally pierced through the gloom of the dawn.

It is perhaps in such times of danger that our senses sharpen and we act before we are even aware of thinking. I found myself drawn to a collapsed stable of sorts, where one end of the thatched roof had fallen nearly to the ground, making a lean-to against the remaining stone wall. I quickly burrowed under, finding straw mixed with dried dung. As I situated myself, I realized I could look out through the thatch in several directions without being seen. After a moment's thought, I pushed the dung out towards the opening where I had entered, then broke several open. I rubbed my cloak with the scat as well. With luck, this would hide my human smell and discourage any nosey dog or fastidious soldier from entering my hole. I thanked The Almighty and the dung beetle spirit that seemed to be guiding me.

For two days I did nothing but watch, stilling my usual impatience. As I should have expected, the walls were patrolled at regular intervals, for the Romans were nothing if not regimented. They were not early risers and always sought shade in the heat of the day. I made a crude sun dial from a stick driven into the ground just outside my lair, and with that I roughly tracked their daytime movements.

The night was feebly lit by braziers fed on the walls by the night guard. The light did not quite reach my den, and I hoped that a good moon might soon help me get closer to where my mother's house had stood. The first night, I crawled out and explored briefly, stopping at one point to relieve myself far from my hiding place. I buried my waste as I had seen dogs do, using my sword to scratch out a hole in the packed earth. I resolved to be like a spirit, leaving no mark of my passage for either man or beast to find.

Dogs. I had ventured out the second night armed with my sword, although I was reluctant to use it lest I leave fresh blood and announce my presence. I had gone out only 100 paces or so before two dark and panting shapes crossed an intersection some thirty paces in front of me. I was downwind, but the beasts must have heard my footsteps, for one stopped long enough for me to see its features in the moonlight. It was a massive, blunt thing that seemed to be wearing spikes around its thick neck. A name something like Molasses or Molossus came to me from my army days. We all had been told about these fierce killing dogs of the Roman army. I had never seen one so close, however, and did not know its capabilities. Could it see in the dark or smell my fear? Could it track me silently and be upon me before I could defend myself? Or would it howl, attracting its handlers? And where was its partner?

I could not wait to find out, and my only choice was to turn my back on it and retreat as quickly as possible. I half-ran, half-stumbled as I picked my way gingerly over rubble and in and out of shadow. The hairs in the back of my neck tingled with death as I imagined razor-sharp teeth closing in on me. I knew that the thatched roof of my retreat would be no protection from the dogs, and that I could not swing my sword in such a confined space. My only hope was to avoid detection. I was the rabbit and they were the hunters.

Crawling into my den, I cannot say how long I shivered with sword drawn, waiting for my discovery and dismemberment. At last I heard some snuffling and low growls, and it seemed as though the beasts were at the entrance. Then. . .. nothing, silence; then. . .. the sound of water splashing.

The dogs had done what dogs do to mark their territory and signal their disdain for other beasts—they had simply peed on the turds I had placed at the entrance to my den. I could hear them padding away into the night, careless of my existence after all. My night excursions were ended.

That left me spent, as one can imagine, and I did not sleep well that night. I awoke at some early hour before the dawn, and could not return to the awful dreams and fitful tossing that had marked my sleep. Foggy from lack of rest, I yet resolved to leave my den, which no longer felt safe since the shadow of death had tracked me there in the shape of those dogs. I did not know when the dogs ended their night prowl, or just what patrols I might encounter, but knew I could not remain a rabbit, trapped far from my destination.

After a quick breakfast, I set off towards the base of the eastern wall. I hoped to cleave to it, making it hard for any watchman to see me pass directly beneath. All I can say is that it was rough going. Many of the houses that abutted the wall had been destroyed in the rebellion, leaving mounds of rubble that I crossed scrabbling like a rat on all four limbs. I could feel my joints and limbs complaining at the effort, and I must have left small splotches of blood on the stones from my knees and hands.

I arrived at the neighborhood described by my aunt just as day was breaking. It was time to hide again, and again I found a destroyed outbuilding from which to observe my surroundings. I could see the ruins of the *Beit HaMikdash* some distance away across an empty and ravaged plaza. From my vantage point I could see the roads that had lead up to the Temple, and it was on these roads that I expected to see the Roman patrols.

But what I did not expect was that I was not alone in the ruins. Ragged, emaciated creatures would creep out of the rubble on their hands and knees when they saw no Romans about, then would set about keening, wailing, and beating their breasts with the very stones that had once surrounded the sacred Ark. They appeared to be mad, their hair wild and blood-stained, with clothing torn and barely covering what used to be the temple of their body. Their faith in Adonai must have been as shattered as their minds.

Without the rules and kohenim to intercede on their behalf with The Almighty, they were as shipwrecked sailors cast adrift on an endless sea of uncertainty. Many were caught unaware by patrols, but instead of running, they rushed on the swords to end their pain.

It was a waking nightmare, like the vision of Sheol that our angry village kohen had tried to pound into our heads. A creeping kind of shame began to grow in me, as I realized the true cost of the war we rebels had brought to all that seemed sacred and beautiful in our country.

Furthermore, I dared do nothing to assuage the starvation and desperation of these lost souls, for they would devour my food and water supplies and alert the Romans to my presence. The sword at my side clearly marked me as a responsible party to the madness. In all my days and nights in that benighted city, I considered throwing it away, but the practical necessity to survive and complete my mission overrode any guilt. That guilt sat in the pit of my stomach like rotten food, and I knew that sooner or later I would have to face its accusations.

Swords. They have a double edge in more than just a martial sense. My damaged sword also served as the very tool I needed to lever through the rubble, chop away the rafters, and ultimately pry up the floor stone that concealed my mother's precious diary. I had crept out of hiding one early morning when the light slanted just so, making the white marble of the Temple and the dew-splashed stones of the surrounding rubble shine in an almost heavenly light. I stood in a half-crouch, momentarily caught between an almost predatory alertness and awe at the beauty of the day, but something was tugging at my vision. Something at the edge of my awareness was telling me it did not belong or fit with the rest.

It was a dark space, an absence where light should have been. I approached cautiously, as I had been disappointed from previous forays in the neighborhood. I then noticed dark, caking flakes on the blackened doorway; this could only be blood, something I sadly recognized from my warring days. I half-expected to find a body buried in the rubble, with this blood showing its final resting place. Instead I found the fish symbol carved on the darkened doorframe and no smell of death or fire. The beauty of the day and my own mounting excitement convinced me that I had found what I had long sought.

I knew that I would only be able to work an hour or two at a time, in between when the Romans made their rounds. It took time, but I was able to shoulder many of the smaller building stones up and out of the way. I used my sword to pry the doorframe off from the wall; these longer timbers served to lever stones I could not lift. Some of the stones were still mortared together, and I had to use my sword to scrape through the grout. The nicks in it turned that sword into a saw, and I smiled to realize that the very damage that had caused the sword's owner to cast it aside had proved so useful. I did not beat that sword into a ploughshare, but it did become the tool I most needed to honor my mother's wishes.

There were times, however, when I could not work at all, and I nearly went mad with idleness in the cramped confines of my hiding place. On the sixth day, I finally was able to clear off enough of the floor to see another fish symbol barely visible as a scratch on one of the stones. I was about to pry it up when a disturbance above me caused me to whirl around with sword in hand. A chunk of stone glanced off the blade and hilt of my sword, crushing my foot as it fell. I leapt backwards in pain, just as another stone fell where I had just been standing. Two ragged and emaciated men were crouched above me, using the stones like some barbarians on the hunt, but their eyes widened in fear when they saw my sword. I let out a muffled roar and feinted to climb up after them, although in truth my foot was in no condition to pursue anyone. The men nearly fell backwards in their fright to escape death, wisely as it turned out, given my fury at being interrupted so close to my goal.

In a panic now that I had been seen and no doubt heard, I turned back to the marked stone, only to find that the last deadly chunk thrown at me had broken it to pieces. A guttural kind of gleeful laugh escaped my lips as I madly pried and scraped away the shards with my sword. There in the debris was a plain dust-covered box that held the prize. Grabbing it with both hands, I shoved it into my travel bag only to hear soft steps approaching.

I grabbed my sword, whirled, and cocked my arm for a killing blow, but my thrust was stayed by a most unexpected cry. There before me, cowering beneath my sword, was the terrified face of a gaunt, unkempt woman holding a swaddled baby. Which of them had cried out, I do not know, but that cry saved them from death. It also saved me from a shame that would have haunted me forever.

All the tension, hopelessness, fear and disgust of these last days fell in on me then, like the very rubble in which I stood. I dropped my sword and fell to my knees, burying my face in my hands to keep from sobbing outright. I bit into the hand that had held the sword, as if to punish it for wanting blood. Neither of us could speak or look at each other, but when I regained enough breath I stammered "I am so, so very sorry, sister. But what in the world are you doing here . . . and what do you want?"

Still not looking at me, she mutely held out her baby, which was making small mewling sounds. "Take her," she finally croaked when I made no move. "I have no more milk and she is dying. I am already dead." Her thin body shook with dry tears and she seemed on the verge of collapse.

Seeing her plight must have roused me from my confusion and shame. I shook my head to clear my thoughts, stood up, and sheathed my sword. I grabbed my bag with its precious cargo and motioned for the woman to follow me.

"Come," I said. "Let us get away before the next patrol arrives. I still have some food and water, and perhaps that will revive you." She stood there a moment unable to move, but I again reached out my hand. In my softest voice, almost a whisper, I said, "Come, sister, let us survive, for your baby's sake if not our own."

With that, she sighed and nodded mutely. We set off through the rubble to my hiding place, passing no one on our way. Each step sent pain racing up my leg from my damaged and bruised foot, but I was relieved not to be cut too badly. I hoped that I would leave no fresh blood or a trail to my retreat.

When we finally arrived, however, the woman was most reluctant to enter that dark space, suspecting the worst of me, I suppose. I had to plead and reassure her that I had no ill intent.

"Sister, please know that I am kin to Jesus of Nazareth, he who preaches love and peace. My family has sent me on a mission to this dead city to retrieve a holy book. By the blessing of God on high, I have what I came for and hope to leave this cursed place tomorrow at dawn. You are welcome to come with me, but first we must hide ourselves from the Romans."

With this, I gave her my most sincere and heartfelt look, then gestured inside. With another of her resigned sighs, she bent down and entered.

True to my word, I gave her much of my remaining food. She nibbled at the bread and cheese like a frightened mouse, stealing glances at me with distrustful eyes. I offered her my waterskin, which she used to soak some bread for her hot, wilted child. Some turgor returned to both of them, and I deemed it time to discuss how to escape the city.

First, I needed to learn who this frightened woman was, and what help or hindrance she might be to my mission.

"So," I began, "now that we are safe for the moment, it is time to introduce ourselves. My name is Gideon. May I ask who you might be?" I waited a moment to see if she would reciprocate, but she just stared at the floor. Not knowing if it was exhaustion or our religious laws that constricted her, I tried again. "Sister, know that as a believer in Jesus, I respect women, as equals even. Please know that you may speak freely to me even though I am a stranger and a man."

Still no response from her, just absent-minded nibbling on a piece of bread. Sensing that she needed more time to come back from whatever horrors she had been through, I settled back against the sidewall of my den. I used my eating knife to cut a strip of cloth off the bottom of my tunic, and wrapped the strip around my foot to relieve its chafing against my sandal. With nothing else to do but wait for the dawn, I stretched out, being careful to avoid crowding or touching the woman. Soon the exhaustion from the day's events took me into a dark, uncertain sleep.

I awoke after the heat of the day had dashed itself against the rocks. The woman was still there at the farther end of the broken room, listlessly wiping the sweat off her newborn. The little girl was too spent to cry or do more than whimper. It was a pitiful sight, but I was grimly relieved that she would not draw the Romans with her cries.

Keeping my voice to a whisper, I again asked the woman's name, but she again declined to answer. "Please look at me while I speak," I finally commanded, trying hard to control the exasperation in my voice, "Since you will not name yourself, I am going to call you L'chaim, 'to life.' I do not know what you have gone through, L'chaim, but it seems to have put a spell on you. Perhaps you think you have nothing to say, or even that there is no future worth living in. You are wrong, L'chaim, you have a future with your baby. This future is as real as the bread and water you had—you only have to want it and take it in when offered, as I am offering it now. Do not sit eating dead or painful memories, for they will only suck the life out of you. Believe me, with so much death about, we need all the life we can muster, L'chaim."

She obediently had kept her empty eyes on me, eyes which now started to mist with tears. Her lips moved up and down a few times, but no words could escape. I gave her more of my precious stock of water, along with some dried figs. She accepted these, but this time looked me right in the eyes, as if measuring me against other men she had known. For the third time, I asked her to introduce herself and to let me know if she wanted to escape the city with me. Her words came out grudgingly, but could not be stopped once she committed to speech.

"My name is Rachael, and my baby is Ava. I had the great misfortune of meeting and following a rebel, although he called himself a soldier of Adonai. Oh, he was handsome enough and seemed so very righteous, at first. He said all his prayers and insisted on following Kosher as best we could while living rough in the countryside. We slept in separate areas, I with the other women who did the cooking and tended to many other camp needs.

"There came a time when a high-ranking man came to the troop and declared that all the women and men should be married, so that no sin would be among us. He said it was needed to please Adonai and assure us of victory. All of the women had more or less attached themselves to only one man, so it seemed somewhat natural to be married. The couples assembled themselves in the parade ground after some attempt at ritual cleansing, but the weddings were ramshackle affairs at best. There had been no time to arrange for dowries or permission from our patriarchs; indeed, it was the high-ranking man himself who served as kohen, as we had no proper one. All this was explained as the necessary result of our being at war.

"My new husband took enthusiastically to his new rights, the moreso after each skirmish. He rejoiced to be alive, but I began to dread his return. He seemed determined to pump as much life into me as he could before he died. I was soon pregnant with Ava; this pleased him mightily, but did not slow his assaults on me.

"In my fifth or sixth month, the troop got orders to march to Jerusalem to relieve the Roman siege. I begged to return to my family so that I could safely deliver Ava, but he slapped me fiercely, accusing me of being a deserter, a shameful wife, and an abomination to The Lord. I was to be obedient unto death for the cause he fought for, for were we not one flesh, joined by The Almighty's commands for His righteous purposes? Apparently, I was to be nothing but flesh for him, with no will or needs of my own. Many of the other women reported the same treatment, and it began to dawn on me that the weddings had been a sham, meant only to keep the men satisfied, fed, and mothered in their desperate need."

Here Rachael laughed bitterly, having learned the painful lesson that most men lose their humanity when bloodlust or the fear of death is upon them. She no doubt saw me with my sword as just another deceitful, bestial man. Although I had done her no wrong personally, yet I felt compelled to keep showing her as much humanity and kindness as I could.

"I thank you, Rachael, for your honesty; know that there is much truth in what you say. I have been on the fringe of war and count it as a blessing that it did not damage my soul too much. And yet, I know how close I came to striking you with my sword. There is but a breath between life and death, and between those who act out of faith or out of madness. I pray we shall escape Jerusalem without having to put our faith to the test." I gave a world-weary sigh to that, which she echoed unconsciously.

I then asked Rachael how she came to be among the haunted survivors of the Roman's revenge. She described the agonies of the siege, and of her delivering her baby with the help of a midwife who was among the war brides. The pain was almost unbearable, as they lacked herbs and anything else to help with the birth. She recounted with renewed bitterness how her husband scoffed at her for producing a female child, saying that only warriors could save Israel. She admitted that she now wished him dead so that he could no longer insult and abuse her.

"I thought to steal his sword in the night and show him just what a woman could do to rid our land of evil men. I built my courage to the point where I did unsheathe it on a dark night with no moon. It was just as I was gathering my resolve for the deed that Ava cried out. He roused himself enough to scream at me to shut her up, then he rolled over. I was able to the resheathe the blade while quieting my daughter. The fool should have blessed Ava for saving his miserable life, which only lasted until the next week anyway. By then, I had started hoarding food and water in hopes of escaping the madness, but the end came so swiftly that all I could do was hide. Even when a kind of deathly peace came over the city, I still feared discovery, either by the Romans or the madmen at the Temple. I had to gag my poor baby to keep her quiet, and many times we were nearly flushed from hiding. I died of fright many times over.

"As you saw, I was almost dead from hunger and thirst when I saw you working in that rubble. You were the first countryman I had seen who did not look mad or starved, so I put my hopes in you." She paused a moment, then added, looking right at me, "As I do now."

A respectful silence grew between us as the import of her trust and hope finally hit me. It had been years since I had had the responsibility for another soul. My wife had died in childbirth, taking an infant son with her. I had basically been afraid to marry or even show any interest in women ever since. Joining the revolt with men from my village was something I understood. There were clear duties and obligations to your fellow soldiers, and what seemed like clear permission from The Lord Above not to care about our enemies. The choices were laid out, sanctified, and rehearsed to the point of habit.

With Rachael and her child, however, I was on most unfamiliar ground. I felt a small duty to help her escape the city, having offered it to her earlier. But beyond that, I had nothing to guide me. She was neither kin nor fellow soldier. I feared she could do little to help me slip out of the city or fight those who would block our way, if it came to that. More than anything, I was too old to have romantic interests, as love or the hope for love often drove men to risk all for a woman.

I finally remembered what Uncle Jesus and his followers had taught about loving your neighbor as yourself. At the time, the saying had conjured up specific neighbors who I knew from my village, so of course I would want to look after and care for them. I thus had given that commandment no further thought. Now it seemed I was to consider this woman to be part of the dire neighborhood I now found myself in. She was a fellow human trying to survive Jerusalem as best she could, and I was her best hope of salvation.

Although I quickly glimpsed that this commandment seemed to have no guidelines and no limit, the urgency of the moment returned me to our own survival. "I know a gap in the northern wall where we might gain release from this dread city. The Romans patrol the walls by day and release foul, monstrous dogs along the roadways during the night. We will have but a brief hour at dawn to make our escape. I fear that your baby will need to be gagged once more if we are to avoid detection. She will fit into this traveling bag, which I need you to carry so that you have both hands to help you over the rubble and down the wall. You may have my staff as well. God willing, we shall be in Beth'el by tomorrow eve."

She nodded solemnly to this, and after taking the last of the food and water, we again prepared ourselves for sleep. I made a pillow after stuffing my now empty bag with my scaling rope and some debris that had blown into our refuge, and spread my cloak out on the packed earth. Imagine my surprise when she joined me on my cloak, although she turned her back and curled herself around her sleeping baby. "It is good not to face the night alone," was all she said.

Having slept alone all these years, it took me considerable time to adjust to the arrangement. All manner of old memories and thoughts crossed my mind, so I found myself smiling as I finally drifted off into a deep, dreamless sleep.

The baby's stirring awoke Rachael well before dawn. She nudged me awake, and I startled abruptly to have another person interrupt my usual solitary sleep. Rachael shushed me before I could cry out, and then did the same with Ava. Even in my fog I could tell that she was not afraid to command me if necessary. I again smiled at how far she had come in trusting me, and in choosing life over death.

"Ava will be hungry soon," she said without other morning greeting. "We have used up all your food and drink, so what do you propose?" *You are her mother and know more than me*, I thought to myself, but I sensed that she wanted to give me some authority in the matter. After a pause, I said, "Why not put her to your breast and see if by miracle your milk has returned?"

Even in the dimness of the fore-dawn, I could see her clearly skeptical look. At length she gave one of her resigned sighs. She pulled up her tunic right in front of me and cautiously put Ava to her breast. The baby eagerly took to it, and there followed a tense, quiet struggle as mother and child sought to reestablish a once familiar rhythm and routine. I held them in my eyes as I yearned with small prayers for their reconciliation. I could see that Rachael's whole body was tense and heard Ava complaining with small mewling sounds. At one point, Rachael's head slumped and her arms moved imperceptibly to push the baby away. Then something released inside both of them, and a kind of warmth and glow seemed to surround them. Quiet sucking sounds filled the room.

I confess that I cried, as did Rachael. I instinctively moved to hug her, and kissed the top of her head. Rachael kept muttering, "Oh, my baby, oh my baby," while I was temporarily lost for words. I had never witnessed such a moment, and sat in awe of what this most basic and life-giving love looked like. I found myself shaking my head back and forth, perhaps ridding my thoughts of doubt. "Thank you, God, thank you, thank you," was all I could say.

Sadly, the moment did not last long. There was only so much of Rachael's milk to be had, but it seemed enough to keep Ava quiet for a time. The three of us sat quietly in each other's arms for several moments, but then Rachael and I roused ourselves to face the day. We both made our toilet in the far corner of the room, and neither of us felt any shame. Rachael carefully placed the sleeping Ava in the bag , which she then slung gently over her shoulder. I checked that my sword slid easily from its scabbard, and strapped it on. Rachael and I then gave each other a lingering kiss, the first I had had in years. I pulled away with a sigh and whispered for her to huddle close behind me under my dark cloak. Like some four-legged beast, we entered the dim light of the new dawn.

It was slow going back over the rubble to where I remembered the gap to be. Rachel could not see well under the cloak, but I was reluctant to lose the protective coloration. She finally whispered, "I am slowing you down, and you know it. If we are to succeed, speed is more important than stealth." Before I could protest, she detached herself from beneath my cloak and scrabbled ahead of me beneath the wall. I had to push myself just to keep up. I learned later that she had marched mils with her putative husband. Out of pride or simple survival, she had developed the stamina to be his equal. This was but one of her remarkable talents.

We got past the Pool without incident, and at length arrived at the base of the gap as the sun was rising. Once again, I wrapped one end of the rope around my sword, and again stuffed it so it would not slide out unexpectedly. After a few practiced throws, the sword lodged above me on some rocks. I was vulnerable without my sword, but needed to climb quickly before any patrol arrived.

It was not a patrol that greeted me at the top of my climb, but a nervous young soldier barely old enough for a beard. He stood at the top of the intact wall, looking down at me as I scrambled to my feet. "What is going on here?" he demanded, in a high-pitched voice that sounded abnormally loud in the stillness of the dawn. There was something in that juvenile voice that gave me the courage to use my age to advantage. "At ease, soldier," I commanded in my most stentorian tone. I spoke loudly enough that Rachael might hear and take precautions. "You have done well to be alert to anyone leaving the city. Your *principale* shall hear of your regard for duty. Your name, soldier?" I paused long enough for him to decide what to tell me, and to gather my thoughts for my next play.

He said something like "Darius Spongopolos," or some such Greek-sounding name. I took him to be a conscript, and felt my confidence grow.

"I have been sent by Centurion Magnus Miriamus to probe weaknesses in our defenses. I came from our legions in the Kidron last night, and had no problem entering the city. I pray that you were not on duty then." With that, I gave him a most probing look, adding "*Were* you on duty then, soldier?"

The lad stammered his response, which, I confess, I did not hear above the beating of my heart and the race of thoughts in my head. He seemed to recover enough of his authority to ask why I was dressed in civilian clothes, but was careful to add 'sir' to his question.

"You can see that I dressed as one of these foul rebels, but only to determine if the wall guard could tell friend from foe. Here, you will see by my scabbard and sword that I am Roman." With that, I bent down to my make-shift grappling hook and made to withdraw my sword and scabbard.

I could not dislodge either one. A heavy weight seemed to be pulling on the hook, pinning it to the rocks where it lay. I tried the hilt, but I had done too good a job wedging the gladius in place. As I tugged futilely on the sword, I swore unconsciously in Hebrew. I could hear young Darius utter an exclamation of his own; he drew his own sword and started looking for a way to climb down to me. Suddenly, I heard Rachael scream out, "Gideon! Here!" It was she whose weight had been pulling on the rope, and she now tossed my staff to me with a free hand. Her scream momentarily distracted young Darius, giving me a second to grab the staff and prepare my defense.

I now had some advantage, with the staff able to keep his sword at bay. Thankfully, he was not as well-trained or confident. As the young are prone to do, he tried to come right at me as he climbed down. One swipe of my staff at his leading foot tumbled the poor lad down heavily onto the jagged rocks of the gap where I stood. This winded and pained him considerably, and also caused him to drop his sword. I was on him with my eating knife in hand before he could recover. A savage heat came on me, fueled both by fear and the knowledge that I was protecting Rachael and her baby as well. I put the knife to his throat and was within a hair's breath of plunging it in when I noticed a cross hung about his neck.

"Are you a Christian, then?" I managed to ask just before the beast in me would have finished him off. He looked at me with utter confusion, as I suppose he expected death and not a question about his religion. In even a higher voice than before, he stammered, "yes, please sir, by the love of Jesus, let me live!"

"Only if you give me your word you will not harm us," I said through gritted teeth, for I found that I had steeled my jaw to make the killing stroke. Indeed, my entire body had tensed into one large muscle in this life and death struggle that was thankfully over before his youth could wear down my age. While he nodded vigorously, I took several deep breaths to unlock my anger. Reaching down, I gathered his fallen sword and pulled his small dagger out from his belt, for I knew enough about Roman weaponry to disarm him fully.

I backed away from him to give him space to sit up, but kept a wary eye on him just the same. I did not know how deep his allegiance was to the Roman cause, even if he was a Christian. He was in no shape for any further trouble, as it turned out, for the fall had bruised him badly. I had time to look around for Rachael, but she was nowhere in sight. I panicked, fearing that she had fallen off the wall in the swift course of events. I need not have worried, as she soon reappeared with her baby again strapped to her back. She was proving to be most brave and resourceful.

I then turned to Darius, who was sitting sullenly on some rocks, massaging his side and legs. "I thank you, Darius, for not alerting your mates to our presence, and, I guess, for being a Christian. I would have hated myself for spilling your young blood, however necessary. Know that I have seen the madness and destruction that comes from war, and wish not to be a part of it. If I may, though, could I ask how you came to be a Christian *and* a Roman soldier?"

Darius' mouth and brows twisted in many directions, and it seemed as though there was an emotional war going on within him. His pride surely had been wounded along with his ribs. There must have been some fear of punishment by his superiors, but also relief to be alive. Perhaps he was weighing whether duty demanded that he attack us even though unarmed. These conflicting feelings merely left him bewildered, I suppose, for at length he just sighed and said in a flat voice, "My grandfather was servant to a Roman Centurion up in Capernaum. Lord Jesus healed my grandfather, and without that neither my mother nor I would have been born. It was grandfather who followed Jesus from that day on, and he passed that faith on to us."

"Well, you can tell your mother and family that you have just now met Gideon, the nephew of Jesus. It was by and for love of Him that we both live. Well, the day has broken and we must go. I cannot return your arms until we are safely on the ground, but I will gladly throw them up to you so that you are not shamed or punished by your company. You may tell them that you fell into this gap in the dark. You may even redeem yourself by saying you fear rebels can enter and exit through here unless the wall is repaired.

"I also would ask this favor of you, that you do not sound the alarm as we leave and that you throw down my battered, useless sword and my rope when we reach the ground. God go with you, young Darius." I saw him nod in agreement, although he would not make eye contact with me. I made the sign of the cross at him anyway, and turned to our escape.

I could see no patrols afoot and quickly repositioned our rope and hook so we could leave this cursed city. True to his word, Darius waited until we were safely down before coming to the edge of the wall. I first tossed up his sheathed dagger, which he caught deftly and returned to his own belt. I dared not throw his sharp sword, so tied the hilt to the loose end of my rope and gestured for him to pull it up. He did so, but when I gestured further for my own sword in return, he merely smiled.

"Know this, Gideon, nephew of Jesus, I serve two masters. Love will have to be your only weapon in the days to come. May our God be with you as well." With that, he gave a small laugh and pulled away, leaving me open-mouthed and momentarily angry.

Perhaps I should have seen that coming, Perhaps I should not have cared how he would look to his comrades. Then again, perhaps one *should* part on good terms with one's enemy, for fortunes change and you might meet again. All I could do now was accept this twist and move on.

I led Rachael, stooping and scuttering as before through the scrub, rocks, and brush back in the general direction of the Northern Road. I heard no cry of alarm behind us, and none ahead. Upon reaching the Road, I hid us behind a screen of brush until I could verify our safety. There were the usual beggars asleep on the verge and only distant sounds of movement. We left hiding and ventured out, becoming just one more dirty, dispirited couple trudging home.

On the long trek to Beth'el, we passed the crucified, the beggars, Roman patrols, and countless reminders of the ruin that our rebellion had brought on ourselves. I struggled with guilt over my part in the madness, yet welcomed how my army training had availed me. I feared for my country, my future, and mostly for Rachael and Ava, they who had started the week as nothing to me. Yet mixed in with these dark and burdensome thoughts was gratitude, even some pride at having succeeded in my mission. It was still too early to know how I truly felt about Rachael, but even that prospect gave the future a tinge of hope.

It was with all this stew of emotion that I finally arrived at our family compound just after the evening meal. Miriam welcomed me tersely, as the entire mission seemingly brought back painful memories of the loss of her sister. She soon retired to the kitchen, grumbling after seeing Rachael and Ava that I had collected two more hungry mouths to add to our troubles.

And we were hungry, having walked the 70 or 80 stadiae from Jerusalem with neither food nor water. We joined a few kin lounging at the house after the meal, and ate every leftover scrap. My kin offered the usual thanks for a safe return, but I could tell that they were tired and had worries of their own.

None questioned Rachael's presence. One of my female cousins had taken some umbrage at Miriam's unkind reception, and offered to settle Rachael and her baby in the women's quarter after they had supped and washed themselves. This left me unburdened for a moment, and with nothing better to do with myself, I went to bed.

I must report that my dreams were as troubled as my waking hours had been. In this instance, at least, that peculiar world of dreams mirrored the nightmare I had just passed through. *Golems,* soldiers, and starving forms with blood dripping from their teeth all pursued me through twisted and broken streets. In vain I searched for something I could not remember wanting or needing. At every corner, there was a child screaming for help that never came, and they too joined the crowd following me. I also cried out for help, from my mother, James, Jesus, and God Himself, but again, no one heard my pleas. The empty sky with its burning sun beat down upon my bare head, and I could feel myself melting into the earth below. I became something like a puddle of mud, and my pursuers trampled me under as they raced to find another victim.

I was awoken by a firm hand on my shoulder, while another hand grabbed my arm as I tried to swing it at whoever had broken into my dreams. It was my cousin Micah, hissing at me to awaken but be silent. My nightmare screams had woken him and others in the house, and a twinge of guilt joined its brethren in the pit of my stomach.

I stammered out my apologies and quickly told him of my horrifying dream. Micah tried to comfort me.

"You are safe now, Gideon. You have fulfilled your promise to your mother, you have done your duty. More than that, you have given new life to a woman and child who most likely would have died without your help. Surely your good deeds must count for something in this battle with your dark forces?"

I could just see his anxious, kindly face leaning over me in the early gloom before dawn, and a wave of some relief did ripple through me. As I recovered my wits, I said, "Thank you, cousin, for your kind words. There seems to be a growing faithlessness within me. God Himself seems to have abandoned Israel to its foolishness, but at least we kin have each other, and for that I am most grateful."

Micah smiled modestly, released my arm, and added that we would talk again in the daylight. He left me then, to reassure those I had awoken that all was well. After a time, the house fell back into an uneasy sleep.

All except for me.

Despite his kind words, I yet feared that my dream of turning into mud was some kind of omen, meant to warn me that I would soon become a *golem*. . .If what? If I doubted God? Doubted our covenant as a special people? Doubted the great words of hope so recently espoused by Uncle Jesus? Maybe it was doubt alone that turned a man's soul into mud, as if all things previously held dear were now soiled, foul, and base.

I knew from Torah that our people had been enslaved over and over again in our history, but each time Adonai had redeemed and freed us, thus keeping His promise. Jesus had also died to redeem his people from sin, and been resurrected by a loving God, whom he called Abba, Father. But against these testimonies and promises stood my actual experiences in Jerusalem, where all was ruin and men were reduced to scavenging beasts. The Romans cared little for our God, yet they had been victorious and we defeated. Where was God then?

I pondered these mysteries until the cockcrow roused the house. I got many a worried look from my kin when I joined them for the morning meal, but one glance at my dark face kept the questions away. I dutifully put on a smile for their benefit, and that seemed to ease the tension around the table. Rachael and her daughter entered behind all the rest, with head down and her ragged cloak pulled tightly across her shoulders. She would have slunk off to a dirty corner if my cousin had not invited her to sit with the other women.

Her presence and my shifting moods dampened speech for a time, but eventually one of my other cousins asked how I found Jerusalem. Micah tried to make light by saying, "He just followed the Northern Road and looked for a jumble of rocks," which provoked a few nervous groans.

"It is truly and utterly a disaster," I replied, after pausing to consider how to give vent to what I had seen and done. "It is a necropolis haunted by madmen. Two of them attacked me just as I was about to unearth Mother's diary, and I would have chased and killed them if they had not lamed me in the attack. I nearly killed Rachael here, who had chosen that dire moment to ask for my help. Rachel did save me from a Roman guard, but I nearly killed him as well, only to discover he was a Christian. It was not an adventure I would care to repeat, but we did get the diary."

That only seemed to whet their curiosity about my mission, but Micah intervened before they could ask more.

"Let us give Gideon some peace, as he surely needs to rest from his labors. It is not time to have him relive his nightmares."

As I finished my meal, thankful for this reprieve, it dawned on me that my mother had not told me what to do with this precious diary. It had been bought with her life, Aunt Miriam's broken spirit, and my own travails. Jesus' followers had scattered due to Sanhedrin persecution, and Aunt Miriam wanted nothing to do with it. I reasoned that I should at least read the thing to gauge its worth and see if it pointed to some person or group to whom it should be directed. Just as Mother had been taught to read by her brother, so she had passed that learning on to me. It was time to put those lessons to use.

I found a quiet corner under the arbor at the back of the house, and went about unrolling the parchments so long hidden from sight. It took some time to arrange them in the proper order, but at least I could tell Mother's writing from Aunt Miriam's. To my eye, Mother's script was as smooth, flowing, and delicate as she was herself. Her words unexpectedly brought tears to my eyes; they held her very voice and thoughts, and seemed therefore to resurrect her spirit from the dead.

What a wonder were these simple scratches and scribbles on skin! What a testament to my mother, who now could be summoned at will from my fading memories by a simple act of reading. And what a delight to be able to read them myself and not have some angry, pompous, or sly kohen hoard and interpret the words for themselves, as if they alone could converse with God.

It was with this unexpected sense of wonder, then, that I began to read what was clearly an eyewitness account of Uncle Jesus' roots and his formative years. I learned about the tragic circumstances of his birth, the near-miraculous presence of his step-mother Mary in the shattered family, and the fortuitous tutelage offered by Rebbe Nathan, himself a rejected scholar and kohen. I shed tears over Mother's identification of her betrayer and her eventual arrest. Her Judas was responsible for her martyrdom, as was Jesus' before her. Was this to be the fate of our whole clan, to be healers and martyrs in an age that only valued power and might?

A strange kind of disquiet began to grow in me as I then read my Aunt Miriam's diary entries. Her doubts and bitter confusion about the nature of God struck a chord in me as well. How could a loving and merciful God allow good people like my mother to suffer? How could we even know what goes on in the mind of God? Jesus preached many times that God was more like a loving Father than a stern, punitive patriarch, but was this merely wishful thinking? Was he just hoping that God was like his own father, Joseph?

Furthermore, it was clear from Mother's reported history that Jesus was born a man like any other, and had healing gifts more as a result of Rebbe Nathan's teaching than by divine grace. So how then could they say he was God's son, from a virgin birth no less? Mary was a virgin, but was not his mother. Why confuse and confound the two women except to elevate Jesus beyond his brief? Why make of him some pure creation and not celebrate his humanity? A godly prophet, yes, and one who was so much more hopeful and loving than his predecessors. But, some kind of creature fathered by God? The more I read and thought about the diary's revelations, the more confused and even suspicious I got.

I was so absorbed in these musings that I barely noticed that the afternoon sun was waning. I had missed the midday meal altogether and had to content myself with its cold remains. Miriam must have sensed the impact that the diaries were having on me. She sat next to me in silence as I toyed with my food, until I saw a tear roll down her cheek.

"I am sorry, Gideon, if my words upset you, but you must know that they came from grief over the loss of your mother. I have not been able to pray to God since that day—there, Salome, I have said His name, just in memory of you. But know that I have lost my faith and that I am the worse for it.

"For a brief time, I had hoped that Jesus' words were true, that God was indeed like a loving spiritual Father who practically inhabited the very air around us. I could tell Him anything and if quiet long enough could almost hear His whispered advice and blessings return to me. What a comfort to believe I was not alone in a cruel and empty world, that my confusion and doubts were known to God, who forgave me my human limitations. It was as if God were a warm glow who surrounded each and every daily event. For a time, I walked without care and with love in my heart. For a time. . ."

Here Miriam gave out a deep, deep sigh; her shoulders slumped and she seemed overcome with the weight of her grief and disappointment in God. Now it was my turn to comfort her, although truth be told, I had my own dark thoughts to contend with.

"Dear Aunt, if it is any solace, you are not alone in your doubts. I saw enough death and destruction in Jerusalem to squeeze out any hopes I had that we are favored of God. When I took up swords against the Romans, I believed what the kohenim said about the righteousness of our cause; but in the end, might proved right and righteousness proved foolish.

"It seems to me that most of what we have been told about God, and even Jesus, is an exaggeration at best, and lies at worst. What we have seen with our own eyes is that gold went into the *Beit HaMikdash* but did not come back out to feed the poor. Is that why the Temple got destroyed, to punish them for their deception, greed, and hardness of heart? I would believe that that was a display of God's justice if only we were better off as a result. We meek have inherited only blood and grief. We must toil even harder than we did before, as we now have whole cities to rebuild."

Miriam nodded in agreement, then added her own thoughts. "As I said in that diary, pain and suffering seem real, but promises of Heaven do not. And yet, I felt better when I did have hope, when I did believe in prophetic words and had a personal god to talk to. Should I trick myself into believing what my own eyes and feelings deny?"

To this, we were both silent, as if one wrong word would tumble our entire existence. My mind drifted to the words of the so-called Cynics. They were men who seemed able to pierce the veils of pretention and artifice that religious and other authorities used to cover up their all-too-human greed, lust, and ambition. There was something powerful and appealing in having such vision, but the few Cynics I had met seemed unhappier than the rest of us. They seemed disinclined to trust anything or anyone except their own thoughts. They were aloof and even isolated in their superior wisdom. Some sought out carnal pleasures, as if words were illusion and only physical sensations had merit and substance. They were then no better than dogs who could talk.

And yet, here were Miriam and I, two disillusioned souls who had seen too much of the dark side of life to believe in what we could not prove to be so. We cared too much about our country and countrymen, perhaps, to drift into cynicism, but we could no longer seek the safe harbor of simplistic promises and airy fantasies.

But I also knew how close I had come in Jerusalem to reverting to the beastliness I had seen around me. In my heart, I could admit that it was only some mixed fear and love of God, and a desire to be righteous, that had stayed my hand. If I removed God from my thoughts and heart, who then could I rely on to stem my animal instincts?

Furthermore, what would happen if our entire country gave up their belief that God would hold them to account for their sins? Would even more chaos and animal lust be loosed upon the damned and innocent alike? Torah told of Sodom and Gomorrah being destroyed by fire due to their depravity, and tales had reached us from distant lands of sacrificial rituals, mass orgies, and other inhumane consequences of a people's lack of faith in a higher moral authority. My people had worshipped Baal or simply forsaken Adonai off and on throughout our history. We were not immune to the lure of the flesh and the glitter of gold and power. It had taken generations to rise above the pagans and barbarians, and that was mainly due to our adherence to the 613 *mitzvot* laws supposedly handed down by God through the Torah and Talmud.

But then I reflected that many of these laws made no sense, even though I knew that we must have lawfulness if we were to survive as a people. The kohenim demanded that all these divine laws be followed scrupulously. They were never to be amended to suit our human whims or even our expanding knowledge of the world around us. Yet it was impossible to live one's life without violating some authority's interpretation or application of these laws. It was as if we were told to constantly strive for a perfection that was forever beyond us. No wonder people abandoned faith after a time, like that proverbial fox of Aesop's who determines that the tantalizing grapes far above him are most likely sour.

Back and forth I went in my mind as the day drew to a close. Miriam by then had drifted off into her afternoon nap. I was getting drowsy myself when my gaze happened to fall on my walking staff, left leaning against the wall after my journey. I looked from it to the scrolls on my lap, and something began to form and fall into place inside me. I realized that there most certainly was a time to believe in God, in the tales of good triumphing over evil, and of what it would take to be a truly righteous human being. One must lean on those stories as one would a stout staff, at least as long as there were bandits on the road and long journeys to make. Lean on God when you are young and not grown to your full strength. Lean on God until you learn to tame your animal nature. Let fear of His wrath chasten you if need-be, but let the love of God be your staff and support as well. Let this love be like a mystery, something to keep your own heart ever open to what life has to yet to teach.

When well-seasoned by the joys and pains of experience, you may release your grip on the staff and see if you can walk more freely. If so, use both hands to do good works in the world, but keep your eyes alert to evil.

Just as staffs come in all shapes and sizes, I realized, so will the gods that other travelers use for their support. Some of Jesus' followers had started to promote him as the only way to attain heavenly rewards, but I suspected that all religions felt the same way. Either all religions were right in their own way, or all were wrong. Jesus had once said that his sheep were the ones who heard his voice; so many different sheep in this world meant that each would hear their shepherd in his (or perhaps even her) own voice. Jesus himself was a voice I myself could heed and follow, as he surely was godly, if not God. His humanity was something I could immediately relate to, moreso than his silent, at times absent God.

I could respect all the different travelers on the godly road of life, as long as we joined together to thwart the bandits and not attack each other. That brought to mind how to handle bandits, and indeed all the armies of the powerful. Kings and their minions use their might to forcibly tilt the course of history in their favor. War itself just seems to lead to more war, as shedding another's blood only lead to more blood in retaliation. There always seem to be those who glory in the sword's power to determine who should live and who should die. I am starting to believe that it should be law and mercy, not brute strength, that ought to weigh these matters. Those of a brutish nature should not be allowed anywhere near swords, as that just releases their inner beast. It is foolish to believe that one can leash and direct such creatures, because blood lust feeds on a power greater than all our words and commands can control.

I had learned in my mission to Jerusalem that my sword had many uses—as a threat, a saw, and a grappling hook. It is good to realize it is only a tool and not a thing to be worshipped. Godly people should be prepared to take up the sword, but hopefully only for protection.

Finally, I looked at the diaries, this time with new eyes. I thought how essential it is to have a record of the truth of things, but perhaps only if one is grounded in love. Love and truth are odd companions indeed, but it is too easy to become cynical if one learns too much without caring about the people whom that wisdom touches.

I have no doubt that there is much boastfulness, exaggeration, myth, and wishful thinking in the Torah and other holy writings, even in the stories circulating about my beloved Jesus. My own mother declared that Jesus was born a man, not a god. I do not know what to make of his resurrection, as that is the one event that suggests intervention from powers greater than mere mortal man. I resolve to explore that story further. In general, though, if one can separate truth from fiction, no one can cast their spell over you or draw you into their own schemes and devices.

I resolve to nurture this ability to pierce through artifice to get at essential truths, but this also requires that I have compassion for those who cling to their beliefs. Perhaps there are nuggets of truth in almost all beliefs, and it is not for me to judge where a person is in their journey. Compassion has its own limits, I suppose, especially if people take up swords against you and others with different beliefs. I had lost my own mother, Uncle Jesus, and many friends to such zealots, and the world as I know it is worse for the killings. Jesus had tried to bring love into the forefront of all we worshipped and held dear, but his message has been cruelly rejected. I know, in my deepest heart, that such love is essential in the battle of good against both evil and death itself, so I am determined to value anyone who values it.

Perhaps this is to be my own new faith, to believe in that which brings good to those around me without stealing it from someone else. How odd but prophetic, perhaps, that "God" and "Good" are only one letter apart. I know that I will need something like a God in my heart if I am not to revert to bestiality and selfishness. However, I will have to be very careful whose image of God I adopt for my own and whose spokesman and prophet I listen to. I will choose to listen to Jesus and see what happens.

It is going to be lonely work charting my own path, but at least now I may have some sort of compass to guide my steps. If not quite reborn, as some of Jesus' followers have started to proclaim, I at least feel on some kind of firmer footing. The dark fog and fatigue of my mission is falling away, leaving me eager to explore this new awareness. I know there will be many false turns and dangers in the terrain ahead, and that I will survive longer if I have companions with whom to share the search along the way. Finding such like-minded people will be delicate work, as my own kin are vehement supporters of Jesus and can hear nothing but praise and adoration whenever his name is mentioned. They are in the blush of a new and powerful love, and I envy them their romance. It is not for me, but it would be cruel to cast doubts and aspersions on their beloved.

I should finish by noting that I never did discover what to do with the two diaries. As I suspected, Miriam wants nothing to do with them, but Micah thinks that he may be able to find one of the original disciples and let them decide on their fate. I warned him in broad terms about the diaries' power to upend the near-mythical stories going around about Jesus. Micah just has that starry look in his eyes and tells me not to worry. "God will decide," he says, but he can not say how God's decision will become known.

I am fairly certain that it will be men who will decide their fate, and that the diaries will be cast aside as some kind of stumbling block to the faithful. As the believers in Christ are being hunted and harassed by our religious authorities, I do not think they can risk their resolve being weakened or challenged.

At least I have survived and found some truths from my mission. And for that I believe I should thank someone or something beyond myself.

XVI

Letter of Eupsychus, A Scribe
To The Council Of Nicea

DEAR AND CHERISHED BROTHERS and sisters in Christ,

May our Lord and Savior continue his blessings upon you and our brethren in Christ. Our Bishop Macarius has asked me to keep you informed of events up here, for it is by the grace of God that I have been chosen as one of the Scribes to this august body of scholars and future saints.

You may have heard that there has been tension—the kindest word I can ascribe—between our brother Bishops Arius and Alexander. Sadly, there are deep divisions in our faith community. Indeed, it is to settle such disputes that Emperor Constantin has convened this council, hoping perhaps that a unified doctrine of faith can co-equally unify his Christian rule. Learned bishops of every persuasion from throughout the Levant, North Africa, Rome, and beyond have struggled and argued over all matters, including who shall scribe their words. I had to bide several weeks in this pleasant town before being chosen. They must have thought I was a neutral party, having come from Scythopolis, a good distance from each of the Sees of Antioch and Alexandria.

It is perhaps also mete that I have walked the very roads trod by our Savior and his Disciples, and have been to many of the sites of his miracles and sermons. It has been some 300 years since his glorious Ascension, but one feels his spirit in these holy places even now. That spirit once gave birth to a glorious flowering of hope and love in our dark world, with brothers and sisters in the faith having planted Jesus' gospel in lands both far and near. What wonderful varieties, what a profusion of visions, miracles, and inspirational speech sprung like a veritable Garden of Eden from his life and glorious death!

It is perhaps this familiarity and feeling of closeness with our Lord Jesus the Christ, however, that prompts grave concern, which I sincerely hesitate to share with you, my brothers and sisters. On the one hand, Brother Paul has urged us to be open with each other, to let nothing fester lest our hearts rot with bile. In another letter, however, he urges us not to speak ill of our brethren, as evil can easily snake into our thoughts and actions, weakening our faith and love. It is a fine line between the two, and I pray to walk it most carefully in this and future letters.

Would that Brother Paul himself were here to make peace between those who battle over the true nature of our Lord Christ! Instead, we have our new brother, Emperor Constantin himself, and his counselor Hosius of Cordova, here to help shepherd the Council towards some resolution of our many differences. The Bishops do not appear outwardly daunted by his royal presence. They are as adamant and contentious as schoolboys, each side promoting their opinions about Jesus' human and divine natures, the extent of each, and what it all says about the Blessed Trinity. I do pray to God that all this bickering and lawyerly debate will not drive the Emperor screaming back to his palace in frustration. His faith may not be strong enough yet to withstand all the charges and counter-charges. I know that I have had to scrape and rescrape these skins with each change of wording, so even my own stamina and faith have been tested!

In brief, a young man named Athanathius argued that Christ was begotten by God, and not made by woman and man. He referenced Matthew's account where Jesus says he is the Son of God, born of Mary. As Mary was a virgin, said Athanasius, Jesus must have been conceived and born in a non-human way—hence Son of God, of one being with The Father. As you may know from my Hellenistic roots, we Greeks are quite used to gods coming down to have congress with humans. Those legates from Antioch and the Levant who have had any contact with Hellenes readily saw this logic.

The few remaining followers of Arius of Alexandria, however, protested vehemently, noting that Jesus said peacemakers could also be called sons of God. They further argued that Jesus was truly a human whose perfect obedience to and oneness with the divine Will elevated him to a kind of equality with God, as a favored son to his father. Athanasius and his group convened for a time, and then argued that Jesus meant that peacemakers could become sons of God through adoption, still favored and in the family, so to speak, but not of the same blood and being. This seemed to answer the Arians' final objections, and the "begotten" wording was approved with nearly unanimous acclaim. Two or three Arians still demurred, however, and they were rudely exiled from the Council. I was not allowed, nor would I have wanted, to scribe the many unkind, threatening, and even hateful words the majority uttered against their fellow delegates. Apparently, only those of one mind with the Council shall be considered the true fruit of the vine.

Some of the younger legates next tried to explain The Trinity to the older believers. One elderly Bishop from Alexandria had timorously questioned how three could be one and one be three, saying, "I have learned some of the new mathematica from our Arab brethren, and even they could not help me understand what you are proposing."

Jesus himself had spoken throughout his ministry of Father, Son, and Holy Spirit, but some in the assembly felt that these were parables, meant to convey in human terms what Jesus felt about God, who remained largely beyond simple human understanding and definition. Some in the assembly had only recently even heard the term, first coined by Tertulian a hundred years ago. A more complete agreement over what is meant by The Trinity was tabled, and another Council has been proposed by Constantin to be held in his capital city, Constantinople.

The bitterly fought agreement about Christ's fully divine nature seemed to exhaust the delegations, and there was still much muttering as all retired to their chambers. I learned the next day that Constantin himself had congratulated young Athanasius, and stated what a fine Bishop he would make some day. Those who follow Bishops Lucian and Arius have fallen into disfavor, and will face ex-communication unless they recant their views. There is talk that all texts and writings from those not hewing to the present understanding will have a similar fate. On the other hand, those who curry Constantin's patronage will do very well in the months and even years to come. I humbly urge the Bishops in Scythopolis and our See of Jerusalem to take heed of these ominous developments and adjust their preaching accordingly.

There was such contentiousness over the "true" nature of Christ that precious else was agreed upon. There were some who wanted priests and deacons to be celibate, as was our Lord. Constantin and others thought this was too much to ask of fallible human beings, as we Christians have only just learned to wear the mantle of Christ. The delegates did agree that bishops, priests, and deacons should not jump from church to church like some hungry wolf looking for new meat. We are to bloom where we are planted, perhaps until such time as our Church's roots are sufficiently strong to handle any adversity or sudden change.

And that was about it. No mention of love, service, healing, the rule of justice and mercy, or the meek inheriting the Kingdom of Heaven. Perhaps the presence of an actual Emperor in their midst daunted the delegates, although all feigned to treat him as just another brother in Christ. Even so, we Scribes were enjoined to give certain personages in the assembly titles and honorifics, such as, "His most Excellent Emperor," "His Holiness," and "The Most Blessed."

This begins to bother me, brethren, for compared to the glory of God in Christ, what mere man should dare to say he is the "most" anything? Surely, we are all equal in our common fallen humanity.

And what of the brothers exiled from the Council and those already labeled anathema for believing and speaking as they did? How do we justify ex-communicating those who focus on the *homoiousios* rather than the *homoousios*?[1] Such furious debate there was over a mere letter difference and a shade of meaning too small for many in the assembly to even notice! Truly, compared to God who created the cosmos, who are we humans to presume to know if Jesus attended the birth of the cosmos, was born divine, or came into divinity during his lifetime? What is time to God? It is not by words that we shall be judged, but by deeds—did these rejected Arians not love The Lord with all their hearts and their neighbors as themselves? Was not Christ himself rejected by the world? I fear we are repeating the sins of an earlier generation, as if a Pharisitical spirit has infested our hearts and souls.

We who have walked where Jesus and the Apostles walked have seen and felt the joy that comes to our brethren when they realize that God indeed cares for them personally, no matter how lowly. In Christ, God humbled Himself in human form, bridging Heaven and Earth. We are forgiven our sins and are free to love God and our neighbors as ourselves.

How glorious was that simple message when first I heard it, but instead the delegates here argued like lawyers over the finest points of inheritance

1. Greek for 'of similar substance' and 'of the same substance.' This debate about the divine nature of Christ lead to the modern phrase, 'Not an iota of difference,' as only the 'iota' or Greek letter 'i' separates the two concepts.

and title. They want Christ to be proven—beyond doubt and second-guessing—to be His only begotten Son, hence the true and sole heir of God's estate. They believe Christ should be exalted above all prophets and earthly powers.

However, Christ himself washed his disciples' feet and urged them to be like the "least of these," like the smallest child of God. He did not say he was King; he did not have his disciples bow down and exalt him. Why should we have to listen to "proofs" when the true nature of Jesus—the very fruit of his time on this earth—is seen in his enduring love of mankind?

I do not presume to know what use God has planned for Constantin, although the Emperor has already blessed our Church in many ways. He has treated the whole assembly graciously, with fine accommodations, food, and wine. He has rooted out those who oppress us and has striven to bring peace between the quarreling factions within the Church.

However, he is a warrior king, with a kingdom to subdue and rule. He appeared among us in all his gold and jewels, and many were taken with him. I fear that he is shaping the Church into one instrument with one voice and one approved profession of faith. The price of peace within the Church seems to have been bought with the sacrifice of many who have traveled a different road to our common God. This Council of Constantin's may be a wedding in which the Bride will sacrifice too much for the ease of living in a palace.

There remains but two more days of this conclave, so I will have more to say then. Peace be with you all.

Your brother in Christ, Eupsychus

LETTER OF ANTICLIUS, SCRIBE TO SECUNDUS OF PTOLEMAIS:

I sad to report to yu, brethrn, of my brothr scryb, Eupsychus, —he spelt it for me—that he got expelt from the Nicae asembly soon after we Ptolies wer expelt. His inks, skins, an' stylus wer taykn. We fundt him beat and bashed near the tan'ng pits of toun. His fingrs ben brokn, hands tyd doun in a barel of foul wayst used to sof'n the lethers. His hands ar no good nou, an' I am ryten for him as he hold ona what helth he got lef.

Plees pardn my rytn, as I am no wher skild and lern as he. Soma his words kina big for me. I was somtym scryb to my Bish Secundus, but dunt kno much Greek. Bish cant read anway, so I stil got job, ha. Maybe them that beet Eup dint kno I scryb an' thats why I kep my oun rytn kit? Tho we wer expelt by the asembly, my Bish had bisnes in toun, so we hid for a week aftr our shaymful treetment. The Bish had sens to disguys lyk a traydsman, els he myt got beet lyk Eup.

So we start to leev toun and foundt Eup. Who don it to yu? I say. Dunt reely kno he say, but thay don me in. Cudda ben Constnntn Empr men. What yu do, I say. I ryt letr to frens an' Empr men dint lyk it. How thay kno what yu ryt? I showd it to my fren, a Judas of my oun I bet. Eup start to cry an' say he scart to think it was them that expelt us that don him in to.

Bish kno a little med and got Eup fixt up a bit. Cleen, fed, and slept him an' such, al the tym look'n for trubl. Bish dont kno if Eup can tayk a hard boat ryd doun to Ptolmais, but Eup say he cant stay heer. God wil decyd, says Eup, if I liv or dy, but you a gud man to help me, Bish. Then Eup giv me the ey an' say, If I dont mayk it, you got to tel my brethrn to hold ona the God of Luv an' dont trust them that took over the Nicae. He dint mary, but want to giv his guds to his brothr an' sistr in Scythopolis, nayma Digenus an' Persphyn. (spelt ryt?)

So off we go doun road to our ship, with Eup kina spral on a donky. He cant hold on to gud cuz his hands bad. Al the tym he tels the Bish an' me not to loos fayth cuz eevn Jesus was rejekt, then kilt. Leest I got breth, Eup says. We stop doun road a bit for nyt, an' Eup ask Bish to tayk his confessun, cuz Eup says he harbr hayt ina his hart. Bish say yes, an' they tauk ryt thru dinr. What do yu kno, they both bleev Jesus reel human cuz reel peepl seen him an' no uon but Moses evr seen God, an' he only seen a burn'ng bush. Yy thay gota get so shur bout Jesus be'ng exac saym as God, Eup say? Why thay do me lyk a hertic? Eup warn the Bish not to ryt anyth'ng lyk he reel feel, but Bish cant ryt no way, ha.

Them as reed this, kno that Eup a gud man an' tauk alot bout yu befor he dy. His hands got green lyk and then resta him. He got to our boat, but dy at see. Last thing aftr we say prayrs, he jok, Gonna swim to our lord, ash to ash, dust to fish. Dyd with a smyl ona his fayc. We rapt him ina old sayl with rox and sent him swim'ng.

Ima send this letr to yu by a man dos Bish bisnes in Yerush. He gud man an' cant reed, so Bish an' me hop we ar safe. Yu to. Plees let his kin kno. Bish say bles yu.

Yur servint in Chryst,
Anticlius

The End